THE GARDEN MURDER CASE

THE GARDEN MURDER CASE

S. S. Van Dine

FELONY & MAYHEM PRESS • NEW YORK

THE GARDEN MURDER CASE

A Felony & Mayhem mystery

PRINTING HISTORY
First edition (Scribner's): 1935

Felony & Mayhem edition: 2020

ISBN: 978-1-63194-205-1

Manufactured in the United States of America

Library of Congress Cataloging-in-Publication Data

Names: Van Dine, S. S., author.
Title: The garden murder case / S.S. Van Dine.
Description: Felony & Mayhem edition. | New York : Felony & Mayhem
    Press, 2020. | Series: Philo Vance ; 9 | Summary: "A classic "house party
    gone wrong" scenario forces Philo Vance to distinguish between suicide
    and murder"-- Provided by publisher.
Identifiers: LCCN 2020045329 | ISBN 9781631942051 (trade paperback) |
    ISBN 9781631942136 (ebook)
Subjects: GSAFD: Mystery fiction.
Classification: LCC PS3545.R846 G32 2020 | DDC 813/.52--dc23
LC record available at https://lccn.loc.gov/2020045329

TO MY MOTHER

An two men ride of a horse,
one must ride behind.
—*Much Ado About Nothing.*

The icon above says you're holding a copy of a book in the Felony & Mayhem "Vintage" category. These books were originally published prior to about 1965, and feature the kind of twisty, ingenious puzzles beloved by fans of Agatha Christie and John Dickson Carr. If you enjoy this book, you may well like other "Vintage" titles from Felony & Mayhem Press.

THE GARDEN MURDER CASE

CHAPTER ONE

The Trojan Horses
(Friday, April 13; 10 p. m.)

THERE WERE TWO reasons why the terrible and, in many ways, incredible Garden murder case—which took place in the early spring following the spectacular Casino murder case*—was so designated. In the first place, the scene of this tragedy was the penthouse home of Professor Ephraim Garden, the great experimental chemist of Stuyvesant University; and secondly, the exact *situs criminis* was the beautiful private roof-garden over the apartment itself.

It was both a peculiar and implausible affair, and one so cleverly planned that only by the merest accident—or, perhaps I should say a fortuitous intervention—was it discovered at all. Despite the fact that the circumstances preceding the crime were entirely in Philo Vance's favor, I cannot help regarding it as one of his greatest triumphs in criminal investigation and

---

* *"The Casino Murder Case"* (Scribners, 1934).

deduction; for it was his quick uncanny judgments, his ability to read human nature, and his tremendous flair for the significant undercurrents of the so-called trivia of life, that led him to the truth.

The Garden murder case involved a curious and anomalous mixture of passion, avarice, ambition and horse-racing. There was an admixture of hate, also; but this potent and blinding element was, I imagine, an understandable outgrowth of the other factors. However, the case was amazing in its subtleties, its daring, its thought-out mechanism, and its sheer psychological excitation.

The beginning of the case came on the night of April 13. It was one of those mild evenings that we often experience in early spring following a spell of harsh dampness, when all the remaining traces of winter finally capitulate to the inevitable seasonal changes. There was a mellow softness in the air, a sudden perfume from the burgeoning life of nature—the kind of atmosphere that makes one lackadaisical and wistful; and, at the same time, stimulates one's imagination.

I mention this seemingly irrelevant fact because I have good reason to believe these meteorological conditions had much to do with the startling events that were imminent that night and which were to break forth, in all their horror, before another twenty-four hours had passed.

And I believe that the reason, with all its subtle innuendoes, was the real explanation of the change that came over Vance himself during his investigation of the crime. Up to that time I had never considered Vance a man of any deep personal emotion, except in so far as children and animals and his intimate masculine friendships were concerned. He had always impressed me as a man so highly mentalized, so cynical and impersonal in his attitude toward life, that an irrational human weakness like romance would be alien to his nature. But in the course of his deft inquiry into the murders in Professor Garden's penthouse, I saw, for the first time, another and softer side of his character. Vance was never a happy man in the conventional sense; but after the Garden murder case there were evidences of an even deeper loneliness in his sensitive nature.

But these sentimental side-lights perhaps do not matter in the reportorial account of the astonishing history I am here setting down, and I doubt if they should have been mentioned at all but for the fact that they gave an added inspiration and impetus to the energy Vance exerted and the risks he ran in bringing the murderer to justice.

As I have said, the case opened—so far as Vance was concerned with it—on the night of April 13. John F.-X. Markham, then District Attorney of New York County, had dined with Vance at his apartment in East 38th Street. The dinner had been excellent—as all of Vance's dinners were—and at ten o'clock the three of us were sitting in the comfortable library, sipping *Napoléon* 1809—that famous and exquisite cognac brandy of the First Empire.*

Vance and Markham had been discussing crime waves in a desultory manner. There had been a mild disagreement, Vance discounting the theory that crime waves are calculable, and holding that crime is entirely personal and therefore incompatible with generalizations or laws. The conversation had then drifted round to the bored young people of postwar decadence who had, for the sheer excitement of it, organized crime clubs whose members tried their hand at murders wherein nothing was to be gained materially. The Loeb-Leopold case naturally was mentioned, and also a more recent and equally vicious case that had just come to light in one of the leading western cities.

It was in the midst of this discussion that Currie, Vance's old English butler and majordomo, appeared at the library door. I noticed that he seemed nervous and ill at ease as he

---

*   *I realize that this statement will call forth considerable doubt, for real* Napoléon *brandy is practically unknown in America. But Vance had obtained a case in France; and Lawton Mackall, an exacting connoisseur, has assured me that, contrary to the existing notion among experts, there are at least eight hundred cases of this brandy in a warehouse in Cognac at the present day.*

waited for Vance to finish speaking; and I think Vance, too, sensed something unusual in the man's attitude, for he stopped speaking rather abruptly and turned.

"What is it, Currie? Have you seen a ghost, or are there burglars in the house?"

"I have just had a telephone call, sir," the old man answered, endeavoring to restrain the excitement in his voice.

"Not bad news from abroad?" Vance asked sympathetically.

"Oh, no, sir; it wasn't anything for me. There was a gentleman on the phone—"

Vance lifted his eyebrows and smiled faintly.

"A gentleman, Currie?"

"He spoke like a gentleman, sir. He was certainly no ordinary person. He had a cultured voice, sir, and—"

"Since your instinct has gone so far," Vance interrupted, "perhaps you can tell me the gentleman's age?"

"I should say he was middle-aged, or perhaps a little beyond," Currie ventured. "His voice sounded mature and dignified and judicial."

"Excellent!" Vance crushed out his cigarette. "And what was the object of this dignified, middle-aged gentleman's call? Did he ask to speak to me or give you his name?"

A worried look came into Currie's eyes as he shook his head.

"No, sir. That's the strange part of it. He said he did not wish to speak to you personally, and he would not tell me his name. But he asked me to give you a message. He was very precise about it and made me write it down word for word and then repeat it. And the moment I had done so he hung up the receiver." Currie stepped forward. "Here's the message, sir." And he held out one of the small memorandum sheets Vance always kept at his telephone.

Vance took it and nodded a dismissal. Then he adjusted his monocle and held the slip of paper under the light of the table lamp. Markham and I both watched him closely, for the incident was unusual, to say the least. After a hasty reading of the paper he gazed off into space, and a clouded look came into his eyes. He read the message again, with more care, and sank back into his chair.

"My word!" he murmured. "Most extr'ordin'ry. It's quite intelligible, however, don't y' know. But I'm dashed if I can see the connection..."

Markham was annoyed. "Is it a secret?" he asked testily. "Or are you merely in one of your Delphic oracle moods?"

Vance glanced toward him contritely.

"Forgive me, Markham. My mind automatically went off on a train of thought. Sorry—really." He held the paper again under the light. "This is the message that Currie so meticulously took down: 'There is a most disturbing psychological tension at Professor Ephraim Garden's apartment, which resists diagnosis. Read up on radioactive sodium. See Book XI of the *Æneid*, line 875. Equanimity is essential.'... Curious—eh, what?"

"It sounds a little crazy to me," Markham grunted. "Are you troubled much with cranks?"

"Oh, this is no crank," Vance assured him. "It's puzzlin', I admit; but it's quite lucid."

Markham sniffed skeptically.

"What, in the name of Heaven, have a professor and sodium and the *Æneid* to do with one another?"

Vance was frowning as he reached into the humidor for one of his beloved *Régie* cigarettes with a deliberation which indicated a mental tension. Slowly he lighted the cigarette. After a deep inhalation he answered.

"Ephraim Garden, of whom you surely must have heard from time to time, is one of the best-known men in chemical research in this country. Just now, I believe, he's professor of chemistry at Stuyvesant University—that could be verified in *Who's Who*. But it doesn't matter. His latest researches have been directed along the lines of radioactive sodium. An amazin' discovery, Markham. Made by Doctor Ernest O. Lawrence, of the University of California, and two of his colleagues there, Doctors Henderson and McMillan. This new radioactive sodium has opened up new fields of research in cancer therapy—indeed, it may prove some day to be the long-looked-for cure for cancer. The new gamma radiation of this sodium is more penetrating than any ever before obtained. On the other hand, radium and radioactive substances can be very dangerous if diffused into the normal tissues of the body and through the blood stream. The chief difficulty in the treatment of cancerous tissue by radiation is to find a selective carrier which will distribute the radioactive substance in the tumor alone. But with the discovery of radioactive sodium tremendous advances have been made; and it will be but a matter of time when this new sodium will be perfected and available in sufficient quantities for extensive experimentation…"*

"That is all very fascinating," Markham commented sarcastically. "But what has it to do with you, or with trouble in the Garden home? And what could it possibly have to do with the *Æneid*? They didn't have radioactive sodium in the time of Æneas."

"Markham old dear, I'm no Chaldean. I haven't the groggiest notion wherein the situation concerns either me or Æneas, except that I happen to know the Garden family slightly. But I've a vague feeling about that particular book of the *Æneid*. As I recall, it contains one of the greatest descriptions of a battle in all ancient literature. But let's see…"

Vance rose quickly and went to the section of his bookshelves devoted to the classics, and, after a few moments' search, took down a small red volume and began to riffle the pages. He ran his eye swiftly down a page near the end of the volume and after a minute's perusal came back to his chair with the book, nodding his head comprehensively, as if in answer to some question he had inwardly asked himself.

"The passage referred to, Markham," he said after a moment, "is not exactly what I had in mind. But it may

---

*   It is interesting to note the recent announcement that a magnetic accelerator of five million volts and weighing ten tons for the manufacture of artificial radium for the treatment of malignant growths, such as cancer, is being built by the University of Rochester.

be even more significant. It's the famous onomatopœic *Quadrupedumque putrem cursu quatit ungula campum*— meanin', more or less literally: 'And in their galloping course the horsehoof shakes the crumbling plain.' "

Markham took the cigar from his mouth and looked at Vance with undisguised annoyance.

"You're merely working up a mystery. You'll be telling me next that the Trojans had something to do with this professor of chemistry and his radioactive sodium."

"No. Oh, no." Vance was in an unusually serious mood. "Not the Trojans. But the galloping horses perhaps."

Markham snorted. "That may make sense to you."

"Not altogether," returned Vance, critically contemplating the end of his cigarette. "There is, nevertheless, the vague outline of a pattern here. You see, young Floyd Garden, the professor's only offspring, and his cousin, a puny chap named Woode Swift—he's quite an intimate member of the Garden household, I believe—are addicted to the ponies. Quite a prevalent disease, by the way, Markham. They're both interested in sports in general—probably the normal reaction to their professorial and ecclesiastical forebears: young Swift's father, who has now gone to his Maker, was a D.D. of sorts. I used to see both young johnnies at Kinkaid's Casino occasionally. But the galloping horses are their passion now. And they're the nucleus of a group of young aristocrats who spend their afternoons mainly in the futile attempt to guess which horses are going to come in first at the various tracks."

"You know this Floyd Garden well?"

Vance nodded. "Fairly well. He's a member of the Far Meadows Club and I've often played polo with him. He's a five-goaler and owns a couple of the best ponies in the country. I tried to buy one of them from him once—but that's beside the point.* The fact is, young Garden has invited me on several

---

* *At one time Vance was a polo enthusiast and played regularly. He too had a five-goal rating.*

occasions to join him and his little group at the apartment when the out-of-town races were on. It seems he has a direct loud-speaker service from all the tracks, like many of the horse fanatics. The professor disapproves, in a mild way, but he raises no serious objections because Mrs. Garden is rather inclined to sit in and take her chances on a horse now and then."

"Have you ever accepted his invitation?" asked Markham.

"No," Vance told him. Then he glanced up with a far-away look in his eyes. "But I think it might be an excellent idea."

"Come, come, Vance!" protested Markham. "Even if you see some cryptic relationship between the disconnected items of this message you've just received, how, in the name of Heaven, can you take it seriously?"

Vance drew deeply on his cigarette and waited a moment before answering.

"You have overlooked one phrase in the message: 'Equanimity is essential,'" he said at length. "One of the great racehorses of today happens to be named Equanimity. He belongs in the company of such immortals of the turf as Man o' War, Exterminator, Gallant Fox, and Reigh Count.[*] Furthermore, Equanimity is running in the Rivermont Handicap tomorrow."

"Still I see no reason to take the matter seriously," Markham objected.

Vance ignored the comment and added: "Moreover, Doctor Miles Siefert[†] told me at the club the other day that Mrs. Garden had been quite ill for some time with a mysterious malady."

Markham shifted in his chair and broke the ashes from his cigar.

---

[*] *When Vance read the proof of this record, he made a marginal notation: "And I might also have mentioned Sir Barton, Sysonby, Colin, Crusader, Twenty Grand, and Equipoise."*

[†] *Miles Siefert was, at that time, one of the leading pathologists of New York, with an extensive practice among the fashionable element of the city.*

"The affair gets more muddled by the minute," he remarked irritably. "What's the connection between all these commonplace data and that precious phone message of yours?" He waved his hand contemptuously toward the paper which Vance still held.

"I happen to know," Vance answered slowly, "who sent me this message."

"Ah, yes?" Markham was obviously skeptical.

"Quite. It was Doctor Siefert."

Markham showed a sudden interest.

"Would you care to enlighten me as to how you arrived at this conclusion?" he asked in a satirical voice.

"It was not difficult," Vance answered, rising and standing before the empty hearth, with one arm resting on the mantel. "To begin with, I was not called to the telephone personally. Why? Because it was someone who feared I might recognize his voice. Ergo, it was someone I know. To continue, the language of the message bears the earmarks of the medical profession. 'Psychological tension' and 'resists diagnosis' are not phrases ordinarily used by the layman, although they consist of commonplace enough words. And there are two such identifying phrases in the message—a fact which eliminates any possibility of a coincidence. Take this example, for instance: the word *uneventful* is certainly a word used by every class of person; but when it is coupled with another ordin'ry word, *recovery*, you can rest pretty much assured that only a doctor would use the phrase. It has a pertinent medical significance—it's a *cliché* of the medical profession… To go another step: the message obviously assumes that I am more or less acquainted with the Garden household and the race-track passion of young Garden. Therefore, we get the result that the sender of the message is a doctor whom I know and one who is aware of my acquaintance with the Gardens. The only doctor who fulfills these conditions, and who, incidentally, is middle-aged and cultured and highly judicial—Currie's description, y' know,—is Miles Siefert. And, added to this simple deduction, I happen to know that Siefert is a Latin scholar—I once encountered him at the Latin Society club-rooms. Another point in my favor is the fact that he is the family physician of the Gardens and would have ample opportunity to know about the galloping horses—and perhaps about Equanimity in particular—in connection with the Garden household."

"That being the case," Markham protested, "why don't you phone him and find out exactly what's back of his cryptography?"

"My dear Markham—oh, my dear Markham!" Vance strolled to the table and took up his temporarily forgotten cognac glass. "Siefert would not only indignantly repudiate any knowledge of the message, but would automatically become the first obstacle in any bit of pryin' I might decide to do. The ethics of the medical profession are most fantastic; and Siefert, as becomes his unique position, is a fanatic on the subject. From the fact that he communicated with me in this roundabout way I rather suspect that some grotesque point of honor is involved. Perhaps his conscience overcame him for the moment, and he temporarily relaxed his adherence to what he considers his code of honor... No, no, that course wouldn't do at all. I must ferret out the matter for myself—as he undoubtedly wishes me to do."

"But what is this matter that you feel called upon to ferret out?" persisted Markham. "Granting all you say, I still don't see how you can regard the situation as in any way serious."

"One never knows, does one?" drawled Vance. "Still, I'm rather fond of the horses myself, don't y' know."

Markham seemed to relax and fitted his manner to Vance's change of mood.

"And what do you propose to do?" he asked good-naturedly.

Vance sipped his cognac and then set down the glass. He looked up whimsically.

"The Public Prosecutor of New York—that noble defender of the rights of the common people—to wit: the Honorable John F.-X. Markham—must grant me immunity and protection before I'll consent to answer."

Markham's eyelids drooped a little as he studied Vance. He was familiar with the serious import that often lay beneath the other's most frivolous remarks.

"Are you planning to break the law?" he asked.

Vance picked up the lotus-shaped cognac glass again and twirled it gently between thumb and forefinger.

"Oh, yes—quite," he admitted nonchalantly. "Jailable offense, I believe."

Markham studied him for another moment.

"All right," he said, without the slightest trace of lightness. "I'll do what I can for you. What's it to be?"

Vance took another sip of the *Napoléon*.

"Well, Markham old dear," he announced, with a half smile, "I'm going to the Gardens' penthouse tomorrow afternoon and play the horses with the younger set."

CHAPTER TWO

Domestic Revelations
(Saturday, April 14; noon.)

As SOON AS Markham had left us that night, Vance's mood changed. A troubled look came into his eyes, and he walked up and down the room pensively.

"I don't like it, Van," he murmured, as if talking to himself. "I don't at all like it. Siefert isn't the type to make a mysterious phone call like that, unless he has a very good reason for doing so. It's quite out of character, don't y' know. He's a dashed conservative chap, and no end ethical. There must be something worrying him deeply. But why the Gardens' apartment? The domestic atmosphere there has always struck me as at least superficially normal—and now a man as dependable as Siefert gets jittery about it to the extent of indulging in shillin'-shocker technique. It's deuced queer."

He stopped pacing the floor and looked at the clock.

"I think I'll make the arrangements. A bit of snoopin' is highly indicated."

He went into the anteroom, and a moment later I heard him dialing a number on the telephone. When he returned to the library he seemed to have thrown off his depression. His manner was almost flippant.

"We're in for an abominable lunch tomorrow, Van," he announced, pouring himself another pony of cognac. "And we must torture ourselves with the viands at a most ungodly hour—noon. What a time to ingest even good food!" He sighed. "We're lunching with young Garden at his home. Woode Swift will be there and also an insufferable creature named Lowe Hammle, a horsy gentleman from some obscure estate on Long Island. Later we'll be joined by various members of the sporting set, and together we'll indulge in that ancient and fascinatin' pastime of laying wagers on the thoroughbreds. The Rivermont Handicap tomorrow is one of the season's classics. That, at any rate, may be jolly good fun..."

He rang for Currie and sent him out to fetch a copy of *The Morning Telegraph*.

"One should be prepared. Oh, quite. It's been years since I handicapped the horses. Ah, gullible Youth! But there's something about the ponies that gets in one's blood and plays havoc with the saner admonitions of the mind...* I think I'll change to a dressing gown."

He finished his *Napoléon*, lingering over it fondly, and disappeared into the bedroom.

Although I was well aware that Vance had some serious object in lunching with young Garden the following day and

---

* Vance at one time owned several excellent race-horses. His Magic Mirror, Smoke Maiden, and Aldeen were well known in their day; and Magic Mirror, as a three-year-old, won two of the most important handicaps on the eastern tracks. But when, in the famous Elmswood Special, this horse broke a leg on entering the backstretch and had to be destroyed, Vance seemed to lose all interest in racing and disposed of his entire stable. He is probably not a true horseman, any more than he is a truly great breeder of Scottish terriers, for his sentiments are constantly interfering with the stern and often ruthless demands of the game.

in participating in the gambling on the races, I had not the slightest suspicion, at the time, of the horrors that were to follow. On the afternoon of April 14 occurred the first grim act of one of the most atrocious multiple crimes of this generation. And to Doctor Siefert must go, in a large measure, the credit for the identification of the criminal, for had he not sent his cryptic and would-be anonymous message to Vance, the truth would probably never have been known.

I shall never forget that fatal Saturday afternoon. And aside from the brutal Garden murder, that afternoon will always remain memorable for me because it marked the first mature sentimental episode, so far as I had ever observed, in Vance's life. For once, the cold impersonal attitude of his analytical mind melted before the appeal of an attractive woman.

Vance was just reentering the library in his deep-red surah-silk dressing gown when Currie brought in the *Telegraph*. Vance took the paper and opened it before him on the desk. To all appearances, he was in a gay and inquisitive frame of mind.

"Have you ever handicapped the ponies, Van?" he asked, picking up a pencil and reaching for a small tablet. "It's as absorbin' an occupation as it is a futile one. At least a score of technical considerations enter into the computations—the class of the horse, his age, his pedigree, the weight he has to carry, the consistency of his past performances, the time he has made in previous races, the jockey that is to ride him, the type of races he is accustomed to running, the condition of the track and whether or not the horse is a mudder, his post position, the distance of the race, the value of the purse, and a dozen other factors—which, when added up, subtracted, placed against one another, and eventually balanced through an elaborate system of mathematical checking and counterchecking, give you what is supposed to be the exact possibilities of his winning the race on which you have been working. However, it's all quite useless. Less than forty percent of favorites—that is, horses who, on paper, should win—verify the result of these calculations. For instance, Jim Dandy beat Gallant Fox in the Travers and paid a hundred to one; and the theoretically invincible Man o' War lost one of his races to a colt named Upset. After all your intricate computations, horse-racing still remains a matter of sheer luck, as incalculable as roulette. But no true follower of the ponies will place a bet until he has gone through the charmin' rigmarole of handicapping the entries. It's little more than abracadabra—but it's three-fourths of the sport."

He gave me a waggish look.

"And that's why I shall sit here for another hour or two at least, indulging one of my old weaknesses. I shall go to the Gardens' tomorrow with every race perfectly calculated—and you will probably make a pin choice and collect the rewards of innocence." He waved his hand in a pleasant gesture. "Cheerio."

I turned in with a feeling of uneasiness.

Shortly before noon the next day we arrived at Professor Garden's beautiful skyscraper apartment, and were cordially, and a little exuberantly, greeted by young Garden.

Floyd Garden was a man in his early thirties, erect and athletically built. He was about six feet tall, with powerful shoulders and a slender waist. His hair was almost black, and his complexion swarthy. His manner, while easy and casual, and with a suggestion of swagger, was in no way offensive. He was not a handsome man: his features were too rugged, his eyes set too close together, his ears protruded too much, and his lips were too thin. But he had an undeniable charm, and there was a quiet submerged competency in the way he moved and in the rapidity of his mental reactions. He was certainly not intellectual, and later, when I met his mother, I recognized at once that his hereditary traits had come down to him from her side of the family.

"There are only five of us for lunch, Vance," he remarked breezily. "The old gentleman is fussing with his test tubes and Bunsen burners at the University; the mater is having a grand time playing sick, with medicos and nurses dashing madly

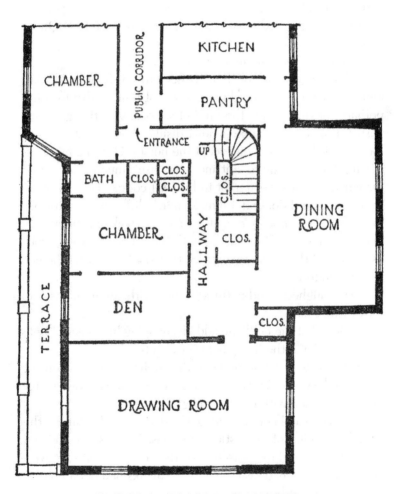

MAIN FLOOR OF GARDEN APARTMENT

back and forth to arrange her pillows and light her cigarettes for her. But Pop Hammle is coming—rum old bird, but a good sport; and we'll also be burdened with beloved cousin Woode with the brow of alabaster and the heart of a chipmunk. You know Swift, I believe, Vance. As I remember, you once spent an entire evening here discussing Ming celadons with him. Queer crab, Woody."

He pondered a moment with a wry face.

"Can't figure out just how he fits into this household. Dad and the mater seem inordinately fond of him—sorry for him, perhaps; or maybe he's the kind of serious, sensitive guy they wish I'd turned out to be. I don't dislike Woode, but we have damned little in common except the horses. Only, he takes his betting too seriously to suit me—he hasn't much money, and his wins or losses mean a lot to him. Of course, he'll go broke in the end. But I doubt if it'll make much difference to him. My loving parents—one of 'em, at least—will stroke his brow with one hand and stuff his pockets with the other. If I went broke as a result of this horse-racing vice they'd tell *me* to get the hell out and go to work."

He laughed good-naturedly, but with an undertone of bitterness.

"But what the hell!" he added, snapping his fingers. "Let's scoop one down the hatch before we victual."

He pushed a button near the archway to the drawing room, and a very correct, corpulent butler came in with a large silver tray laden with bottles and glasses and ice.

Vance had been watching Garden covertly during this rambling recital of domestic intimacies. He was, I could see, both puzzled and displeased with the confidences: they were too obviously in bad taste. When the drinks had been poured, Vance turned to him coolly.

"I say, Garden," he asked casually, "why all the family gossip? Really, y' know, it isn't being done."

"My social blunder, old man," Garden apologized readily. "But I wanted you to understand the situation, so you'd feel at ease. I know you hate mysteries, and there's apt to be some funny things happening here this afternoon. If you're familiar with the set-up beforehand, they won't bother you so much."

"Thanks awfully and all that," Vance murmured. "Perhaps I see your point."

"Woode has been acting queer for the past couple of weeks," Garden continued, "as if some secret sorrow was gnawing at his mind. He seems more bloodless than ever. He suddenly goes sulky and distracted for no apparent reason. I mean to say, he acts moonstruck. Maybe he's in love. But he's a secretive duffer. No one'll ever know, not even the object of his affections."

"Any specific psychopathic symptoms?" Vance asked lightly.

"No-o." Garden pursed his lips and frowned thoughtfully. "But he's developed a curious habit of going upstairs to the roof-garden as soon as he's placed a large bet, and he remains there alone until the result of the race has come through."

"Nothing very unusual about that." Vance made a deprecatory motion with his hand. "Many gamblers, d' ye see, are like that. The emotional element, don't y' know. Can't bear to be on view when the result comes in. Afraid of spillin' over. Prefer to pull themselves together before facing the multitude. Mere sensitiveness. Oh, quite. Especially if the result of the wager means much to them... No...no. I wouldn't say that your cousin's retiring to the roof at such tense moments is remarkable, after what you've volunteered about him. Quite logical, in fact."

"You're probably right," Garden admitted reluctantly. "But I wish he'd bet moderately, instead of plunging like a damned fool whenever he's hot for a horse."

"By the by," asked Vance, "why do you particularly look for strange occurrences this afternoon?"

Garden shrugged.

"The fact is," he replied, after a short pause, "Woody's been losing heavily of late, and today's the day of the big Rivermont

Handicap. I have a feeling he's going to put every dollar he's got on Equanimity, who'll undoubtedly be the favorite... Equanimity!" He snorted with undisguised contempt. "That rail-lugger! Probably the second greatest horse of modern times—but what's the use? When he does come in he's apt to be disqualified. He's got wood on his mind—in love with fences. Put a fence across the track a mile ahead, with no rails to right or left, and he'd very likely do the distance in 1:30 flat, making Jamestown, Roamer and Wise Ways look like cripples.* He had to cede the win to Vanderveer in the Youthful Stakes. He cut in toward the rail on Persian Bard at Bellaire; and he was disqualified for the same thing in Colorado, handing the race over to Grand Score. In the Urban he tried the same rail-diving, with the result that Roving Flirt won by a nose... How's anyone to know about him? And there's always the chance he'll lose, rail or no rail. He's not a young horse any more, and he's already lost eighteen races to date. He's up against some tough babies today—some of the greatest routers from this country and abroad. I'd say he was a pretty bad bet; and yet I know that nut cousin of mine is going to smear him on the nose with everything he owns."

He looked up solemnly.

"And that, Vance, means trouble if Equanimity doesn't come in. It means a blow-up of some kind. I've felt it coming for over a week. It's got me worried. To tell you the truth, I'm glad you picked this day to sit in with us."

Vance, who had been listening intently and watching Garden closely as he talked, moved to the front window where he stood smoking meditatively and gazing out over Riverside Park twenty stories below, at the sun-sprayed water of the Hudson River.

"Very interestin' situation," he commented at length. "I agree in the main with what you say regarding Equanimity.

---

*   *These three horses were the first to better, by fractions of a second, Jack High's 1:35 record for the mile at Belmont.*

But I think you're too harsh, and I'm not convinced that he's a rail-lugger because of any innate passion for wood. Equanimity always had shelly feet and a quarter crack or two, and as a result often lost his plates. And, in addition, he had a bad off fore-ankle, which, when it began to sting at the close of a gruelling race, caused him to bear in toward the rail. But he's a great horse. He could do whatever was asked of him at any distance on any kind of track. As a two-year-old he was the leading money-winner of his age; as a three-year-old he already had foot trouble and was started only three times; but as a four-year-old he came back with a new foot and won ten important races. The remarkable thing about Equanimity is that he could either go right to the front and take it on the Bill Daly, or come from behind and win in the stretch. In the Futurity, when he was left at the post and entered the stretch in last place, he dropped two of his plates and, in spite of this, ran over Grand Score and Sublimate to win going away. It was a bad foot that kept him from being the world's outstanding champion."

"Well, what of it?" retorted Garden dogmatically. "Excuses are easy to find, and if, as you say, he has a bad foot, that's all the more reason for not playing him today."

"Oh, quite," agreed Vance. "I myself wouldn't wager a farthing on him in this big Handicap. I spent some time porin' over the charts last night after I phoned you, and I decided to stay off Equanimity in today's feature. My method of fixing the ratings is no doubt as balmy as any other system, but I couldn't manipulate the ratios in his favor..."

"What horse do you like there?" Garden asked with interest.

"Azure Star."

"Azure Star!" Garden was as contemptuous as he was astonished. "Why, he's almost an outsider. He'll be twelve or fifteen to one. There's hardly a selector in the country who's given him a play. An ex-steeplechaser from the bogs of Ireland! His legs are too weak from jumping to stand the pace today. And at a mile and a quarter! He can't do it! Personally, I'd rather put my money on Risky Lad. There's a horse with great possibilities."

"Risky Lad checks up as unreliable," said Vance. "Azure Star beat him badly at Santa Anita this year. Risky Lad entered the stretch in the lead and then tired to finish fifth. And he certainly didn't run a good mile race at the same track when he finished fifth again in a field of seven. If I remember correctly, he weakened in last year's Classic and was out of the money. His stamina is too uncertain, I should say..." Vance sighed and smiled. "Ah, well, *chacun à son cheval*... But as you were sayin', the psychological situation hereabouts has you worried. I gather there's a super-charged atmosphere round this charmin' aerie."

"That's it, exactly," Garden answered almost eagerly. "Super-charged is right. Nearly every day the mater asks, 'How's Woody?' And when the old gentleman comes home from his lab at night he greets me with a left-handed 'Well, my boy, have you seen Woody today?'... But *I* could die of the hoof-and-mouth disease without stirring up such solicitude in my immediate ancestors."

Vance made no comment on these remarks. Instead he asked in a peculiarly flat voice: "Do you consider this recent hypertension in the household due entirely to your cousin's financial predicament and his determination to risk all he has on the horses?"

Garden started slightly and then settled back in his chair. After he had taken another drink he cleared his throat.

"No, damn it!" he answered a little vehemently. "And that's another thing that bothers me. A lot of the golliwogs we're harboring are due to Woode's cuckoo state of mind; but there are other queer invisible animals springing up and down the corridors. I can't figure it out. The mater's illness doesn't make sense either, and Doc Siefert acts like a pompous old Buddha whenever I broach the subject. Between you and me, I don't think he knows what to make of it himself. And there's funny business of some kind going on among the gang that drifts in here nearly every afternoon to play the races. They're all right, of course—belong to 'our set,' as the phrase goes, and spring from eminently respectable, if a trifle speedy, environments..."

At this moment we heard the sound of light footsteps coming up the hall, and in the archway, which constituted the entrance from the hall into the drawing room, appeared a slight, pallid young man of perhaps thirty, his head drawn into his slightly hunched shoulders, and a melancholy, resentful look on his sensitive, sallow face. Thick-lensed *pince-nez* glasses emphasized the impression he gave of physical weakness.

Garden waved his hand cheerily to the newcomer.

"Greetings, Woody. Just in time for a spot before lunch. You know Vance, the eminent sleuth; and this is Mr. Van Dine, his patient and retiring chronicler."

Woode Swift acknowledged our presence in a strained but pleasant manner, and listlessly shook hands with his cousin. Then he picked up the bottle of Bourbon and poured himself a double portion, which he drank at one gulp.

"Good Heavens!" Garden exclaimed good-humoredly. "How you have changed, Woody!... Who's the lady now?"

The muscles of Swift's face twitched, as if he felt a sudden pain.

"Oh, pipe down, Floyd," he pleaded irritably.

Garden shrugged indifferently. "Sorry. What's worrying you today besides Equanimity?"

"That's enough worry for one day." Swift managed a sheepish grin; then he added aggressively: "I can't possibly lose." And he poured himself another drink. "How's Aunt Martha?"

Garden narrowed his eyes.

"She's pretty fair. Nervous as the devil this morning, and smoking one cigarette after another. But she's sitting up. She'll probably be in later to take a crack or two at the prancing steeds..."

At this point Lowe Hammle arrived. He was a heavy-set short man of fifty or thereabouts, with a round ruddy face and closely cropped gray hair. He was wearing a black-and-white checked suit, a gray shirt, a brilliant green four-in-hand, a chocolate-colored waistcoat with leather buttons, and tan blucher shoes the soles of which were inordinately thick.

"The Marster of 'Ounds, b' Gad!" Garden greeted him jovially. "Here's your Scotch-and-soda; and here also are Mr. Philo Vance and Mr. Van Dine."

"Delighted—delighted!" Hammle exclaimed heartily, coming forward. He extended his hands effusively to Vance. "Been a long time since I saw you, sir... Let me see... Ah, yes. Broadbank. You hunted with me that morning. Nasty spill you got. Warned you in advance that horse couldn't take the fences. But you were in at the kill—yes, by George! Recollect?"

"Oh, quite. Jolly affair. A good fox. Never fancied your bolting him from that drain into the jaws of the pack after the sport he showed."* Vance's manner was icy—obviously he did not like the man—and he turned immediately to Swift and began chatting amiably about the day's big race. Hammle busied himself with his Scotch-and-soda.

In a few minutes the butler announced lunch. The meal was heavy and tasteless, and the wine of dubious vintage— Vance had been quite right in his prognostication.

The conversation was almost entirely devoted to horses, the history of racing, the Grand National, and the possibilities of the various entrants in the afternoon's Rivermont Handicap. Garden was dogmatic in stating his opinions but eminently pleasant and informative: he had made a careful study of modern racing and had an amazing memory.

Hammle was voluble and suave, and harked back to the former glories of racing and to famous dead heats—Attila and Acrobat in the Travers, Springbok and Preakness in the Saratoga Cup, St. Gatien and Harvester in the English Derby, Pardee and Joe Cotton at Sheepshead Bay, Kingston and Yum-Yum

---

* *In America, where earths are not stopped, not more than one fox in twenty is actually killed in the open, and it is very unpopular—and by many considered unsportsmanlike—to force a fox out of a place in which he has taken refuge, in order to kill him. But this practice is regularly resorted to in England, for various reasons; and occasionally an American Master will ape the English to this extent in order to boast that he had killed his fox and not merely accounted for him.*

at Gravesend, Los Angeles and White in the Latonia Derby,*
Domino and Dobbins at Sheepshead Bay, Domino again and
Henry of Navarre at Gravesend, Arbuckle and George Kessler in
the Hudson Stakes, Sysonby and Race King in the Metropolitan
Handicap, Macaw and Nedana at Aqueduct, and Morshion
and Mate, also at Aqueduct. He spoke of the great upsets on
the track, both here and abroad—of that early winning of the
Epsom Derby by an unnamed outsider known as the "Fidget
colt"; of the lone success of Amato over Grey Momus, forty-one
years later; of the lucky win of Aboyeur in 1913, when Craganour
was disqualified; and of the recent win of April the Fifth. He
discussed the Kentucky Derby—the unlooked-for success of
Day Star as a result of the poor ride given Himyar, and the
tragic failure to win of Proctor Knott. And he talked of the great
strategy of "Snapper" Garrison in bringing Boundless home in
the World's Fair Derby of 1893; of the two lucky races of Plucky
Play when he won over Equipoise in the Arlington Handicap and
over Faireno in the Hawthorne Gold Cup. He mentioned the
fateful ride that Coltiletti gave Sun Beau at Agua Caliente, losing
the race to Mike Hall. He had a fund of historic information and,
despite his prejudices, knew his subject well.

Swift, nervous and somewhat peevish, had little to say,
and though he assumed an outward attitude of attention, I got
the impression that other and more urgent matters were occu-
pying his mind. He ate little and drank too much wine.

Vance contented himself mainly with listening and studying
the others at the table. When he spoke at all, it was to mention
with regret some of the great horses that had recently been
destroyed because of accidents—Black Gold, Springsteel, Chase
Me, Dark Secret and others. He spoke of the tragic and unexpected death of Victorian after his courageous recovery, and the
accidental poisoning of the great Australian horse, Phar Lap.

---

*   *"Lucky" Baldwin, the owner of Los Angeles, insisted upon a run-off
(which was the privilege of the owners of dead-heat winners up to
1932), and Los Angeles won.*

We were nearing the end of the luncheon when a tall, well-built and apparently vigorous woman, who looked no more than forty (though I later learned that she was well past fifty), entered the room. She wore a tailored suit, a silver-fox scarf and a black felt toque.

"Why, mater!" exclaimed Garden. "I thought you were an invalid. Why this spurt of health and energy?"

He then presented me to his mother: both Vance and Hammle had met her on previous occasions.

"I'm tired of being kept in bed," she told her son querulously, after nodding graciously to the others. "Now you boys sit right down—I'm going shopping, and just dropped in to see if everything was going all right… I think I'll have a *crème de menthe frappé* while I'm here."

The butler drew up a chair for her beside Swift, and went to the pantry.

Mrs. Garden put her hand lightly on her nephew's arm.

"How goes it with you, Woody?" she asked in a spirit of *camaraderie*. Without waiting for his answer, she turned to Garden again. "Floyd, I want you to place a bet for me on the big race today, in case I'm not back in time."

"Name your poison," smiled Garden.

"I'm playing Grand Score to win and place—the usual hundred."

"Right-o, mater." Garden glanced sardonically at his cousin. "Less intelligent bets have been made in these diggins full many a time and oft… Sure you don't want Equanimity, mater?"

"Odds are too unfavorable," returned Mrs. Garden, with a canny smile.

"He's quoted in the over-night line at five to two."

"He won't stay there." There was authority and assurance in the woman's tone and manner. "And I'll get eight or ten to one on Grand Score. He was one of the greatest in his younger days, and the old spark may still be there—if he doesn't go lame, as he did last month."

"Right you are," grinned Garden. "You're on the dog for a century win and place."

The butler brought the *crème de menthe*, and Mrs. Garden sipped it and stood up.

"And now I'm going," she announced pleasantly. She patted her nephew on the shoulder. "Take care of yourself, Woody... Good afternoon, gentlemen." And she went from the room with a firm, masculine stride.

After a soggy *Baba au Rhum*, Garden led the way back to the drawing room and the butler followed for further instructions.

"Sneed," Garden ordered, "fix the set-up as usual."

I glanced at the electric clock on the mantel: it was exactly ten minutes after one.

CHAPTER THREE

The Rivermont Races
(Saturday, April 14; 1:10 p. m.)

"FIXING THE SET-UP" was a comparatively simple procedure, but a more or less mysterious operation for anyone unfamiliar with the purpose it was to serve. From a small closet in the hall Sneed first wheeled out a sturdy wooden stand about two feet square. On this he placed a telephone connected to a loud-speaker which resembled a midget radio set. As I learned later, it was a specially constructed amplifier to enable everyone in the room to hear distinctly whatever came over the telephone.

On one side of the amplifier was attached a black metal switch box with a two-way key. In its upright position this key would cut off the voice at the other end of the line without interfering with the connection; and throwing the key forward would bring the voice on again.

"I used to have earphones for the gang," Garden told us, as Sneed rolled the stand back against the wall beside the archway and plugged the extension wires into jacks set in the baseboard.

The butler then brought in a well-built folding card table and opened it beside the stand. On this table he placed another telephone of the conventional French, or hand, type. This telephone, which was gray, was plugged into an additional jack in the baseboard. The gray telephone was not connected with the one equipped with the amplifier, but was on an independent line.

When the two instruments and the amplifier had been stationed and tested, Sneed brought in four more card tables and placed them about the drawing room. At each table he opened up two folding chairs. Then, from a small drawer in the stand, he took out a long manila envelope which had evidently come through the mail, and, slitting the top, drew forth a number of large printed sheets approximately nine by sixteen inches. There were fifteen of these sheets—called "cards" in racing parlance—and after sorting them he spread out three on each of the card tables. Two neatly sharpened pencils, a well-stocked cigarette box, matches and ashtrays completed the equipment on each table. On the table holding the gray telephone was one additional item—a small, much-thumbed ledger.

The final, but by no means least important, duty of Sneed in "fixing the set-up" was to open the doors of a broad, low cabinet in one corner of the room, revealing a miniature bar inside.

A word about the "cards": These concentrated racing sheets were practically duplicates of the programs one gets at a race track, with the exception that, instead of having each race on a separate page, all the races at one track were printed, one after the other, across a single sheet. There were only three tracks open that month, and the cards on each table were the equivalent of the three corresponding programs. Each of the printed columns covered one race, giving the post position of the horses,* the name of each entry and the weights carried.

---

*   On the "cards" for New York State, however, the numbers do not correspond to the post positions, as here these positions are drawn shortly before the races begin, except in stake races.

At the top of each column were the number and distance of the race, and at the bottom were ruled spaces for the pari-mutuel prices. At the left of each column was a space for the odds; and between the names of the horses there was sufficient room to write in the jockeys' names when that information was received. (On the day in question, race number Four was that memorable Rivermont Handicap which was to prove the vital primary factor in the terrible tragedy that took place in Professor Garden's home that afternoon.)

When Sneed had arranged everything he started from the room, but hesitated significantly in the archway. Garden grinned broadly and, sitting down at the table with the gray telephone, opened the small ledger before him and picked up a pencil.

"All right, Sneed," he said, "on what horse do you want to lose your easily earned money today?"

Sneed coughed discreetly.

"If you don't mind, sir, I'd like to risk five dollars on Roving Flirt to show."

Garden made a notation in the ledger.

"All right, Sneed; you're on Roving Flirt for a V at third."

With an apologetic "Thank you, sir," the butler disappeared into the dining room. When he had gone Garden glanced at the clock and reached for the black telephone connected with the amplifier.

"The first race today," he said, "is at two-thirty, and I'd better hop to it and get the line-up. Lex* will be coming on in a few minutes; and the boys and girls will want to be knowing everything and a little bit more when they arrive with their usual high hopes and misgivings."

He lifted the receiver from the hook of the telephone and dialed a number. After a pause he spoke into the transmitter:

"Hello, Lex. B-2-9-8. Waiting for the dope." And, laying the receiver down on the stand, he threw the switch key forward.

---

*   *Alexis Flint was the service announcer at the central news station.*

A clear-cut, staccato voice came through the amplifier: "*O. K., B-2-9-8.*" Then there was a click, followed by several minutes of silence. Finally the same voice began speaking: "*Everybody get ready. The exact time now is one-thirty and a quarter.—Three tracks today. The order will be Rivermont, Texas, and Cold Springs. Just as you have them on the cards. Here we go. Rivermont: weather clear and track fast. Clear and fast. First post, 2:30. And now down the line. First race: 20, Barbour; 4, Gates; 5, Lyons; 3, Shea; scratch twice; 3, Denham; 20, Z. Smythe—that's S-m-y-t-h-e; 10, Gilly; 10, Deel; 15, Carr.—And the Second race: 4, Elkind; 20, Barbour; 4, Carr; 20, Hunter; 10, Shea; scratch number 6; 20, Gedney, and make the weight 116; scratch number 8; 3 to 5, Lyon; 4, Martinson.—And the Third race: The top one is 10, with Huron; scratch twice; 20, Denham; 20, J. Briggs—that's Johnny Briggs; 20, Hunter; 4, Gedney; even money, Deel; 20, Landseer. And now race number Four. The Rivermont Handicap. The top one is 8, with Shelton; 15, Denham; 10, Redman; 6, Baroco; 20, Gates; 20, Hunter; 6, Cressy; 5, Barbour; 12, J. Briggs—that's Johnny Briggs; 5, Elkind; 4, Martinson; scratch number 12; 20, Gilly; 2-1/2, Birken.—And the Fifth: 6, Littman; 12, Huron...*"

The incisive voice continued with the odds and jockeys and scratches on the two remaining races at Rivermont Park. As the announcements came over, Garden attentively and rapidly filled in the data on his card. When the last entrant of the closing race at Rivermont Park had been reached there was a slight pause. Then the announcements continued:

"*Now everybody go to Texas. At Texas, weather cloudy and track slow. Cloudy and slow. In the First: 4, Burden; 10, Lansing—*"

Garden leaned over and threw the amplifier switch up, and there was silence in the room.

"Who cares about Texas?" he remarked negligently, rising from his chair and stretching. "No one around here plays those goats anyway. I'll pick up the Cold Springs dope later. If I don't,

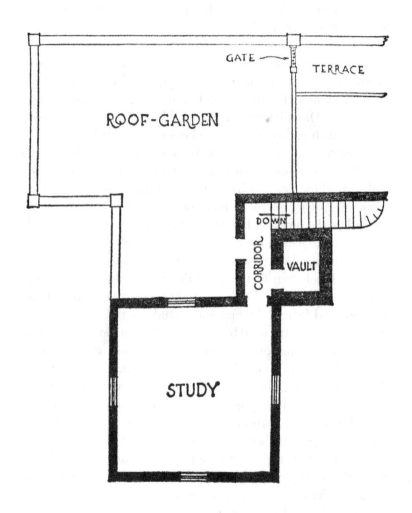

someone's sure to ask for it, just to be contrary." He turned to his cousin. "Why don't you take Vance and Mr. Van Dine upstairs and show them around the garden?... They might," he added with good-natured sarcasm, "be interested in your lonely retreat on the roof, where you listen in to your fate. Sneed has probably got it arranged for you."

Swift rose with alacrity.

"Damned glad of the chance," he returned surlily. "Your manner today rather annoys me, Floyd." And he led the way down the hall and up the stairs to the roof-garden, Vance and I following. Hammle, who had settled himself in an easy chair with a Scotch-and-soda, remained below with our host.

The stairway was narrow and semicircular, and led upward from the hallway near the front entrance. In glancing back up the hall, toward the drawing room, I noticed that no section of that room was visible from the stair end of the hall. I made this mental note idly at the time, but I mention it here because the fact played a very definite part in the tragic events which were to follow.

At the head of this narrow stairway we turned left into a corridor, barely four feet wide, at the end of which was a door leading into a large room—the only room on the roof. This spacious and beautifully appointed study, with high windows on all four sides, was used by Professor Garden, Swift informed us, as a library and private experimental laboratory. Near the door to this room, on the left wall of the corridor, was another door, of kalamein, which, I learned later, led into a small store-room built to hold the professor's valuable papers and data.

Halfway down the corridor, on the right, was another large kalamein weather door which led out to the roof. This door had been propped open, for the sun was bright and the day mild. Swift preceded us into one of the loveliest skyscraper gardens I have ever seen. It covered a space about forty feet square and was directly over the drawing room, the den and the reception hall. In the center was a beautiful rock pool. Along the low brick balustrade were rows of thick privet and evergreens. In front of these were boxed flowerbeds, in which

the crocuses, tulips and hyacinths were already blooming in
a riot of color. That part of the garden nearest the study was
overhung by a gay stationary awning, and various pieces of
comfortable garden furniture were arranged in its shade.

We walked leisurely about the garden, smoking. Vance
seemed deeply interested in two or three rare evergreens,
and chatted casually about them. At length he turned, strolled
back toward the awning, and sat down in a chair facing the
river. Swift and I joined him. The conversation was desultory:
Swift was a difficult man to talk to, and as the minutes went
by he became more and more *distrait*. After a while he got up
nervously and walked to the other end of the garden. Resting
his elbows on the balustrade, he looked for several minutes
down into Riverside Park; then, with a sudden jerky movement,
almost as if he had been struck, he straightened up and came
back to us. He glanced apprehensively at his wristwatch.

"We'd better be going down," he said. "They'll be coming
out for the first race before long."

Vance gave him an appraising look and rose.

"What about that *sanctum sanctorum* of yours which your
cousin mentioned?" he asked lightly.

"Oh, that…" Swift forced an embarrassed smile. "It's that
red chair over there against the wall, next to the small table…
But I don't see why Floyd should spoof about it. The crowd
downstairs always rags me when I lose, and it irritates me. I'd
much rather be alone when I get the results."

"Quite understandable," nodded Vance with sympathy.

"You see," the man went on rather pathetically, "I frankly play
the ponies for the money—the others downstairs can afford to take
heavy losses, but I happen to need the cash just now. Of course, I
know it's a hell of a way to try to make money. But you either make
it in a hurry or lose it in a hurry. So what's the difference?"

Vance had stepped over to the little table on which stood
a desk telephone which had, instead of the ordinary receiver,
what is known as a head receiver—that is, a flat disk earphone
attached to a curved metal band to go over the head.

"Your retreat is well equipped," commented Vance.

"Oh, yes. This is an extension of the news-service phone downstairs; and there's also a plug-in for a radio, and another for an electric plate. And floodlights." He pointed them out to us on the study wall. "All the comforts of a hotel," he added with a sneer.

He took the earphone from the hook and, adjusting the band over his head, listened for a moment.

"Nothing new yet at Rivermont," he mumbled. He removed the earphone with nervous impatience and tossed it to the table. "Anyway we'd better get down." And he walked toward the door by which we had come out in the garden.

When we reached the drawing room we found two newcomers—a man and a woman—seated at one of the tables, poring over the racing cards and making notations. Vance and I were casually introduced to them by Garden.

The man was Cecil Kroon, about thirty-five, immaculately attired and sleek, with smooth, regular features and a very narrow waxed mustache. He was quite blond, and his eyes were a cold steely blue. The woman, whose name was Madge Weatherby, was about the same age as Kroon, tall and slender, and with a marked tendency toward theatricalism in both her attire and her makeup. Her cheeks were heavily rouged and her lips crimson. Her eyelids were shaded with green, and her eyebrows had been plucked and replaced with fine penciled lines. In a spectacular way she was not unattractive.

Hammle had moved from his easy chair to one of the card tables at the end of the room nearest the entrance, and was engaged in checking over the afternoon's entries.

Swift went to the same table and, nodding to Hammle, sat down opposite him. He removed his glasses, wiped them carefully, reached for one of the cards, and glanced over the races.

Garden looked up and motioned to us—he was holding the receiver of the black telephone to his ear.

"Choose a table, Vance, and see how accurate, or otherwise, your method of handicapping is. They'll be coming to the post for the first race in about ten minutes, and we'll be getting a new line shortly."

Vance strolled over to the table nearest Garden's, and seating himself, drew from his pocket a sheet of notepaper on which were written rows of names and figures and computations—the results of his labors, the night before, with the past performance charts of the horses in that day's races. He adjusted his monocle, lighted a fresh cigarette, and appeared to busy himself with the Rivermont race card. But I could see that he was covertly studying the occupants of the room more intently than he was the racing data.

"It won't be long now," Garden announced, the receiver still at his ear. "Lex is repeating the Cold Springs and Texas lines for some subscribers who were late calling in."

Kroon went to the small bar and mixed two drinks which he took back to his table, setting one down before Miss Weatherby.

"I say, Floyd," he called out to Garden; "Zalia coming today?"

"Absolutely," Garden told him. "She was all stirred up when she phoned this morning. Full of sure things. Bulging with red-hot tips direct from trainers and jockeys and stable-boys and all the other phony sources of misinformation."

"Well, what about it?" came a vivacious feminine voice from down the hall; and the next moment a swaggering, pretty girl was standing in the archway, her hands on her muscular boyish hips. "I've concluded I can't pick any winners myself, so why not let the other guy pick 'em for me?... Hello, everybody," she threw in parenthetically. "But Floyd, old thing, I really have a humdinger in the First at Rivermont today. This tip didn't come from a stable-boy, either. It came from one of the stewards—a friend of dad's. And am I going to smear that hay-burner!"

"Right-o, Baby-face," grinned Garden. "Step into our parlor."

She started forward, and hesitated momentarily as she caught sight of Vance and me.

"Oh, by the way, Zalia,"—Garden put the receiver down and rose—"let me present Mr. Vance and Mr. Van Dine... Miss Graem."

The girl staggered back dramatically and lifted her hands to her head in mock panic.

"Oh, Heaven protect me!" she exclaimed. "Philo Vance, the detective! Is this a raid?"

Vance bowed graciously.

"Have no fear, Miss Graem," he smiled. "I'm merely a fellow criminal. And, as you see, I'm dragging Mr. Van Dine along the downward path with me."

The girl flashed me a whimsical glance.

"But that isn't fair to Mr. Van Dine. Where would you be without him, Mr. Vance?"

"I admit I'd be unknown and unsung," returned Vance. "But I'd be a happier man—an obscure, but free, spirit. And I'd never have unconsciously provided the inspiration for Ogden Nash's poetic masterpiece."*

Zalia Graem smiled broadly, and then pouted.

"It was horrid of Nash to write that jingle," she said. "Personally, I think you're adorable." She went toward the unoccupied card table. "But after all, Mr. Vance," she threw back over her shoulder, "you *are* terribly stingy with your g's."

At this moment Garden, who was again listening through the receiver, announced:

"The new line's coming. Take it down if you want it."

He pressed forward the key on the switch box, and in a moment the voice we had heard earlier was again coming through the amplifier.

"*Coming out at Rivermont, and here's the new line: 20, 6, 4, 8 to 5, scratch twice, 3, 20, 15, 10, 15... Who was it wanted the run-down at Texas—?*"

Garden cut out the amplifier.

"All right, boys and girls," he sang out, drawing the ledger to him. "What's on your mind? Be speedy. Only two minutes to post time. Any customers?... How about your hot tip, Zalia?"

---

* Vance was referring to Nash's famous couplet: "Philo Vance Needs a kick in the pance."

"Oh, I'm playing it, all right," Miss Graem answered seriously. "And he's ten to one. I want fifty on Topspede to win—and...seventy-five on him to show."

Garden wrote rapidly in the ledger.

"So you don't quite trust your hot tip?" he gloated. "Covering, as it were... Who else?"

"I'm playing Sara Bellum," Hammle spoke up. "Twenty-five across the board."

"And I want Moondash—twenty on Moondash, to show." This bet came from Miss Weatherby.

"Any others?" asked Garden. "It's now or never."

"Give me Miss Construe—fifty to win," said Kroon.

"How about you, Vance?" asked Garden.

"I had Fisticuffs and Black Revel down as about equal choices, so I'll take the one with the better odds—but not to win. Make it a hundred on Black Revel to place."

Garden turned to his cousin. "And you, Woody?"

Swift shook his head. "Not this race."

"Saving it all for Equanimity, eh? Right-o. I'm staying off this race myself."

Garden reached for the gray telephone and dialed a number... "Hello, Hannix.* This is Garden... Feeling fine, thanks... Here's the book for the First at Rivermont:—Topspede, half a hundred—0—seventy-five. Sara Bellum, twenty-five across the board. Moondash, twenty to show. Miss Construe, half a hundred to win. Black Revel a hundred to place... Right."

He hung up the receiver and cut in the amplifier. There was a momentary silence. Then:

"I got 'em at the post at Rivermont. At the post, Rivermont. Topspede is making trouble... They've taken him to the outside... And there they go! Off at Rivermont at 2:32 and a half... At the quarter: it's Topspede, by a length; Sara Bellum, by a head; and Miss Construe... At the half: Sara Bellum, half a length; Black Revel, a length; and Topspede... In the stretch:

---

*   *Hannix was Floyd Garden's book-maker.*

Black Revel, a length; Fisticuffs, a head and gaining; and Sara Bellum… AND the Rivermont winner: Fisticuffs. The winner is Fisticuffs. Black Revel is second. Sara Bellum is third. The numbers are 4, 7, and 3. Winner closed at eight to five. Hold on for the official O.K. and the muts*…"

"Well, well, well!" chortled Garden. "That was a grand race for Hannix as far as this crowd was concerned. They came in like little trained pigs. Even our two winners here didn't nick the old fox for much. Pop Hammle chiseled out a bit of show money, but he has to deduct fifty dollars. And Vance probably picked about even money at place on Black Revel… What about that humdinger of yours, Zalia? Oh, trusting child, will you never learn?…"

"Well, anyway," protested the girl good-naturedly, "wasn't Topspede a length ahead at the quarter? And he was still in the money at the half. I had the right idea."

"Sure," returned Garden. "Topspede made a noble effort, but I suspect he's a blood-brother of Morestone and a boyfriend of Nevada Queen—the world's most eminent folder-uppers.[†] He'd probably go big at three furlongs on the Nursery Course."

"Who cares?" retorted Zalia Graem. "I'm still young and healthy…"

The voice over the amplifier came back:

"O.K. at Rivermont. Official. They got off at 2:32 and a half. Winner: number 4, Fisticuffs; second, number 7, Black Revel; third, number 3, Sara Bellum. The running time, 1:24… And here are the muts: Fisticuffs paid $5.60—$3.10—$2.90. Black Revel paid $3.90 and $3.20. Sara Bellum paid $5.80…

---

* *The pari-mutuel prices.*

† *David Alexander, the entertaining turf chronicler, wrote an item about these two horses recently. "Morestone," said Mr. Alexander, "could run plenty fast—up to six furlongs. But after six furlongs he flagged the horse ambulance. Morestone could quit in track record time. Nothing like it had been seen since they tried to make Nevada Queen go more than a half-mile a few years ago. There were two mysteries about Morestone. One was how he could run so fast, and the other was how he could quit so fast."*

Post time for the second race 3:05. The line: 3; 15, 5, 20, 12, scratch, 15, scratch, 4 to 5, 6... They're coming out at Cold Springs. And here's a new line—"

Garden cut out the amplifier again.

"Well, Vance," he said, "you're the only winner on the first race. You made ninety-five dollars—all entered up in the ledger. And you, Pop, lose two dollars and a half."*

Since no one present was interested in the Texas or Cold Springs meets, there was approximately a half hour between races. During these intervals the members of the party moved from table to table, chatting, discussing horses, and indulging in pleasant, intimate give-and-take; and there was considerable traffic to and from the bar. Occasionally Garden cut in the amplifier to pick up any late scratches, changes of odds, and other flashes from the tracks.

Vance, while apparently mingling casually with the alternately gay and serious groups, was closely watching everything that went on. I could plainly see that he was far less interested in the races than in the human and psychological relationships of those present.

Despite the superficial buoyancy of the gathering, I could detect an undercurrent of extreme tension and expectancy;

---

* *Mutuel prices are figured on the basis of a two-dollar bet made at the track, and already paid in there. Therefore, away from the track, where the money wagered has not actually been passed over, the two dollars is subtracted from the mutuel price and the remainder is then divided by two to ascertain the exact odds which the horse paid on one dollar. In this particular race, Vance's horse paid $3.90 to come in second, or place. Two dollars subtracted from this leaves $1.90, and this amount divided by two gives ninety-five cents—that is, in the position in which Vance played him, Black Revel paid ninety-five cents on the dollar. Hence, Vance, having wagered $100 on the horse to place, won $95. In Hammle's case, the horse paid $5.80 in third place, so that the net odds were $1.90 to the dollar in that position. And, since he bet $25 on the horse to come in third, he won $47.50. But, from this must be deducted the $25 he played on the horse to win, and the $25 he put on the same horse to come in second—both of which bets he lost. This left him minus $2.50.*

and I made mental note of various little occurrences during the first hour or so. I noticed, for instance, that from time to time Zalia Graem joined Cecil Kroon and Madge Weatherby and engaged them in serious low-toned conversation. Once the three strolled out on the narrow balcony which ran along the north side of the drawing room.

Swift was by turns hysterically gay and dejected, and he made frequent trips to the bar. His inconsistent moods impressed me unpleasantly; and several times I noticed Garden watching him with shrewd concern.

One incident connected with Swift puzzled me greatly. I had noticed that he and Zalia Graem had not spoken to each other during the entire time they had been in the drawing room. Once they had brushed against each other near Garden's table, and each, as if instinctively, had drawn resentfully to one side. Garden had cocked his head at them irritably and said:

"Aren't you two on speaking terms yet—or is this feud to be permanent?... Why don't you kiss and make up and let the gaiety of the party be unanimous?"

Miss Graem had proceeded as if nothing had happened, and Swift had merely given his cousin a quick, indignant glance. Garden had then smiled sourly, shrugged his shoulders, and turned back to the ledger.

Hammle maintained his complacent, jovial manner throughout the afternoon; but even he seemed ill at ease at times, and his gaze drifted repeatedly to Kroon and Miss Weatherby. Once when Zalia Graem was at their table, he strolled over and boisterously slapped Kroon on the back. Their conversation ceased abruptly, and Hammle filled in the sudden silence with a pointless anecdote about Salvator's race against time at Monmouth Park in 1890.

Garden did not leave his seat at the telephones, and, with the exception of an occasional furtive scrutiny of his cousin, he paid little attention to his guests...

The Second race at Rivermont Park, which went off at eight minutes after three, brought the group better results than the first. Only Kroon lost—he had played the odds-on favorite, Invulnerable, heavily to win; and Invulnerable, though in the lead coming into the stretch, quit badly. However, the next race—which took place a few minutes after half-past three— was a disappointment to everyone. The even-money favorite was bumped at the stretch turn and barely managed to finish third, and an outsider, Ogowan, won the race and paid $86.50. Luckily, no large amount had been placed on the race by any of those present. Swift, incidentally, made no wagers on any of the first three races.

The following race, the Fourth—the post time of which was announced as 4:10—was the Rivermont Handicap; and Garden had no more than cut out the amplifier after the third race, then I felt a curiously subdued and electrified atmosphere in the room.

CHAPTER FOUR

The First Tragedy
(Saturday, April 14; 3:45 p. m.)

"THE GREAT MOMENT approaches!" Garden announced, and though he spoke with sententious gaiety, I could detect signs of strain in his manner. "Hannix's phone is going to be pretty busy during the last ten minutes of this momentous intermission, and I'd advise all of you to get your bets in before the post line comes across. There won't be any material changes, anyway; so speed the hopeful wagers."

There was silence for several moments, and then Swift, looking up from his card, said in a peculiarly flat voice:

"Get the latest run-down, Floyd. We haven't had one since the opening line, and there may be some shifts in the odds or a late scratch."

"Anything you say, dear cousin," Garden acceded in a cynical, yet troubled, tone, as he drew down the switch to cut in the amplifier and picked up the black receiver. He waited for a pause in the announcements from Texas and Cold Springs, and then spoke into the transmitter:

"Hello, Lex. Give me the run-down on the big one at Rivermont."

From the amplifier came the now familiar voice:

"*I just gave the latest line there. Where've YOU been?... All right, here it is, but listen this time—6, 12, 12, 5, 20, 20, 10, 6, 10, 6, 4, scratch, 20, 2. Post, 4:10...*"

Garden cut out the amplifier and looked down at the new row of figures he had hastily scribbled beside the earlier odds.

"Not very different from the morning line," he commented. "Heat Lightning, down two; Train Time, down three; Azure Star, up two; Roving Flirt, down one; Grand Score up from six to ten—what a picnic for the mater if *he* comes in! Risky Lad, up one—and that helps *me*. Head Start, down two; Sarah Dee, up one; and the rest as they were. Except Equanimity." He shot a quick look at his cousin. "Equanimity has gone from two-and-a-half to two, and I doubt if he'll pay even that much. Too many hopeful but misguided enthusiasts shoveling coarse money into the tote*."

Garden got up, mixed himself a highball, and carried it back to the table. Having disposed of it, he turned about in his chair.

"Well, aren't any of the master minds present made up?" He was a little impatient now.

Kroon rose, finished the drink which stood on the table before him, and dabbing his mouth with a neatly folded handkerchief which he took from his breast pocket, he moved toward the archway.

"My mind was made up yesterday." He spoke across the room, as if including everyone. "Put me down in your fateful little book for one hundred on Hyjinx to win and two hundred on the same filly to place. And you can add two hundred on Head Start to show. Making it, all told, half a grand. That's my contribution to the afternoon's festivities."

---

*   *Short for totalizer, an electrical automatic betting device used at mutuel tracks.*

"Head Start's a bad actor at the post," advised Garden, as he entered the bets in the ledger.

"Oh, well," sighed Kroon, "maybe he'll be a smart little boy and beat the barrier today." And he turned into the hall.

"Not deserting us, are you, Cecil?" Garden called after him.

"Frightfully sorry," Kroon answered, looking back. "I'd love to stay for the race, but a legal conference at a maiden aunt's is scheduled for four-thirty, and I've got to be there. Papers to sign, and such rubbish. I'll try to get back, though, if I don't have to read the bally documents." He waved his hand and, with a "Cheerio," continued down the hall.

Madge Weatherby immediately picked up her cards and moved to Zalia Graem's table, where the two women began a low, whispered conversation.

Garden's inquiring glance moved from one to another of the party.

"Is that the only bet I'm to give Hannix?" he asked impatiently. "I'm warning you not to wait too long."

"Put me down for Train Time," Hammle rumbled ponderously. "I've always liked that bay colt. He's a grand stretch runner—but I don't think he'll win today. Therefore, I'm playing him place and show. Make it a hundred each."

"It's in the book," said Garden, nodding to him. "Who's next?"

At this moment a young woman of unusual attractiveness appeared in the archway and stood there hesitantly, looking shyly at Garden. She wore a nurse's uniform of immaculate white, with white shoes and stockings, and a starched white cap set at a grotesque angle on the back of her head. She could not have been over thirty; yet there was a maturity in her calm, brown eyes, and evidence of great capability in the reserve of her expression and in the firm contour of her chin. She wore no makeup, and her chestnut hair was parted in the middle and brushed back simply over her ears. She presented a striking contrast to the two other women in the room.

"Hello, Miss Beeton," Garden greeted her pleasantly. "I

thought you'd be having the afternoon off, since the mater's well enough to go shopping... What can I do for you? Care to join the madhouse and hear the races?"

"Oh, no. I've too many things to do." She moved her head slightly to indicate the rear of the house. "But if you don't mind, Mr. Garden," she added timidly, "I would like to bet two dollars on Azure Star to win, and to come in second, and to come in third."

Everyone smiled covertly, and Garden chuckled.

"For Heaven's sake, Miss Beeton," he chided her, "whatever put Azure Star in your mind?"

"Oh, nothing, really," she answered with a diffident smile. But I was reading about the race in the paper this morning, and I thought that Azure Star was such a beautiful name. It—it appealed to me."

"Well, that's one way of picking 'em." Garden smiled indulgently. "Probably as good as any other. But I think you'd be better off if you forgot the beautiful name. The horse hasn't a chance. And besides, my book-maker doesn't take any bet less than five dollars."

Vance, who had been watching the girl with more interest than he usually showed in a woman, leaned forward.

"I say, Garden, just a moment." He spoke incisively. "I think Miss Beeton's choice is an excellent one—however she may have arrived at it." Then he nodded to the nurse. "Miss Beeton, I'll be very happy to see that your bet on Azure Star is placed." He turned again to Garden. "Will your book-maker take two hundred dollars across the board on Azure Star?"

"Will he? He'll grab it with both hands," Garden replied. "But why—?"

"Then it's settled," said Vance quickly. "That's my bet. And two dollars of it in each position belongs to Miss Beeton."

"That's perfect with me, Vance." And Garden jotted down the wager in his ledger.

I noticed that during the brief moments that Vance was speaking to the nurse and placing his wager on Azure Star, Swift was glowering at him through half-closed eyes. It was not until later that I understood the significance of that look.

The nurse cast a quick glance at Swift, and then spoke with simple directness.

"You are very kind, Mr. Vance." Then she added: "I will not pretend I don't know who you are, even if Mr. Garden had not called you by name." She stood looking straight at Vance with calm appraisal; then she turned and went back down the hall.

"Oh, my dear!" exclaimed Zalia Graem in exaggerated rapture. "The birth of Romance! Two hearts with but a single horse. How positively stunning!"

"Never mind the jealous persiflage," Garden rebuked the girl impatiently. "Choose your horse, and say how much."

"Oh, well, I can be practical, if subpœnaed," the girl returned. "I'm taking Roving Flirt to win... Let's see—say, two hundred. And there goes my new spring suit!... And I might as well lose my sport coat too; so put another two hundred on him to place... And now I think I'll have a bit of liquid sustenance." And she went to the bar.

"How about you, Madge?" Garden asked, turning to Miss Weatherby. "Are you in on this classic?"

"Yes, I'm in on it," the woman answered with affected concern. "I want Sublimate, fifty across."

"Any more customers?" Garden asked, entering the bet. "I myself, if anyone is interested, am pinning my youthful hopes on Risky Lad—one, two, and three hundred." He looked across the room apprehensively to his cousin. "What about you, Woody?"

Swift sat hunched in his chair, studying the card before him and smoking vigorously.

"Give Hannix the bets you've got," he said without raising his head. "Don't worry about me—I won't miss the race. It's only four o'clock."

Garden looked at him a moment and scowled. "Why not get it off your chest now?" As there was no response, he drew the gray telephone toward him and dialed a number. A moment later he was relaying to the book-maker the various bets entered in his ledger.

Swift stood up and walked to the cabinet with its array of bottles. He filled a whiskey glass with Bourbon and drank it down. Then he walked slowly to the table where his cousin sat. Garden had just finished the call to Hannix.

"I'll give you my bet now, Floyd," Swift said hoarsely. He pressed one finger on the table, as if for emphasis. *"I want ten thousand dollars on Equanimity to win."*

Garden's eyes moved anxiously to the other.

"I was afraid of that, Woody," he said in a troubled tone. "But if I were you—"

"I'm not asking you for advice," Swift interrupted in a cold steady voice; "I'm asking you to place a bet."

Garden did not take his eyes from the man's face. He said merely:

"I think you're a damned fool."

"Your opinion of me doesn't interest me either." Swift's eyelids drooped menacingly, and a hard look came into his set face. "All I'm interested in just now is whether you're going to place that bet. If not, say so; and I'll place it myself."

Garden capitulated.

"It's your funeral," he said, and turning his back on his cousin, he took up the gray hand set again and spun the dial with determination.

Swift walked back to the bar and poured himself another generous drink of Bourbon.

"Hello, Hannix," Garden said into the transmitter. "I'm back again, with an additional bet. Hold on to your chair or you'll lose your balance. I want ten grand on Equanimity to win… Yes, that's what I said: ten G-strings—ten thousand iron men. Can you handle it? Odds probably won't be over two to one… Right-o."

He replaced the receiver and tilted back in his chair just as Swift, headed for the hall, was passing him.

"And now, I suppose," Garden remarked, without any indication of raillery, "you're going upstairs so you can be alone when the tidings come through."

"If it won't break your heart—yes." There was a resentful note in Swift's words. "And I'd appreciate it if I was not disturbed." His eyes swept a little threateningly over the others in the room, all of whom were watching him with serious intentness. Slowly he turned and went toward the archway.

Garden, apparently deeply perturbed, kept his eyes on the retreating figure. Then, as if on sudden impulse, he stood up quickly and called out: "Just a minute, Woody. I want to say a word to you." And he stepped after him.

I saw Garden put his arm around Swift's shoulder as the two disappeared down the hall.

Garden was gone from the room for perhaps five minutes, and in his absence very little was said, aside from a few constrained conventional remarks. A tension seemed to have taken possession of everyone present: there was a general feeling that some unexpected tragedy was impending—or, at least, that some momentous human factor was in the balance. We all knew that Swift could not afford his extravagant bet— that, in fact, it probably represented all he had. And we knew, too, or certainly suspected, that a serious issue depended upon the outcome of his wager. There was no gaiety now, none of the former light-hearted atmosphere. The mood of the gathering had suddenly changed to one of sombre misgiving.

When Garden returned to the room his face was a trifle pale, and his eyes were downcast. As he approached our table, he shook his head dejectedly.

"I tried to argue with him," he remarked to Vance. "But it was no use; he wouldn't listen to reason. He turned nasty... Poor devil! If Equanimity doesn't come in he's done for." He looked directly at Vance. "I wonder if I did the right thing in placing that bet for him. But, after all, he's of age."

Vance nodded in agreement.

"Yes, quite," he murmured dryly, "—as you say. Really, y'know, you had no alternative."

Garden took a deep breath and, sitting down at his own

table, picked up the black receiver and held it to his ear.

A bell rang somewhere in the apartment, and a few moments later Sneed appeared in the archway.

"Pardon me, sir," he said to Garden, "but Miss Graem is wanted on the other telephone."

Zalia Graem stood up quickly and raised one hand to her forehead in a gesture of dismay,

"Who on earth or in the waters under the earth can that be?" Her face cleared. "Oh, I know." Then she stepped up to Sneed. "I'll take the call in the den." And she hurried from the room.

Garden had paid little attention to this interruption: he was almost oblivious to everything but his telephone, waiting for the time to switch on the amplifier. A few moments later he turned in his chair and announced:

"They're coming out at Rivermont. Say your prayers, children… Oh, I say, Zalia," he called out in a loud voice, "tell the fascinating gentleman on the phone to call you back later. The big race is about to start."

There was no response, although the den was but a few steps down the hall.

Vance rose and, crossing the room, looked down the hallway, but returned immediately to his table.

"Thought I'd inform the lady," he murmured, "but the den door is closed."

"She'll probably be out—she knows what time it is," commented Garden casually, reaching forward to throw on the amplifier.

"Floyd darling," spoke up Miss Weatherby, "why not get this race on the radio? It's being broadcast by WXZ. Don't you think it'll be more exciting that way? Gil McElroy is announcing it."

"Bully suggestion," seconded Hammle. He turned to the radio, which was just behind him, and tuned in.

"Can Woody still get it upstairs?" Miss Weatherby asked Garden.

"Oh, sure," he answered. "This key on the amplifier

doesn't interfere with any of the extension phones."

As the radio tubes warmed up, McElroy's well-known voice gained in volume over the loudspeaker:

"...and Equanimity is now making trouble at the post. Took the cue from Head Start... Now they're both back in their stalls—it looks as if we might get a—Yes! They're off! And to a good even start. Hyjinx has dashed into the lead; Azure Star comes next; and Heat Lightning is close behind. The others are bunched. I can't tell one from the other yet. Wait a second. Here they come past us—we're up on the roof of the grandstand here, looking right down on them—and it's Hyjinx on top now, by two lengths; and behind her is Train Time; and—yes, it's Sublimate, by a head, or a nose, or a neck—it doesn't matter—it's Sublimate anyway. And there's Risky Lad creeping up on Sublimate... And now they're going round the first turn, with Hyjinx still in the lead. The relative positions of the ones out front haven't changed yet... They're in the backstretch, and Hyjinx is still ahead by half a length; Train Time has moved up and holds his second position by a length and a half ahead of Roving Flirt, who's in third place. Azure Star is a length behind Roving Flirt. Equanimity is pocketed but he's coming around on the outside now; he's far behind but gaining; and just behind him is Grand Score, making a desperate effort to get in the clear..."

At this point in the broadcast Zalia Graem appeared suddenly in the archway and stood with her eyes fixed on the radio, her hands sunk in the pockets of her tailored jacket. She rocked a little back and forth, her head slightly to one side, wholly absorbed in the description of the race.

"...They're rounding the far turn. Equanimity has improved his position and is getting into his famous stride. Hyjinx has dropped back and Roving Flirt has taken the lead by a head, with Train Time second, by a length, in front of Azure Star, who is running third and making a grand effort... And now they're in the stretch. Azure Star has come to the front and is a full length in the lead. Train Time is making a great bid for this classic and is still in second place, a length behind Azure Star. Roving Flirt is *right behind him. Hyjinx has dropped back and it looks as if she was no longer a serious contender. Equanimity is pressing hard and is now in sixth place. He hasn't much time, but he's running a beautiful race and may come up front yet. Grand Score is falling by the wayside. Sublimate is far out in front of both of them but is not gaining. And I guess the rest are out of the running... And here they come to the finish. The leaders are straight out—there won't be much change. Just a second. Here they come... AND...the winner is AZURE STAR by two lengths. Next is Roving Flirt. And a length behind him is Train Time. Upper Shelf finished fourth... Wait a minute. Here come the numbers on the board—Yes, I was right. It's 3, 4, and 2. Azure Star wins the great Rivermont Handicap. Second is Roving Flirt. And third is Train Time..."*

Hammle swung around in his chair and shut off the radio.

"Well," he said, releasing a long-held breath, "I was partly right, at that."

"Not such a hot race," Miss Graem remarked with a toss of her head. "I'll just about break even. Anyway, I won't have to join a nudist colony this spring... Now I'll go and finish my phone call." And she turned back down the hall.

Garden seemed ill at ease and, for the second time that afternoon, mixed himself a highball.

"Equanimity wasn't even in the money," he commented, as if to himself... "But the results aren't official yet. Don't let your hopes rise too high—and don't despair. The winners won't be official for a couple of minutes—and there's no telling what may happen. Remember the final race on the get-away day of the Saratoga meet, when all three placed horses were disqualified?..."*

---

*   *Garden was referring to the last race of the final day of a recent Saratoga season, when Anna V. L., Noble Spirit, and Semaphore finished in that order, and all were disqualified, Anna V. L. for swerving sharply at the start and causing other horses to take up, Noble Spirit for swerving badly at the eighth pole, and Semaphore for alleged interference with Anna V. L. The official placing, after the disqualifications, was Just Cap, first; Celiba, second; and Bahadur,*

Just then Mrs. Garden bustled into the room, her hat, fox scarf, and gloves still on, and two small packages tucked under her arm.

"Don't tell me I'm too late!" she pleaded excitedly. "The traffic was abominable—three-quarters of an hour from 50th Street and Fifth Avenue... Is the big race over?"

"All over but the O.K., mater," Garden informed her.

"And what did I do?" The woman came forward and dropped wearily into an empty chair.

"The usual," grinned Garden. "A Grand Score? Your noble steed didn't score at all. Condolences. But it's not official yet. We'll be getting the O.K. in a minute now."

"Oh, dear!" sighed Mrs. Garden despondently. "The only foul claimed in a race I bet on is against my horse when he wins— and it's always allowed. Nothing can save me now. And I've just spent an outrageous sum on a Brussels lace luncheon set."

Garden cut in the amplifier. There were several moments of silence, and then:

"It's official at Rivermont. O.K. at Rivermont. Off at 4:16. The winner is number 3, Azure Star. Number 4, Roving Flirt, second; and number 2, Train Time, third. That's 3, 4, and 2— Azure Star, Roving Flirt, and Train Time. The running 2:02 and one-fifth—a new track record. And the muts: Azure Star paid $26.80; $9.00 and $6.60. Roving Flirt, $5.20 and $4.60. Train Time, $8.40... Next post at 4:40..."

"Well, there it is," said Garden glumly, throwing back the switch and making rapid notations in his ledger. "Sneed, our admirable Crichton, makes six and a half dollars. The absent Mr. Kroon loses five hundred, and the present Miss Weatherby loses one hundred and fifty. Our old fox hunter is ahead just two hundred and twenty dollars, with part of which he can buy me a good dinner tomorrow. And you, mater, lose your two hundred dollars—very sad. I myself was robbed of six hundred berries. Zalia—who gets her sizzling tips from the

---

third—the only other three horses in the race.

friend of a friend of a distant relative of the morganatic wife of a double-bug rider—is one hundred and twenty dollars to the good—enough to get shoes and a hat and a handbag to match her new spring outfit. And Mr. Vance, the eminent dopester of crimes and ponies, can now take a luxurious vacation. He's the possessor of thirty-six hundred and forty dollars—of which thirty-six dollars and forty cents goes to our dear nurse... And Woody; of course..." His voice trailed off.

"What did Woody do?" demanded Mrs. Garden, sitting up stiffly in her chair.

"I'm frightfully sorry, mater,"—her son groped for words—"but Woody didn't use his head. I tried to dissuade him, but it was no go..."

"Well, what *did* Woody do?" persisted Mrs. Garden. "Did he lose much?"

Garden hesitated, and before he could formulate an answer, a paralyzing sound, like a pistol shot, broke the tense silence.

Vance was the first on his feet. His face was grim as he moved rapidly toward the archway. I followed him, and just behind came Garden. As I turned into the hallway I saw the others in the drawing room get up and move forward. Had the report not been preceded by so electric an atmosphere, I doubt if it would have caused any particular perturbation; but, in the circumstances, everyone, I think, had the same thought in mind when the detonation of the shot was heard.

As we hurried down the hall Zalia Graem opened the den door.

"What was that?" she asked, her frightened eyes staring at us.

"We don't know yet," Vance told her.

In the bedroom door, at the lower end of the hall, stood the nurse, with a look of inquiring concern on her otherwise placid face.

"You'd better come along, Miss Beeton," Vance said, as he started up the stairs two at a time. "You may be needed."

Vance swung into the upper corridor and stopped momentarily at the door on the right, which led out upon the roof. This door was still propped open, and after a hasty preliminary survey through it, he stepped quickly out into the garden.

The sight that met our eyes was not wholly unexpected. There, in the low chair which he had pointed out to us earlier that afternoon, sat Woode Swift, slumped down, with his head thrown back at an unnatural angle against the rattan headrest, and his legs straight out before him. He still wore the earphones. His eyes were open and staring; his lips were slightly parted; and his thick glasses were tilted forward on his nose.

In his right temple was a small ugly hole beneath which two or three drops of already coagulating blood had formed. His right arm hung limp over the side of the chair, and on the colored tiling just under his hand lay a small pearl-handled revolver.

Vance immediately approached the motionless figure, and the rest of us crowded about him. Zalia Graem, who had forced her way forward and was now standing beside Vance, swayed suddenly and caught at his arm. Her face had gone pale, and her eyes appeared glazed. Vance turned quickly and, putting his arm about her, half led and half carried her to a large wicker divan nearby. He made a beckoning motion of his head to Miss Beeton.

"Look after her for a moment," he requested. "And keep her head down." Then he returned to Swift. "Everyone please keep back," he ordered. "No one is to touch him."

He took out his monocle and adjusted it carefully. Then he leaned over the crumpled figure in the chair. He cautiously scrutinized the wound, the top of the head, and the tilted glasses. When this examination was over he knelt down on the tiling and seemed to be searching for something. Apparently he did not find what he sought, for he stood up with a discouraged frown and faced the others.

"Dead," he announced, in an unwontedly sombre tone. "I'm taking charge of things temporarily."

Zalia Graem had risen from the divan, and the nurse was

supporting her with a show of tenderness. The dazed girl was apparently oblivious to this attention and stood with her eyes fixed on the dead man. Vance stepped toward her so that he shut out the sight that seemed to hold her in fascinated horror.

"Please, Miss Beeton," he said, "take the young lady downstairs immediately." Then he added, "I'm sure she'll be all right in a few minutes."

The nurse nodded, put her arm firmly about Miss Graem, and led her into the passageway.

Vance waited until the two young women were gone: then he turned to the others.

"You will all be so good as to go downstairs and remain there until further orders."

"But what are you going to do, Mr. Vance?" asked Mrs. Garden in a frightened tone. She stood rigidly against the wall, with half-closed eyes fixed in morbid fascination on the still body of her nephew. "We must keep this thing as quiet as possible... My poor Woody!"

"I'm afraid, madam, we shall not be able to keep it quiet at all." Vance spoke with earnest significance. "My first duty will be to telephone the District Attorney and the Homicide Bureau."

Mrs. Garden gasped, and her eyes opened wide in apprehension.

"The District Attorney? The Homicide Bureau?" she repeated distractedly. "Oh, no!... Why must you do that? Surely, anyone can see that the poor boy took his own life."

Vance shook his head slowly and looked squarely at the distressed woman.

"I regret, madam," he said, "that this is not a case of suicide... It's murder!"

CHAPTER FIVE

A Search in the Vault
(Saturday, April 14; 4:30 p. m.)

FOLLOWING VANCE'S UNEXPECTED announcement there was a sudden silence. Everyone moved reluctantly toward the door to the passageway. Only Garden remained behind.

"I say, Vance,"—he spoke in a shocked, confidential tone— "this is really frightful. Are you sure you're not letting your imagination run away with you? Who could possibly have wanted to shoot poor Woody? He must have done it himself. He was always a weakling, and he's talked about suicide more than once."

Vance looked at the man coldly for a moment.

"Thanks awfully for the information, Garden." His voice was as cold as his glance. "But it won't get us anywhere now, don't y' know. Swift was murdered; and I want your help, not your skepticism."

"Anything I can do, of course," Garden mumbled hastily, apparently abashed by Vance's manner.

"Is there a telephone up here?" Vance asked.

"Yes, certainly. There's one in the study."

Garden brushed past us with nervous energy, as if glad of the opportunity for action. He threw open the door at the end of the passageway and stood aside for us to enter the study.

"Over there," he said, pointing to the desk at the far end of the room, on which stood a hand telephone. "That's an open line. No connection with the one we use for the ponies, though it's an extension of the phone in the den." He stepped swiftly behind the desk and threw a black key on the switch box that was attached to the side of the desk. "By leaving the key in this position, you are disconnected from the extension downstairs, so that you have complete privacy."

"Oh, quite," Vance nodded with a faint smile. "I use the same system in my own apartment. Thanks awfully for your thoughtfulness... And now please join the others downstairs and try to keep things balanced for a little while—there's a good fellow."

Garden took his dismissal with good grace and went toward the door.

"Oh, by the way, Garden," Vance called after him. "I'll want a little chat with you in private, before long."

Garden turned, a troubled look on his face.

"I suppose you'll be wanting me to rattle all the family skeletons for you? But that's all right. I want to be as useful as I possibly can—you believe that, I hope. I'll come back the minute you want me. I'll be down there pouring oil on the troubled waters, and when you're ready for me you've only to press that buzzer on the bookshelves there, just behind the desk." He indicated a white push-button set flush in the center of a small square japanned box on the upright between two sections of the bookshelves. "That's part of the inter-communicating system between this room and the den. I'll see that the den door is left open so that I can hear the buzzer wherever I am."

Vance nodded curtly, and Garden, after a momentary hesitation, turned and went from the room.

As soon as Garden could be heard making his way down the stairs, Vance closed the door and went immediately to the telephone. A moment later he was speaking to Markham.

"The galloping horses, old dear," he said. "The Trojans are riding roughshod. Equanimity was needed, but came in too far behind. Result, a murder. Young Swift is dead. And it was as clever a performance as I've yet seen... No, Markham"— his voice suddenly became grave—"I'm not spoofing. I think you'd better come immediately. And notify Heath,* if you can reach him, and the Medical Examiner. I'll carry on till you get here..."

He replaced the receiver slowly. Taking out his cigarette case, he lighted a *Régie* with that studied deliberation which, from long observation, I had come to recognize as the indication of a distressed and groping frame of mind.

"This is a subtle crime, Van," he meditated. "Too subtle for my peace of mind. I don't like it—I don't at all like it. And I don't like this intrusion of horse-racing. Sheer expediency..."

He looked about the study appraisingly. It was a room nearly twenty-five feet square, lined with books and pamphlets and filing cabinets. On some of the shelves and in cabinets and atop every available piece of furniture were specimens of a unique collection of ancient pharmacists' paraphernalia— mortars and pestles of rare earthenware, brass, and bronze, chiseled and ornamented with baluster motives, mascarons, lion herms, leafage, cherub heads, Renaissance scrollings, bird figures, and *fleurs de lis*—Gothic, Spanish, French, Flemish, many of them dating back to the sixteenth century; ancient apothecary's scales of brass and ivory, with round columns on plinths, with urn finials, supporting embossed scale pans on straight and bow-shaped, steel arms—many of them of late eighteenth-century French design; numerous early

---

* *Sergeant Edward Heath of the Homicide Bureau, who had had charge of the various criminal investigations with which Vance had been associated.*

pharmacy jars of various shapes, cylindrical, ovoglobular, ring-molded barrel, incurvate octagonal, ovoid, and one inverted pear, in faïence, majolica, and priceless porcelains, exquisitely decorated and lettered; and various other rare and artistic pharmaceutical items—a collection bespeaking years of travel and laborious searching.*

Vance walked round the room, pausing here and there before some unique vase or jar.

"An amazin' collection," he murmured. "And not without significance, Van. It gives one an insight into the nature of the man who assembled it—an artist as well as a scientist—a lover of beauty and also a seeker for truth. Really, y' know, the two should be synonymous. However..."

He went thoughtfully to the north window and looked out on the garden. The rattan chair with its gruesome occupant could not be seen from the study, as it was far to the left of the window, near the west balustrade.

"The crocuses are dying," he murmured, "giving place to the hyacinths and daffodils; and the tulips are well on their way. Color succeeds color. A beautiful garden. But there's death every hour in a garden, Van, or else the garden itself would not live... I wonder..."

He turned from the window abruptly and came back to the desk.

"A few words with the colorless Garden are indicated, before the minions of the law arrive."

He placed his finger on the white button in the buzzer box and depressed it for a second. Then he went to the door and opened it. Several moments went by, but Garden did not appear, and Vance again pressed the button. After a full minute or two had passed without any response to his summons, Vance started down the passageway to the stairs, beckoning me to follow.

---

*　*This collection was later sold at auction, and many of the items are now in the various museums of the country.*

As he came to the vault door on the right, he halted abruptly. He scrutinized the heavy kalamein door for a moment or two. At first glance it seemed to be closed tightly, but as I looked at it more closely, I noticed that it was open a fraction of an inch, as if the spring catch, which locked it automatically, had failed to snap when the door had last been shut. Vance pushed on the door gently with the tips of his fingers, and it swung inward slowly and ponderously.

"Deuced queer," he commented. "A vault for preserving valuable documents—and the door unlocked. I wonder..."

The light from the hall shone into the dark recess of the vault, and as Vance pushed the door further inward a white cord hanging from a ceiling light became visible. To the end of this cord was attached a miniature brass pestle which acted as a weight. Vance stepped immediately inside and jerked the cord, and the vault was flooded with light.

"Vault" hardly describes this small storeroom, except that the walls were unusually thick, and it had obviously been constructed to serve as a burglar-proof repository. The room was about five by seven feet, and the ceiling was as high as that of the hallway. The walls were lined with deep shelves from floor to ceiling, and these were piled with all manner of papers, documents, pamphlets, filing cases, and racks of test tubes and vials labeled with mysterious symbols. Three of the shelves were devoted to a series of sturdy steel cash and security boxes. The floor was overlaid with small squares of black and white ceramic tile.

Although there was ample room for us both inside the vault, I remained in the hallway, watching Vance as he looked about him.

"Egoism, Van," he remarked, without turning toward me. "There probably isn't a thing here that any thief would deign to steal. Formulæ, I imagine—the results of experimental researches—and such abstruse items, of no value or interest to anyone but the professor himself. Yet he builds a special storeroom to keep them locked away from the world..."

Vance leaned over and picked up a batch of scattered typewritten papers which had evidently been brushed down from one of the shelves directly opposite the door. He glanced at them for a moment and carefully replaced them in the empty space on the shelf.

"Rather interestin', this disarray," he observed. "The professor was obviously not the last person in here, or he would certainly not have left his papers on the floor..." He wheeled about. "My word!" he exclaimed in a low tone. "These fallen papers and that unlatched door...it could be, don't y' know." There was a suppressed excitement in his manner. "I say, Van, don't come in here: and, above all, don't touch this doorknob."

He took out his monocle and adjusted it carefully. Then he knelt down on the tiled floor and began a close inspection of the small squares, as if he were counting them. His action reminded me of the way he had inspected the tiling on the roof near the chair in which we had found young Swift. It occurred to me that he was seeking here what he had failed to find in the garden. His next words confirmed my surmise.

"It should be here," he murmured, as if to himself. "It would explain many things—it would form the first vague outline of a workable pattern..."

After searching about for a minute or two, he stopped abruptly and leaned forward eagerly. Then he took a small piece of paper from his pocket and adroitly flicked something onto it from the floor. Folding the paper carefully, he tucked it away in his waistcoat pocket. Although I was only a few feet from him and was looking directly at him, I could not see what it was that he had found.

"I think that will be all for the moment," he said, rising and pulling the cord to extinguish the light. Coming out into the hallway, he closed the vault door by carefully grasping the shank of the knob. Then he moved swiftly down the passageway, stepped through the door to the garden, and went directly to the dead man. Though his back was turned to me as he bent over the figure, I could see that he took the folded paper from his waistcoat pocket and opened it. He glanced repeatedly from the paper in his hand to the limp figure in the chair. At length he nodded his head emphatically, and rejoined me in the hallway. We descended the stairs to the apartment below.

Just as we reached the lower hall, the front door opened and Cecil Kroon entered. He seemed surprised to find us in the hall, and asked somewhat vaguely, as he threw his hat on a bench:

"Anything the matter?"

Vance studied him sharply and made no answer; and Kroon went on:

"I suppose the big race is over, damn it! Who won it—Equanimity?"

Vance shook his head slowly, his eyes fixed on the other.

"Azure Star won the race. I believe Equanimity came in fifth or sixth."

"And did Woody go in on him up to the hilt, as he threatened?"

Vance nodded. "I'm afraid he did."

"Good Gad!" Kroon caught his breath. "That's a blow for the chap. How's he taking it?" He looked away from Vance as if he would rather not hear the answer.

"He's not taking it," Vance returned quietly. "He's dead."

"No!" Kroon sucked in his breath with a whistling sound, and his eyes slowly contracted. When he had apparently recovered from the shock he spoke in a hushed voice: "So he shot himself, did he?"

Vance's eyebrows went up slightly.

"That's the general impression," he returned blandly. "You're not psychic—are you? I didn't mention how Swift died, but the fact is he did die by a revolver shot. Superficially, I admit, it looks like suicide." Vance smiled coldly. "Your reaction is most interestin'. Why, for instance, did you assume that he shot himself, instead of—let us say—jumping off the roof?"

Kroon set his mouth in a straight line, and a look of anger came into his narrowed eyes. He fumbled in his pocket for a cigarette, and finally stammered:

"I don't know—exactly...except that—most people shoot themselves nowadays."

"Oh, quite." Vance's lips were still set in a stern smile. "Not an uncommon way of assisting oneself out of this troublous world. But, really y' know, I didn't mention suicide at all. Why do you take it for granted that his death was self-inflicted?"

Kroon became aggressive. "He was healthy enough when I left here. No one's going to blow a man's brains out in public like this."

"Blow his brains out?" Vance repeated. "How do you know he wasn't shot through the heart?"

Kroon was now obviously flustered.

"I—I merely assumed—"

Vance interrupted the man's embarrassment.

"However," he said, without relaxing his calculating scrutiny, "your academic conclusions regarding a more or less public murder are not without some logic. But the fact remains, someone did actually shoot Swift through the head and practically in public. Things like that do happen, don't y' know. Logic has very little bearing on life and death—and horse-racing. Logic is the most perfect artificial means of arriving at a false conclusion." He held a light to Kroon's cigarette. "However, I could bear to know just where you've been and just when you returned to the apartment house here."

Kroon's gaze wandered, and he took two deep puffs on his cigarette before he answered.

"I believe I remarked before I went out," he said, with an attempt at serenity, "that I was going to a relative's to sign some silly legal documents—"

"And may I have the name and address of your relative— an aunt, I believe you said?" Vance requested pleasantly. "I'm in charge of the situation here until the officials arrive."

Kroon took the cigarette from his mouth with a forced air of nonchalance and drew himself up haughtily.

"I cannot see," he replied stiffly, "that that information concerns anyone but myself."

"Neither can I," admitted Vance cheerfully. "I was merely hopin' for frankness. But I can assure you, in view of what has happened here this afternoon, that the police will want to know exactly when you returned from your mysterious signing of documents."

Kroon smirked. "You surely don't think that I've been lingering outside in the hall, do you? I arrived a few minutes ago and came directly up here."

"Thanks awfully," Vance murmured. "And now I must ask you to join the others in the drawing room, and to wait there until the police arrive. I trust you have no objections."

"None whatever, I assure you," Kroon returned with a display of cynical amusement. "The regular police will be a relief, after this amateur hocus-pocus." He swaggered up the hall toward the archway, with his hands thrust deep in his trousers pockets.

When Kroon had disappeared into the drawing room, Vance went immediately to the front door, opened it quietly and, walking down the narrow public corridor, pressed the elevator button. A few moments later the sliding door opened and a dark, thin, intelligent-looking boy of perhaps twenty-two, in a light-blue uniform, looked out enquiringly.

"Going down?" he said respectfully.

"I'm not going down," Vance replied. "I merely wanted to ask you a question or two. I'm more or less connected with the District Attorney's office."

"I know you, Mr. Vance." The boy nodded alertly.

"A little matter has come up this afternoon," Vance said, "and I think you may be able to help me…"

"I'll tell you anything I know," agreed the boy.

"Excellent! Do you know a Mr. Kroon who visits the Garden apartment?—The gentleman is blond and has a waxed mustache."

"Sure, I know him," the boy returned promptly. "He comes up here nearly every afternoon. I brought him up today."

"About what time was that?"

"Two or three o'clock, I guess." The boy frowned. "Isn't he in there?"

Vance answered the question by asking another.

"Have you been on the car all afternoon?"

"Sure I have—since noon. I don't get relieved till seven o'clock."

"And you haven't seen Mr. Kroon since you brought him up here early this afternoon?"

The boy shook his head. "No, sir; I haven't."

"I was under the impression," said Vance, "that Mr. Kroon went out about an hour ago and just returned."

Again the boy shook his head, and gave Vance a puzzled look.

"No. I only brought him up once today; and that was at least two hours ago. I haven't seen him since, going up or down."

The annunciator buzzed, and Vance quickly handed the boy a folded bill.

"Many thanks," he said. "That's all I wanted to know."

The boy pocketed the money and released the door as we turned back to the apartment.

When we reentered the front hall, the nurse was standing in the doorway of the bedroom at the right of the entrance. There was a worried, inquisitive look in her eyes.

Vance closed the door softly and was about to start up the hall, but he hesitated and turned toward the girl.

"You look troubled, Miss Beeton," he said kindly. "But, after all, you should be accustomed to death."

"I am accustomed to it," she answered in a low voice. "But this is so different. It came so suddenly—without any warning... Although," she added, "Mr. Swift always impressed me as more or less the suicidal type."

Vance looked at the nurse appraisingly. "Your impression may have been correct," he said. "But it happens that Swift did not commit suicide."

The girl's eyes opened wide: she caught her breath and leaned against the casing of the door. Her face paled perceptibly.

"You mean someone shot him?" Her words were barely audible. "But who—who—?"

"We don't know." Vance's voice was matter-of-fact. "But we must find that out... Would you like to help me, Miss Beeton?"

She drew herself up; her features relaxed; and she was once more the unperturbed and efficient nurse.

"I'd be very glad to." There was more than a suggestion of eagerness in her words.

"Then I would like you to stand guard, as it were," he said, with a faint friendly smile. "I want to talk to Mr. Garden, and I don't want anyone to go upstairs. Would you mind taking your post in this chair and notifying me immediately if anyone should attempt to go up?"

"That's so little to ask," the girl replied, as she seated herself in a chair at the foot of the stairs.

Vance thanked her and proceeded to the den. Inside Garden and Zalia Graem were sitting close together on a tapestry davenport and talking in low, confidential tones. An indistinct murmur of voices from beyond the archway indicated that the other members of the group were in the drawing room.

Garden and Miss Graem drew apart quickly as we stepped into the den. Vance ignored their apparent embarrassment and addressed Garden as if he were unaware that he had interrupted a *tête-à-tête*.

"I've called the District Attorney, and he has notified the police. They should be here any minute now. In the meantime, I'd like to see you alone." He turned his head to Miss Graem and added: "I hope you won't mind."

The girl stood up and arched her eyebrows.

"Pray, don't consider me," she replied. "You may be as mysterious as you wish."

Garden rebuked her peevishly.

"Never mind the *hauteur*, Zalia." Then he turned to Vance. "Why didn't you ring the buzzer for me? I would have come up. I purposely stayed here in the den because I thought you might be wanting me."

"I did ring, don't y' know," Vance told him. "Twice, in fact. But as you didn't come up, I came down."

"There was no signal here," Garden assured him. "And I've been right here ever since I came downstairs."

"I can vouch for that," put in Miss Graem.

Vance's eyes rested on her for a moment, and there was the trace of a sardonic smile at the corners of his mouth.

"I'm dashed grateful for the corroboration," he murmured.

"Are you sure you pressed the button?" Garden asked Vance. "It's damned funny. That system hasn't failed in six years. Wait a minute..."

Going to the door he called loudly for Sneed, and the butler came into the room almost immediately.

"Go upstairs to the study, Sneed," Garden ordered, "and push the buzzer button."

"The buzzer is out of order, sir," the butler told him imperturbably. "I've already notified the telephone company and asked them to send a man to fix it."

"When did you know about it?" Garden demanded angrily.

The nurse, who had heard the conversation, left her chair and came to the doorway.

"I discovered this afternoon that the buzzer wasn't working," she explained; "so I told Sneed about it and suggested that he notify the telephone company."

"Oh, I see. Thank you, Miss Beeton." Garden turned back to Vance. "Shall we go upstairs now?"

Miss Graem, who had been looking on with a cynical and somewhat amused expression, started from the room.

"Why go upstairs?" she asked. "I'll fade into the drawing room, and you can talk to your heart's content right here."

Vance studied the girl for a few seconds, and then bowed slightly.

"Thank you," he said. "That will be much better." He stood aside as she strolled leisurely into the hall and closed the door after her.

Vance dropped his cigarette into a small ashtray on the tabouret before the davenport and, moving swiftly to the door, reopened it. From where I stood in the den, I could see that Miss Graem, instead of going toward the drawing room, was walking rapidly in the opposite direction.

"Just a moment, Miss Graem!" Vance's voice was peremptory. "Please wait in the drawing room. No one is to go upstairs just now."

She swung about. "And why not?" Her face was flushed with anger, and her jaw protruded with defiance. "I have a right to go up," she proclaimed spiritedly.

Vance said nothing but shook his head in negation, his eyes holding hers.

She returned his look, but could not resist the power of his scrutiny. Slowly she came back toward him. A sudden change seemed to have come over her. Her eyes dimmed, and tears sprang into them.

"But you don't understand," she protested, in a broken voice. "I'm to blame for this tragedy—it wasn't the race. If it hadn't been for me Woody would be alive now. I—I feel terrible about it. And I wanted to go upstairs—to see him."

Vance put his hand on the girl's shoulder.

"Really," he said softly, "there's nothing to indicate that you're to blame."

Zalia Graem looked up at Vance searchingly.

"Then what Floyd has been trying to tell me is true—that Woody didn't shoot himself?"

"Quite true," said Vance.

The girl drew a deep breath, and her lips trembled. She took a quick impulsive step toward Vance, and resting her head against his arm, burst into tears.

Vance placed his hands on her arms and held her away from him.

"I say, stop this nonsense," he admonished her sternly. "And don't try to be so deuced clever. Run along to the drawing room and have a highball. It'll buck you up no end."

The girl's face suddenly became cynical, and she drew up her shoulders in an exaggerated shrug.

"*Bien*, Monsieur Lecoq," she retorted with a toss of the head. And brushing past him, she swaggered up the hall toward the drawing room.

CHAPTER SIX

An Interrupted Interview
(Saturday, April 14; 4:50 p. m.)

VANCE WATCHED HER disappear. Then he turned and met the half wistful, half indignant gaze of Miss Beeton. He smiled at her a bit grimly and started back into the den. At this moment Mrs. Garden came through the archway with a look of resentful determination, and strode aggressively down the hall.

"Zalia has just told me," she said angrily, "that you forbade her to go upstairs. It's an outrage! But surely *I* may go up. This is my house, remember. You have no right whatever to prevent me from spending these last minutes with my nephew."

Vance turned to confront her. There was a pained look on his face, but his eyes were cold and stern.

"I have every right, madam," he said. "The situation is a most serious one, and if you will not accept that fact, it will be necess'ry for me to assume sufficient authority to compel you to do so."

"This is unbelievable!" the woman remonstrated indignantly.

Garden stepped to the den door.

"For Heaven's sake, mater," he pleaded, "be reasonable. Mr. Vance is quite right. And, anyway, what possible reason could you have for wanting to be with Woody now? We're in for enough scandal as it is. Why involve yourself further?"

The woman looked squarely at her son, and I had a feeling that some telepathic communication passed between them.

"It really doesn't make any particular difference," she conceded with calm resignation. But as she turned her eyes to Vance the look of cynical resentment returned. "Where, sir," she asked, "do you prefer that I remain until your policemen arrive?"

"I don't wish to seem too exacting, madam," Vance returned quietly; "but I would deeply appreciate it if you remained in the drawing room."

The woman raised her eyebrows, shrugged her shoulders, and, turning indifferently, went back up the hall.

"Frightfully sorry, Vance," apologized Garden. "The mater is a dowager. Not accustomed to taking orders. And she resents it. I doubt if she really has the slightest desire to sit by Woody's stiffening body. But she hates to be told what to do and what not to do. She'd probably have spent the day in bed, if Doc Siefert hadn't firmly told her not to get up."

"That's quite all right." Vance spoke indifferently, gazing with perplexed meditation at the tip of his cigarette. Then he came quickly to the den door. "Let's have our little chat—eh, what?" He stood aside for Garden to enter the room; then he followed and closed the door.

Garden sat down wearily at one end of the davenport and took a pipe from a small drawer in the tabouret. He got out his tobacco and slowly packed the pipe, while Vance walked to the window and stood looking out over the city.

"Garden," he began, "there are a few things that I'd like to have cleared up before the District Attorney and the police arrive." He turned about leisurely and sat down at the desk, facing Garden. The latter was having some difficulty getting his pipe lighted. When he had finally succeeded he looked up dejectedly and met Vance's gaze.

"Anything I can do to help," he mumbled, sucking on his pipe.

"A few necess'ry questions, don't y' know," Vance went on. "Hope they won't upset you, and all that. But the fact is, Mr. Markham will probably want me to take a hand in the investigation, since I was a witness to the preamble of this distressin' tragedy."

"I hope he does," Garden returned. "It's a damnable affair, and I'd like to see the axe fall, no matter whom it might behead." His pipe was still giving him trouble. "By the way, Vance," he went on quietly, "how did you happen to come here today? I've asked you so often to join our racing séance—and you pick the one day when the roof blows off the place."

Vance kept his eyes on Garden for a moment.

"The fact is," he said at length, "I got an anonymous telephone message last night, vaguely outlining the situation here and mentioning Equanimity."

Garden jerked himself up to keener attention. His eyes opened wide, and he took the pipe from his mouth.

"The devil you say!" he exclaimed. "That's a queer one. Man or woman?"

"Oh, it was a man," Vance replied casually.

Garden pursed his lips and, after a moment's meditation, said quietly:

"Well, anyway, I'm damned glad you did come... What can I tell you that might be of help? Anything you want, old man."

"First of all, then," asked Vance, "did you recognize the revolver? I saw you looking at it rather apprehensively when we came out on the roof."

Garden frowned, busied himself for a moment with his pipe, and finally answered, as if with sudden resolution:

"Yes! I did recognize it, Vance. It belongs to the old gentleman—"

"Your father?"

Garden nodded grimly. "He's had it for years. Why he ever got it in the first place, I don't know—he probably hasn't the slightest idea how to use it..."

"By the by," Vance put in, "what time does your father generally return home from the University?"

"Why—why—" Garden hesitated and then continued: "On Saturdays he's always here early in the afternoon—rarely after three. Gives himself and his staff a half-holiday... But," he added, "father's very erratic..." His voice trailed off nervously.

Vance took two deep inhalations on his cigarette: he was watching Garden attentively. Then he asked in a soft tone:

"What's on your mind?—Unless, of course, you have good reason for not wanting to tell me."

Garden took a long breath and stood up. He seemed to be deeply troubled as he walked across the room and back.

"The truth is, Vance," he said, as he resumed his place on the davenport, "I don't even know where the pater is this afternoon. As soon as I came downstairs after Woody's death, I called him to give him the news. I thought he'd want to get here as soon as possible, in the circumstances. But I was told that he'd locked up the laboratory and left the University about two o'clock." Garden looked up quickly. "He's probably gone to the library for some research work. Or he may have swung round to Columbia. He spends a good bit of his time there."

I could not understand the man's perturbation; and I could see that it puzzled Vance as well. Vance endeavored to put him at his ease.

"It really doesn't matter," he said, as if dismissing the subject. "It may be just as well that your father doesn't learn of the tragedy till later." He smoked for a moment. "But to get back to the revolver: where was it usually kept?"

"In the center drawer of the desk upstairs," Garden told him promptly.

"And was the fact generally known to the other members of the household, or to Swift himself?"

Garden nodded. "Oh, yes. There was no secret about it. We often joked with the old gentleman about his 'arsenal.' Only last week, at dinner, he thought he heard someone in the garden and ran upstairs to see who it was. The mater called after him spoofingly: 'At last you may have a chance to use your precious revolver.' The old gentleman returned in a few minutes rather sheepishly. One of the flowerpots had been blown over and had rolled across the tiles. We all rode him good-naturedly for the rest of the meal."

"And the revolver was always loaded?"

"So far as I know, yes."

"And was there an extra supply of cartridges?"

"As to that I cannot say," Garden answered; "but I don't think so."

"And here's a very important question, Garden," Vance went on. "How many of the people that are here today could possibly have known that your father kept this loaded revolver in his desk? Now, think carefully before answering."

Garden meditated for several moments. He looked off into space and puffed steadily on his pipe.

"I am trying to remember," he said reminiscently, "just who was here the day Zalia came upon the gun—"

"What day was that?" Vance cut in sharply.

"It was about three months ago," Garden explained. "You see, we used to have the telephone set-up connected upstairs in the study. But some of the western races came in so late that it began to interfere with the old gentleman's routine when he came home from the University. So we moved the paraphernalia down into the drawing room. As a matter of fact, it was more convenient; and the mater didn't object—in fact, she rather enjoyed it—"

"But what happened on this particular day?" insisted Vance.

"Well, we were all upstairs in the study, going through the whole silly racing rigmarole that you witnessed this afternoon, when Zalia Graem, who always sat at the old gentleman's desk, began opening the drawers, looking for a piece of scratch paper on which to figure mutuels. She finally opened the center drawer and saw the revolver. She brought it out with a flourish and, laughing like a silly schoolgirl, pointed it around the room. Then she made some comments about the perfect gambling accommodations, drawing a parallel between the presence of the gun and the suicide room at Monte Carlo. 'All the conveniences of the Riviera,' she babbled. Or something to that effect. 'When you've lost your chemise, you can blow out your brains.' I reprimanded her—rather rudely, I'm afraid—and ordered her to put the revolver back in its place, as it was loaded—and just then a race came over the amplifier, and the episode was ended."

"Most interestin'," murmured Vance. "And can you recall how many of those present today were likewise present at Miss Graem's little *entr'acte*?"

"I rather think they were all there, if my memory is correct."

Vance sighed.

"A bit futile—eh, what? No possible elimination along that line."

Garden looked up, startled.

"Elimination? I don't understand. We were all downstairs here this afternoon except Kroon—and he was out—when the shot was fired."

"Quite—oh, quite," agreed Vance, leaning back in his chair. "That's the puzzlin' and distressin' part of this affair. No one could have done it, and yet someone did. But let's not tarry over the point. There are still one or two matters I want to ask you about."

"Go right ahead." Garden seemed completely perplexed...

At this moment there was a slight commotion in the hallway. It sounded as if a scuffle of some kind was in process, and a shrill, protesting voice mingled with the calm but determined tones of the nurse. Vance went immediately to the door and threw it open. There, just outside the den door, only a short distance from the stairway, were Miss Weatherby and Miss Beeton. The nurse had a firm hold on the other woman and was calmly arguing with her. As Vance stepped toward them, Miss Weatherby turned to face him and drew herself up arrogantly.

"What's the meaning of this?" she demanded. "Must I be mauled by a menial because I wish to go upstairs?"

"Miss Beeton has orders that no one is to go upstairs," Vance said sternly. "And I was unaware that she is a menial."

"But why can't I go upstairs?" the woman asked with dramatic emphasis. "I want to see poor Woody. Death is so beautiful; and I was very fond of Woody. By whose orders, pray, am I being denied this last communion with the departed?"

"By my orders," Vance told her coldly. "Furthermore, this particular death is far from beautiful, I assure you. Unfortunately, we are not living in a Maeterlinckian era. Swift's death is rather a sordid one, don't y' know. And the police will be here any minute. Until then no one will be permitted to disturb anything upstairs."

Miss Weatherby's eyes flashed.

"Then why," she demanded with histrionic indignation, "was this—this woman"—she glanced with exaggerated contempt at the nurse—"coming down the stairs herself when I came into the hall?"

Vance made no attempt to hide a smile of amusement.

"I'm sure I don't know. I may ask her later. But she happens to be under instructions from me to let no one go upstairs. Will you be so good, Miss Weatherby," added, almost harshly, "as to return to the drawing room and remain there until the officials arrive?"

The woman glared superciliously at the nurse, and then, with a toss of the head, strode toward the archway. There she turned and, with a cynical smirk, called back in an artificial tone:

"Blessings upon you, my children." Whereupon she disappeared into the drawing room.

The nurse, obviously embarrassed, turned to resume her post, but Vance stopped her.

"Were you upstairs, Miss Beeton?" he asked in a kindly tone.

She was standing very erect, her face slightly flushed. But, for all her apparent mental disturbance, she was like a symbol of poise. She looked Vance frankly and firmly in the eye and slowly shook her head.

"I haven't left my post, Mr. Vance," she said quietly. "I understand my duty."

Vance returned her gaze for moment, and then bowed his head slightly.

"Thank you, Miss Beeton," he said.

He came back into the den, and closing the door, addressed Garden again.

"Now that we have disposed temporarily of the theatrical queen,"—he smiled sombrely—"suppose we continue with our little chat."

Garden chuckled mildly and began repacking his pipe.

"Queer girl, Madge; always acting like a tragedienne—but I don't think she's ever really been on the stage. Suppressed theatrical ambition and that sort of thing. Dreams of herself as another Nazimova. And morbid as they come. Outside of that, she's a pretty regular sort. Takes her losses like an old general— and she's lost plenty the last few months..."

"You heard her tell me she was particularly fond of Swift," remarked Vance. "Just what did she mean by that?"

Garden shrugged. "Nothing at all, if you ask me. She didn't know that Woody was on earth, so to speak. But dead, Woody becomes a dramatic possibility."

"Yes, yes—quite," murmured Vance. "Which reminds me: what was the tiff between Swift and Miss Graem about? I noticed your little peace-maker advances this afternoon."

Garden became serious.

"I haven't been able to figure that situation out myself. I know they were pretty soft on each other some time ago— that is, Woody was pretty deep in the new-mown hay as far as Zalia went. Hovered round her all the time, and took all her good-natured bantering without a murmur. Then, suddenly, the embryonic love affair—or whatever it was—went sour. I'll-never-speak-to-you-again stuff. Like two kids. Both of them carrying around at least a cord of wood on each shoulder whenever the other was present. Obviously something had happened, but I never got the straight of it. It may have been a new flame on Woody's part—I rather imagine it was something of the kind. As for Zalia, she was never serious about it anyway. And I have an idea that Woody wanted that extra twenty thousand today for some reason connected with Zalia..." Garden stopped speaking abruptly and slapped his thigh. "By George! I wouldn't be surprised if that hard-bitten little gambler had turned Woody down because he was comparatively hard up. You can't tell about these girls today. They're as practical as the devil himself."

Vance nodded thoughtfully.

"Your observations rather fit with the remarks she made to me a little while ago. She, too, wanted to go upstairs to see Swift. Gave as her excuse the fact that she felt she was to blame for the whole sordid business."

Garden grinned.

"Well, there you are." Then he remarked judicially: "But you can never tell about women. One minute Zalia gives the impression of being superficial; and the next minute she'll make some comment that would almost lead you to believe she were an octogenarian philosopher. Unusual girl. Infinite possibilities there."

"I wonder." Vance smoked in silence for a moment. Then he went on: "There's another matter in connection with Swift which you might be able to clear up for me. Could you suggest any reason why, when I placed the bet on Azure Star for Miss Beeton this afternoon, Swift should have looked at me as if he would enjoy murdering me?"

"I saw that too," Garden nodded. "I can't say it meant anything much. Woody was always a weak sister where any woman was concerned. It took damned little to make him think he'd fallen in love. He may have become infatuated with the nurse—he'd been seeing her around here for the past few months. And now that you mention it, he's been somewhat poisonous toward me on several occasions because she was more or less friendly with me and ignored him entirely. But I'll say this for Woody: if he did have ideas about Miss Beeton, his taste is improving. She's an unusual girl—different..."

Vance nodded his head slowly and gazed with peculiar concentration out the window.

"Yes," he murmured. "Quite different." Then, as if bringing himself back from some alien train of thought, he crushed out his cigarette and leaned forward. "However, we'll drop speculation for the moment... Suppose you tell me something about the vault upstairs."

Garden glanced up in evident surprise.

"There's nothing to tell about that old catch-all. It's neither mysterious nor formidable. And it's really not a vault at all. Several years ago the pater found that he had accumulated a lot of private papers and experimental data that he didn't want casual callers messing in. So he had this fireproof storeroom built to house these scientific treasures of his. The vault, as you call it, was built as much for mere privacy as for actual safekeeping. It's just a very small room with shelves around the walls."

"Has everyone in the house access to it?" asked Vance.

"Anyone so inclined," replied Garden. "But who, in the name of Heaven, would want to go in there?"

"Really, y' know, I haven't the groggiest notion," Vance returned, "except that I found the door to it unlatched when I was coming downstairs a little while ago."

Garden shrugged carelessly, as if the matter was neither important nor unusual.

"Probably," he suggested, "the pater didn't shut the door tightly when he went out this morning. It has a spring lock."

"And the key?"

"The key is a mere matter of form. It hangs conveniently on a small nail at the side of the door."

"Accordingly," mused Vance, "the vault is readily accessible to anyone in the household who cares to enter it."

"That's right," nodded the other. "But what are you trying to get at, Vance? What's the vault to do with poor Woody's death?"

"I'm not sure," returned Vance slowly, rising and going again to the window. "I wish I knew. I'm merely tryin' not to overlook any possibility."

"Your line of inquiry sounds pretty far-fetched to me," Garden commented indifferently.

"One never knows, does one?" Vance murmured, going to the door. "Miss Beeton," he called, "will you be good enough to run upstairs and see if the key to the vault door is in its place?"

A few moments later the nurse returned and informed Vance that the key was where it was always kept. Vance thanked her and, closing the den door, turned again to Garden.

"There's one more rather important matter that you can clear up for me—it may have a definite bearing on the situation." He sat down in a low green leather chair and took out his cigarette case. "Can the garden be entered from the fire exit opening on the roof?"

"Yes, by George!" The other sat up with alacrity. "There's a gate in the east fence of the garden, just beside the privet hedge, which leads upon the terrace on which the fire exit of the building opens. When we had the fence built we were required to put this gate in because of the fire laws. But it's rarely used, except on hot summer nights. Still, if anyone came up the main stairs to the roof and went out the emergency fire door, he could easily enter our garden by coming through that gate in the fence."

"Don't you keep the gate locked?" Vance was studying the tip of his cigarette with close attention.

"The fire regulations don't permit that. We merely have an old-fashioned barn-door lift-latch on it."

"That's most interestin'," Vance commented in a low voice. "Then, as I understand it, anyone coming up the main stairway could walk out through the fire exit to the terrace, and enter your garden. And, of course, return the same way."

"That's true." Garden narrowed his eyes questioningly. "Do you really think that someone may have entered the garden that way and popped poor Woody off while we were all down here?"

"I'm doing dashed little thinking at the present moment," Vance answered evasively. "I'm trying to gether some material to think about, don't y' know..."

We could hear the sharp ringing of the entrance bell, and a door opening somewhere. Vance stepped out into the hall. A moment later the butler admitted District Attorney Markham and Sergeant Heath, accompanied by Snitkin and Hennessey.[*]

---

[*] *Snitkin and Hennessey were two detectives of the Homicide Bureau, who had worked as associates of Sergeant Heath on the various criminal cases with which Vance had previously been connected.*

(HAPTER SEVEN

Evidence of Murder
(*Saturday, April 14; 5:10 p. m.*)

"WELL, WHAT'S THE trouble, Vance?" Markham demanded brusquely. "I phoned Heath, as you requested, and brought him up with me."

"It's a bad business," Vance returned. "Same like I told you. I'm afraid you're in for some difficulties. It's no ordin'ry crime. Everything I've been able to learn so far contradicts everything else." He looked past Markham and nodded pleasantly to Heath. "Sorry to make you all this trouble, Sergeant."

"That's all right, Mr. Vance." Heath held out his hand in solemn good nature. "Glad I was in when the Chief called. What's it all about, and where do we go from here?..."

Mrs. Garden came bustling energetically down the hallway.

"Are you the District Attorney?" she asked, eyeing Markham ferociously. Without waiting for an answer, she went on: "This whole thing is an outrage. My poor nephew shot himself and this gentleman here"—she looked at Vance with supreme contempt—"is trying to make a scandal out of it." Her eyes swept over Heath and the two detectives. "And I suppose you're the police. There's no reason whatever for your being here."

Markham looked steadfastly at the woman and seemed to take in the situation immediately.

"Madam, if things are as you say," he promised in a pacifying, yet grave, tone, "you need have no fear of any scandal."

"I'll leave the matter entirely in your hands, sir," the woman returned with calm dignity. "I shall be in the drawing room, and I trust you will notify me the moment you have done what is necessary." She turned and walked back up the hall.

"A most tryin' and complicated state of affairs, Markham." Vance took the matter up again. "I admit the chap upstairs appears to have killed himself. But that, I think, is what everyone is *supposed to believe*. Tableau superficially correct. Stage direction and *décor* fairly good. But the whole far from perfect. I observed several discrepancies. As a matter of fact, the chap did not kill himself. And there are several people here who should be questioned later. They're all in the drawing room now—except Floyd Garden."

Garden, who had been standing in the doorway to the den, came forward, and Vance introduced him to Markham and Heath. Then Vance turned to the Sergeant.

"I think you'd better have either Snitkin or Hennessey remain down here and see that no one leaves the apartment for a little while." He addressed Garden. "I hope you won't mind."

"Not at all," Garden replied complacently. "I'll join the others in the drawing room. I feel the need of a highball, anyway." He included us all in a curt bow and moved up the hall.

"We'd better go up to the roof now, Markham," said Vance. "I'll run over the whole matter with you. There are some strange angles to the case. I don't at all like it. Rather sorry I came today. It might have passed for a nice refined suicide, with no bother or suspicion—everyone smugly relieved. But here I am. However…"

He moved down the hall, and Markham and Heath and I followed him. But before he mounted the stairs he stopped and turned to the nurse.

"You needn't keep watch here any longer, Miss Beeton," he said. "And thanks for your help. But one more favor: when the Medical Examiner comes, please bring him directly upstairs."

The girl inclined her head in acquiescence and stepped into the bedroom.

We went immediately up to the garden. As we stepped out on the roof, Vance indicated the body of Swift slumped in the chair.

"There's the johnnie," he said. "Just as he was found."

Markham and Heath moved closer to the huddled figure and studied it for a few moments. At length Heath looked up with a perplexed frown.

"Well, Mr. Vance," he announced querulously, "it looks like suicide, all right." He shifted his cigar from one corner of his mouth to the other.

Markham too turned to Vance. He nodded his agreement with the Sergeant's observation.

"It certainly has the appearance of suicide, Vance," he remarked.

"No—oh, no," Vance sighed. "Not suicide. A deuced brutal crime—and clever no end."

Markham smoked a while, still staring at the dead man skeptically; then he sat down facing Vance.

"Let's have the whole story before Doremus* gets here," he requested, with marked irritation.

Vance remained standing, his eyes moving aimlessly about the garden. After a moment he recounted succinctly, but carefully, the entire sequence of events of the afternoon, describing the group of people present, with their relationships and temperamental clashes; the various races and wagers; Swift's retirement to the garden for the results of the big Handicap;

---

*   *Doctor Emanuel Doremus, the Chief Medical Examiner of New York.*

and, finally, the shot which had aroused us all and brought us upstairs. When he had finished, Markham worried his chin for a moment.

"I still can't see a single fact," he objected, "that does not point logically to suicide."

Vance leaned against the wall beside the study window and lighted a *Régie*.

"Of course," he said, "there's nothing in the outline I've given you to indicate murder. Nevertheless, it was murder; and that outline is exactly the concatenation of events which the murderer wants us to accept. We are supposed to arrive at the obvious conclusion of suicide. Suicide as the result of losing money on horses is by no means a rare occurrence, and only recently there has been an account of such a suicide in the papers.* It is not impossible that the murderer's scheme was influenced by this account. But there are other factors, psychological and actual, which belie this whole superficial and deceptive structure." He drew on his cigarette and watched the thin blue ribbon of smoke disperse in the light breeze from the river. "To begin with," he went on, "Swift was not the suicidal type. A trite observation—and one that is often untrue. But there can be little doubt of its truth in the present instance, despite the fact that young Garden has taken pains to convince me to the contr'ry. In the first place, Swift was a weakling and a highly imaginative one. Moreover, he was too hopeful and ambitious—too sure of his own judgment and good luck—to put himself out of the world simply because he had lost all his money. The fact that Equanimity might not win the race was an eventuality which, as a confirmed gambler, he would have taken into consideration before hand. In addition, his nature was such that, if he were greatly disappointed, the result would be self-pity and hatred of others. He might, in an emergency,

---

* *Vance was referring to the suicide of a man in Houston, Texas, who left the following note: "To the public—Race horses caused this. The greatest thing the Texas Legislature can do is to repeal and enforce the gambling law."*

have committed a crime—but it would not have been against himself. Like all gamblers, he was trusting and gullible; and I think it was these temperamental qualities which probably made him an easy victim for the murderer..."

"But see here, Vance." Markham leaned forward protestingly. "No amount of mere psychological analysis can make a crime out of a situation as seemingly obvious as this one. After all, this is a practical world; and I happen to be a member of a practical profession. I must have more definite reasons than you have given me before I would be justified in discarding the theory of suicide."

"Oh, I dare say," nodded Vance. "But I have more tangible evidence that the johnnie did not eliminate himself from this life. However, the psychological implications of the man's nature—the contradictions, so to speak, between his character and the present situation—were what led me in the first place to look for more specific and demonstrable evidence that he was not unassisted in his demise."

"Well, let's have it." Markham fidgeted impatiently in his chair.

"*Imprimis*, my dear Justinian, a bullet wound in the temple would undoubtedly cause more blood than you see on the brow of the deceased. There are, as you notice, only a few partly coagulated drops, whereas the vessels of the brain cannot be punctured without a considerable flow of blood. And there is no blood either on his clothes or on the tiles beneath his chair. Meanin' that the blood had been, perhaps, spilled elsewhere before I arrived on the scene—which was, let us say, within thirty seconds after we heard the shot—"

"But good Heavens, man!—"

"Yes, yes; I know what you're going to say. And my answer is that the gentleman did not receive the bullet in his temple as he sat in yonder chair with the headphone on. He was shot elsewhere and brought here."

"A far-fetched theory," muttered Markham. "All wounds don't bleed the same."

Vance ignored the District Attorney's objection.

"And please take a good look at the poor fellow as he sits there, freed from all the horrors of the struggle for existence. His legs are stretched forward at an awkward angle. The trousers are twisted out of place and look most uncomfortable. His coat, though buttoned, is riding his shoulders, so that his collar is at least three inches above his exquisite mauve shirt. No man could endure to have his clothes so outrageously askew, even on the point of suicide—he would have straightened them out almost unconsciously. The *corpus delicti* shows every indication of having been dragged to the chair and placed in it."

Markham's eyes were surveying the limp figure of Swift as Vance talked.

"Even that argument is not entirely convincing," he said dogmatically, though his tone was a bit modified; "especially in view of the fact that he still wears the earphone..."

"Ah, exactly!" Vance took him up quickly. "That's another item to which I would call your attention. The murderer went a bit too far—there was a trifle too much thoroughness in the setting of the stage. Had Swift shot himself in that chair, I believe his first impulsive movement would have been to remove the headphone, as it very easily could have interfered with his purpose. And it certainly would have been of no use to him after he had heard the report of the race. Furthermore, I seriously doubt if he would have come upstairs to listen to the race with his mind made up in advance that he was going to commit suicide in case his horse didn't come in. And, as I have explained to you, the revolver is one belonging to Professor Garden and was always kept in the desk in the study. Consequently, if Swift had decided, after the race had been run, to shoot himself, he would hardly have gone into the study, procured the gun, then come back to his chair on the roof and put the headphone on again, before ending his life. Undoubtedly he would have shot himself right there in the study—at the desk from which he had obtained the revolver."

Vance moved forward a little as if for emphasis.

"Another point about that headphone—the point that gave me the first hint of murder—is the fact that the receiver at present is over Swift's right ear. Earlier today I saw Swift put the headphone on for a minute, and he was careful to place the receiver over his left ear—the custom'ry way. The telephone receiver, d' ye see, Markham, has always been placed on the left side of the phone box, in order to leave the right hand free to make notations or for other emergencies. The result is, the left ear has adapted itself to hearing more distinctly over the wire than the right ear. And humanity, as a result, has accustomed itself to holding a telephone receiver to the left ear. Swift was merely conforming to custom and instinct when he placed the receiving end of the headphone on the left side of his head. But now the headphone is on in reversed position, and therefore unnatural. I'm certain, Markham, that headphone was placed on Swift after he was dead."

Markham meditated on this for several moments.

"Still, Vance," he said at length, "reasonable objections could be raised to all the points you have brought up. They are based almost entirely on the theory and not on demonstrable facts."

"From a legal point of view, you're right," Vance conceded. "And if these had been my only reasons for believing that a crime had been committed, I wouldn't have summoned you and the doughty Sergeant. But, even so, Markham, I can assure you the few drops of blood you see on the chappie's temple could not have thickened to the extent they had when I first saw the body—they must have been exposed to the air for several minutes. And, as I say, I was up here approximately thirty seconds after we heard the shot."

"But that being the case," returned Markham in astonishment, "how can you possibly explain the fact?"

Vance straightened a little and looked at the District Attorney with unwonted gravity.

"Swift," he said, "*was not killed by the shot we heard.*"

"That don't make sense to me, Mr. Vance," Heath interposed, scowling.

"Just a moment, Sergeant." Vance nodded to him in friendly fashion. "When I realized that the shot that wiped out this john- nie's existence was not the shot that we had heard, I tried to figure out where the fatal shot could have been fired without our hearing it below. And I've found the place. It was in a vault- like storeroom—practically soundproof, I should say—on the other side of the passageway that leads to the study. I found the door unlocked and looked for evidence of some activity there..."

Markham had risen and taken a few nervous steps around the pool in the center of the roof.

"Did you find any evidence," he asked, "to corroborate your theory?"

"Yes—unmistakable evidence." Vance walked over to the still figure in the chair and pointed to the thick-lensed glasses tipped forward on the nose. "To begin with, Markham, you will notice that Swift's glasses are in a position far from normal, indicatin' that they were put on hurriedly and inaccurately by someone else—just as was the headphone."

Markham and Heath leaned over and peered at the glasses.

"Well, Mr. Vance," agreed the Sergeant, "they certainly don't look as if he had put 'em on himself."

Markham straightened up, compressed his lips, and nodded slowly.

"All right," he said; "what else?"

"Perpend, Markham." Vance pointed with his cigarette. "The left lens of the glasses—the one furthest from the punc- tured temple—is cracked at the corner, and there's a very small V-shaped piece missing where the crack begins—an indication that the glasses have been dropped and nicked. I can assure you that the lens was neither cracked nor nicked when I last saw Swift alive."

"Couldn't he have dropped his glasses on the roof here?" asked Heath.

"Possible, of course, sergeant," Vance returned. "But he didn't. I carefully looked over the tiles round the chair, and the missin' bit of glass was not there."

Markham looked at Vance shrewdly.

"And perhaps you know where it is."

"Yes—oh, yes." Vance nodded. "That's why I urged you to come here. That piece of glass is at present in my waistcoat pocket."

Markham showed a new interest.

"Where did you find it?" he demanded brusquely.

"I found it," Vance told him, "on the tiled floor in the vault across the hall. And it was near some scattered papers which could easily have been knocked to the floor by someone falling against them."

Markham's eyes opened incredulously, and he turned and studied the dead man again meditatively. At length he took a deep breath and pursed his lips.

"I'm beginning to see why you wanted me and the Sergeant here," he said slowly. "But what I don't understand, Vance, is that second shot that you heard. How do you account for it?"

Vance drew deeply on his cigarette.

"Markham," he answered, with quiet seriousness; "when we know how and by whom that second shot—which was obviously intended for us to hear—was fired, we will know who murdered Swift..."

At this moment the nurse appeared in the doorway leading to the roof. With her was Doctor Doremus, and behind the Medical Examiner were Captain Dubois and Detective Bellamy, the fingerprint men, and Peter Quackenbush, the official police photographer.

CHAPTER EIGHT

Disconnected Wires
(Saturday, April 14; 5:30 p. m.)

M ISS BEETON INDICATED our presence on the roof with a professional nod as she stepped to one side, and the Medical Examiner strolled briskly toward us, with a "Thank you, my dear," thrown over his shoulder to the nurse.

"If I can be of any help—" the young woman offered.

"Not at the moment, thank you," replied Vance with a friendly smile: "though we may call on you later."

With an inclination of her head she indicated that she understood, and made her way back downstairs.

Doremus acknowledged our joint greetings with a breezy wave of the hand, and halted jauntily in front of Heath.

"Congratulations, Sergeant," he said in a bantering falsetto. "By Gad, congratulations!"

The Sergeant was immediately on his guard—he knew the peppery little Medical Examiner of old.

"Well, what's it all about, doc?" Heath grinned.

"For once in your life," Doremus went on jocularly, "you picked the right time to summon me. Positively amazin', as Mr. Vance here would say. I wasn't eating or sleeping when your call came in. Nothing to do—bored with life, in fact. For the first time in history, you haven't dragged me away from my victuals or out from under my downy quilt. Why this sudden burst of charitable consideration?... Not a minim of vinegar in my system today. Bring on your corpses and I'll look 'em over without rancor."

Heath was amused in spite of his annoyance.

"I ain't arranging murders for your convenience. But if I caught you in an idle moment this time, it's fine with me... There's the fellow in the chair over there. It's Mr. Vance's find—and Mr. Vance has got ideas about it."

Doremus pushed his hat further back on his head, thrust his hands deep in his trousers pockets and stepped leisurely to the rattan chair with its lifeless occupant. He made a cursory examination of the limp figure, scrutinized the bullet hole, tested the arms and legs for *rigor mortis*, and then swung about to face the rest of us.

"Well, what about it?" he asked, in his easy cynical manner. "He's dead; shot in the head with a small-calibre bullet; and the lead's probably lodged in the brain. No exit hole. Looks as if he'd decided to shoot himself. There's nothing here to contradict the assumption. The bullet went into the temple, and is at the correct angle. Furthermore, there are powder marks, showing that the gun was held at very close range— almost a contact wound, I should say. There's an indication of singeing around the orifice."

He teetered on his toes and leered at the Sergeant.

"You needn't ask me how long he's been dead, for I can't tell you. The best I can do is to say that he's been dead somewhere between thirty minutes and a couple of hours. He isn't cold yet, and *rigor mortis* hasn't set in. The blood from the wound is only slightly coagulated, but the variations of this process—especially in the open air—do not permit an accurate estimate of the time involved... What else do you want me to tell you?"

Vance took the cigarette from his mouth and addressed Doremus.

"I say, doctor; speakin' of the blood on the johnnie's temple, what would you say about the amount?"

"Too damned little, I'd say," Doremus returned promptly. "But bullet wounds have a queer way of acting sometimes. Anyway, there ought to be a lot more gore."

"Precisely," Vance nodded. "My theory is that he was shot elsewhere and brought to this chair."

Doremus made a wry face and cocked his head to one side.

"*Was* shot? Then you don't think it was suicide?" He pondered a moment. "It could be, of course," he decided finally. "There's no reason why a corpse can't be carried from one place to another. Find the rest of the blood and you'll probably know where his death occurred."

"Thanks awfully, doctor." Vance smiled faintly. "That did flash through my mind, don't y' know; but I believe the blood was wiped up. I was merely hopin' that your findings would substantiate my theory that he did not shoot himself while sitting in that chair, without anyone else around."

Doremus shrugged indifferently.

"That's a reasonable enough assumption," he said. "There really ought to be more blood. And I can tell you that he didn't mop it up himself after the bullet was fired. He died instantly."

"Have you any other suggestions?" asked Vance.

"I may have when I've gone over the body more carefully after these babies"—he waved his hand toward the photographer and the fingerprint men—"finish their hocus-pocus."

Captain Dubois and Detective Bellamy had already begun their routine, with the telephone table as the starting point; and Quackenbush was adjusting his small metal tripod.

Vance turned to Dubois. "I say, Captain, give your special attention to the headphone, the revolver, and the glasses. Also the doorknob of the vault across the hall inside."

Dubois nodded with a grunt, and continued his delicate labors.

Quackenbush, his camera having been set up, took his pictures and then waited by the passageway door for further instructions from the fingerprint officers.

When the three men had gone inside, Doremus drew in an exaggerated sigh and spoke to Heath impatiently. "How about getting your *corpus delicti* over on the settee? Easier to examine him there."

"O.K., doc."

The Sergeant beckoned to Snitkin with his head, and the two detectives lifted Swift's limp body and placed it on the same wicker divan where Zalia Graem had laid when she collapsed at the sight of the dead man.

Doremus went to work in his usual swift and efficient fashion. When he had finished the task, he threw a steamer rug over the dead man, and made a brief report to Vance and Markham.

"There's nothing to indicate a violent struggle, if that's what you're hoping for. But there's a slight abrasion on the bridge of the nose, as if his glasses had been jerked off; and there's a slight bump on the left side of his head, over the ear, which may have been caused by a blow of some kind, though the skin hasn't been broken."

"How, doctor," asked Vance, "would the following theory square with your findings:—that the man had been shot elsewhere, had fallen to a tiled floor, striking his head against it sharply, that his glasses had been torn off when the left lens came in contact with the floor, and that he was carried out here to the chair, and the glasses replaced on his nose?"

Doremus pursed his lips and inclined his head thoughtfully.

"That would be a very reasonable explanation of the lump on his head and the abrasion on the bridge of his nose." He jerked his head up, raised his eyebrows, and smirked. "So this is another of your cock-eyed murders, is it? Well, it's all right with me. But I'll tell you right now, you won't get an autopsy report tonight. I'm bored and need excitement; and I'm going to Madison Square Garden to see Strangler Lewis and Londos have it out on the mat." He thrust his chin out in good-natured belligerence at Heath. "And I'm not going to leave my seat number at the box office either. That's fair warning to you, Sergeant. You can either postpone your future casualties until tomorrow, or worry one of my assistants."

He made out an order for the removal of the body, readjusted his hat, waved a friendly good-by which included all of us, and disappeared swiftly through the door into the passageway.

Vance led the way into the study, and the rest of us followed him. We were barely seated when Captain Dubois came in and reported that there were no fingerprints on any of the objects Vance had enumerated.

"Handled with gloves," he finished laconically, "or wiped clean."

Vance thanked him. "I'm not in the least surprised," he added.

Dubois rejoined Bellamy and Quackenbush in the hall, and the three made their way down the stairs.

"Well, Vance, are you satisfied?" Markham asked.

Vance nodded. "I hadn't expected any fingerprints. Cleverly thought-out crime. And what Doremus found fills some vacant spots in my own theory. Stout fella, Doremus. For all of his idiosyncrasies, he understands his business. He knows what is wanted and looks for it. There can be no question that Swift was in the vault when he was shot; that he fell to the floor, brushing down some of the papers; that he struck his head on the tiled floor, and broke the left lens of his glasses—you noted, of course, that the lump on his head is also on the left side—; and that he was dragged into the garden and placed in the chair. Swift was a small, slender man; probably didn't weigh over a hundred and twenty pounds; and it would have been no great feat of strength for someone to have thus transported him after death..."

There were footsteps in the corridor and, as our eyes involuntarily turned toward the door, we saw the dignified elderly figure of Professor Ephraim Garden. I recognized him immediately from pictures I had seen.

He was a tall man, despite his stooped shoulders; and, though he was very thin, he possessed a firmness of bearing which made one feel that he had retained a great measure of the physical power that had obviously been his in youth. There was benevolence in the somewhat haggard face, but there was also shrewdness in his gaze; and the contour of his mouth indicated a latent hardness. His hair, brushed in a pompadour, was almost white and seemed to emphasize the sallowness of his complexion. His dark eyes and the expression of his face were like his son's; but he was a far more sensitive and studious type than young Garden.

He bowed to us with an old-fashioned graciousness and took a few steps into the study.

"My son has just informed me," he said in a slightly querulous voice, "of the tragedy that has occurred here this afternoon. I'm sorry that I did not return home earlier, as is my wont on Saturdays, for in that event the tragedy might have been averted. I myself would have been in the study here and would probably have kept an eye on my nephew. In any event, no one could then have got possession of my revolver."

"I am not at all sure, Doctor Garden," Vance returned grimly, "that your presence here this afternoon would have averted the tragedy. It is not nearly so simple a matter as it appears at first glance."

Professor Garden sat down in a chair of antique workmanship near the door and, clasping his hands tightly, leaned forward.

"Yes, yes. So I understand. And I want to hear more about this affair." The tension in his voice was patent. "Floyd told me that Woode's death had all the appearances of suicide, but that you do not accept that conclusion. Would it be asking too much if I requested further details with regard to your attitude in this respect?"

"There can be no doubt, sir," Vance returned quietly, "that your nephew was murdered. There are too many indications that contradict the theory of suicide. But it would be inadvisable, as well as unnecess'ry, to go into details at the moment. Our investigation has just begun."

"Must there be an investigation?" Professor Garden asked in tremulous protest.

"Do you not wish to see the murderer brought to justice?" Vance retorted coldly.

"Yes—yes; of course." The professor's answer was almost involuntary; but as he spoke his eyes drifted dreamily to the window overlooking the river, and he sank dejectedly a little lower into his chair. "It's most unfortunate, however," he murmured. Then he looked appealingly to Vance. "But are you sure you are right and that you are not creating unnecessary scandal?"

"Quite," Vance assured him. "Whoever committed the murder made several grave miscalculations. The subtlety of the crime was not extended through all phases of it. Indeed, I believe that some fortuitous incident or condition made certain revisions necess'ry at the last moment... By the by, doctor, may I ask what detained you this afternoon?—I gathered from your son that you usually return home long before this time on Saturdays."

"Of course, you may," he replied with seeming frankness; but there was a startled look in his eyes as he gazed at Vance. "I had some obscure data to look up before I could continue with an experiment I'm making; and I thought today would be an excellent time to do it, since I close the laboratory and let my assistants go on Saturday afternoons."

"And where were you, doctor?" Vance went on, "between the time you left the laborat'ry and the time of your arrival here?"

"To be quite specific," Professor Garden answered, "I left the University at about two and went to the public library where I remained until half an hour ago. Then I took a cab and came directly home."

"You went to the library alone?" asked Vance.

"Naturally I went alone," the professor answered tartly. "I don't take assistants with me when I have research work to do." He stood up suddenly. "But what is the meaning of all this questioning? Am I, by any chance, being called upon to furnish an alibi?"

"My dear doctor!" said Vance placatingly. "A serious crime has been committed in your home, and it is essential that we know—as a matter of routine—the whereabouts of the various persons in any way connected with the unfortunate situation."

"I see what you mean." Professor Garden inclined his head courteously and moved to the front window where he stood looking out to the low purple hills beyond the river, over which the first crepuscular shadows were creeping.

"I am glad you appreciate our difficulties," Vance said; "and I trust you will be equally considerate when I ask you just what was the relationship between you and your nephew?"

The man turned slowly and leaned against the broad sill.

"We were very close," he answered, without hesitation or resentment. "Both my wife and I have regarded Woode almost as a son, since his parents died. He was not a strong person morally, and he needed both spiritual and material assistance. Perhaps, because of this fundamental weakness in his nature, we have been more lenient with him than with our own son. In comparison with Woode, Floyd is a strong-minded and capable man, fully able to take care of himself."

Vance nodded with understanding.

"That being the case, I presume that you and Mrs. Garden have provided for young Swift in your wills."

"That is true," Professor Garden answered after a slight pause. "We have, as a matter of fact, made Woode and our son equal beneficiaries."

"Has your son," asked Vance, "any income of his own?"

"None whatever," the professor told him. "He has made a little money here and there, on various enterprises—largely connected with sports—but he is entirely dependent on the allowance my wife and I give him. It's a very liberal one—too liberal, perhaps judged by conventional standards. But I see no reason not to indulge the boy. It isn't his fault that he hasn't the temperament for a professional career, and has no flair for business. And I see no point in his pursuing some uncongenial commercial routine, since there is no necessity for it. Both Mrs. Garden and I inherited our money; and while I have always regretted that Floyd had no interest in the more serious phases of life, I have never been inclined to deprive him of the things which apparently constitute his happiness."

"A very liberal attitude, doctor," Vance murmured; "especially for one who is himself so wholeheartedly devoted to the more serious things of life as you are... But what of Swift: did he have an independent income?"

"His father," the professor explained, "left him a very comfortable amount; but I imagine he squandered it or gambled most of it away."

"There's one more question," Vance continued, "that I'd like to ask you in connection with your will and Mrs. Garden's: were your son and nephew aware of the disposition of the estate?"

"I couldn't say. It's quite possible they were. Neither Mrs. Garden nor I have regarded the subject as a secret... But what, may I ask,"—Professor Garden gave Vance a puzzled look—"has this to do with the present terrible situation?"

"I'm sure I haven't the remotest idea," Vance admitted frankly. "I'm merely probin' round in the dark, in the hope of findin' some small ray of light."

Hennessey, the detective whom Heath had ordered to remain on guard below, came lumbering up the passageway to the study.

"There's a guy downstairs, Sergeant," he reported, "who says he's from the telephone company and has got to fix a bell or somethin'. He's fussed around downstairs and couldn't find anything wrong there, so the butler told him the trouble might be up here. But I thought I'd better ask you before I let him come up. How about it?"

Heath shrugged and looked inquiringly at Vance.

"It's quite all right, Hennessey," Vance told the detective. "Let him come up."

Hennessey saluted half-heartedly and went out.

"You know, Markham," Vince said, slowly and painstakingly lighting another cigarette, "I wish this infernal buzzer hadn't gone out of order at just this time. I abominate coincidences—"

"Do you mean," Professor Garden interrupted, "that intercommunicating buzzer between here and the den downstairs?... It was working all right this morning—Sneed summoned me to breakfast with it as usual."

"Yes, yes," nodded Vance. "That's just it. It evidently ceased functioning after you had gone out. The nurse discovered it and reported it to Sneed who called up the telephone company."

"It's not of any importance," the professor returned with a lackadaisical gesture of his hand. "It's a convenience, however, and saves many trips up and down the stairs."

"We may as well let the man attend to it, since he's here. It won't disturb us." Vance stood up. "And I say, doctor, would you mind joining the others downstairs? We'll be down presently, too."

The professor inclined his head in silent acquiescence and, without a word, went from the room.

Presently a tall, pale, youthful man appeared at the door to the study, He carried a small black tool-kit.

"I was sent here to look over a buzzer," he announced with surly indifference. "I didn't find the trouble downstairs."

"Maybe the difficulty is at this end," suggested Vance. "There's the buzzer behind the desk." And he pointed to the small black box with the push-button.

The man went over to it, opened his case of tools and, taking out a flashlight and a small screwdriver, removed the outer shell of the box. Fingering the connecting wires for a moment, he looked up at Vance with an expression of contempt.

"You can't expect the buzzer to work when the wires ain't connected," he commented.

Vance became suddenly interested. Adjusting his monocle, he knelt down and looked at the box.

"They're both disconnected—eh, what?" he remarked.

"Sure they are," the man grumbled. "And it don't look to me like they worked themselves loose, either."

"You think they were deliberately disconnected?" asked Vance.

"Well, it looks that way." The man was busy reconnecting the wires. "Both screws are loose, and the wires aren't bent— they look like they been pulled out."

"That's most interestin'." Vance stood up, and returned the monocle to his pocket meditatively. "It might be, of course. But I can't see why anyone should have done it... Sorry for your trouble."

"Oh, that's all in the day's work," the man muttered, read-justing the cover of the box. "I wish all my jobs were as easy as this one." After a few moments he stood up. "Let's see if the buzzer will work now. Anyone downstairs who'll answer if I press this?"

"I'll take care of that," Heath interposed, and turned to Snitkin. "Hop down to the den, and if you hear the buzzer down there, ring back."

Snitkin hurried out, and a few moments later, when the button was pressed, there came two short answering signals.

"It's all right now," the repair man said, packing up his tools and going toward the door. "So long." And he disappeared down the passageway.

Markham had been scrutinizing Vance closely for several minutes.

"There's something on your mind," he said seriously. "What's the point of this disconnected buzzer?"

Vance smoked for a moment in silence, looking down at the floor. Then he walked to the north window and looked out meditatively into the garden.

"I don't know, Markham. It's dashed mystifyin'. But I have a notion that the same person who fired the shot we heard disconnected those wires…"

Suddenly he stepped to one side behind the draperies and crouched down, his eyes still peering out cautiously into the garden. He raised a warning hand to us to keep back out of sight.

"Deuced queer," he said tensely. "That gate in the far end of the fence is slowly opening… Oh, my aunt!" And he swung swiftly into the passageway leading to the garden, beckoning to us to follow.

CHAPTER NINE

Two Cigarette Stubs
(Saturday, April 14; 6 p. m.)

VANCE RAN PAST the covered body of Swift on the settee, and crossed to the garden gate. As he reached it he was confronted by the haughty and majestic figure of Madge Weatherby. Evidently her intention was to step into the garden, but she drew back abruptly when she saw us. Our presence, however, seemed neither to surprise nor to embarrass her.

"Charmin' of you to come up, Miss Weatherby," said Vance. "But I gave orders that everyone was to remain downstairs."

"I had a right to come here!" she returned, drawing herself up with almost regal dignity.

"Ah!" murmured Vance. "Yes, of course. It might be, don't y' know. But would you mind explainin'?"

"Not at all." Her expression remained unchanged, and her voice was hollow and artificial. "I wished to ascertain if *he* could have done it."

"And who," asked Vance, "is this mysterious 'he'?"

"Who?" she repeated, throwing her head back sarcastically. "Why, Cecil Kroon!"

Vance's eyelids drooped, and he studied the woman narrowly for a brief moment. Then he said lightly:

"Most interestin'. But let that wait a moment. How did you get up here?"

"That was very simple." She tossed her head negligently. "I pretended to be faint and told your minion I was going into the butler's pantry to get a drink of water. I went out through the pantry door into the public hallway, came up the main stairs, and out on this terrace."

"But how did you know that you could reach the garden by this route?"

"I didn't know." She smiled enigmatically. "I was merely reconnoitering. I was anxious to prove to myself that Cecil Kroon could have shot poor Woody."

"And are you satisfied that he could have?" asked Vance quietly.

"Oh, yes," the woman replied with bitterness. "Beyond a doubt. I've known for a long time that Cecil would kill him sooner or later. And I was quite certain when you said that Woody had been murdered that Cecil had done it. But I did not understand how he could have gotten up here, after leaving us this afternoon. So I endeavored to find out."

"And why, may I ask," said Vance, "would Mr. Kroon desire to dispose of Swift?"

The woman clasped her hands theatrically against her breast. Taking a step forward, she said in a histrionically sepulchral voice:

"Cecil was jealous—frightfully jealous. He's madly in love with me. He has tortured me with his attentions..." One of her hands went to her forehead in a gesture of desperation. "There has been nothing I could do. And when he learned that I cared for Woody, he became desperate. He threatened me. I was horribly frightened. I didn't dare break everything off with him—I didn't know what he might do. So I humored him: I went about with him, hoping, hoping that this madness of his would subside. For a time I thought he was becoming more normal and rational. And then—today—this terrible crime!..." Her voice trailed off in an exaggerated sigh.

Vance's keen regard showed neither the sympathy her pompous recital called for, nor the cynicism which I knew he felt. There was only a studied interest in his gaze.

"Sad—very sad," he mumbled.

Miss Weatherby jerked her head up and her eyes flashed.

"I came up here to see if it were possible that Cecil could have done this thing. I came up in the cause of justice!"

"Very accommodatin'." Vance's manner had suddenly changed. "We're most appreciative, and all that sort of thing. But I must insist, don't y' know, that you return downstairs and wait there with the others. And you will be so good as to come through the garden and go down the apartment stairs."

He was brutally matter-of-fact as he drew the gate shut and directed the woman to the passageway door. She hesitated a moment and then followed his indicating finger. As she passed the wicker settee she stopped suddenly and sank to her knees.

"Oh, Woody, Woody!" she wailed dramatically. "It was all my fault!" She covered her face with her hands and bent her head far forward in an attitude of abject misery.

Vance heaved a deep sigh, threw away his cigarette and, taking her firmly by one arm, lifted per to her feet.

"Really, y' know, Miss Weatherby," he said brusquely, leading her toward the door, "this is not a melodrama."

She straightened up with a stifled sob and went down the passageway toward the stairs.

Vance turned to the detective and nodded toward the entrance.

"Snitkin," he said wearily, "go downstairs and tell Hennessey to keep an eye on Sarah Bernhardt till we need her."

Snitkin grinned and followed Miss Weatherby below.

When we were back in the study Vance sank into a chair and yawned.

"My word!" he complained. "The case is difficult enough without these amateur theatricals."

Markham, I could see, had been both impressed and puzzled by the incident.

"Maybe it's not all dramatics," he suggested. "The woman made some very definite statements."

"Oh, yes. She would. She's the type." Vance took out his cigarette case. "Definite statements, yes. And misleadin'. Really, y' know, I don't for a moment believe she regards Kroon as the culprit."

"Well, what then?" snapped Markham.

"Nothing—really nothing." Vance sighed. "Vanity and futility. The lady is vanity—we're futility. Neither leads anywhere."

"But she certainly has something on her mind," protested Markham.

"So have we all. I wonder... But if we could read one person's mind completely, we'd probably understand the universe. Akin to omniscience, and that sort of thing."

"God Almighty!" Markham stood up and planted himself belligerently in front of Vance. "Can't you be rational?"

"Oh, Markham—my dear Markham!" Vance shook his head sadly. "What is rationality? However... As you say. There is something back of the lady's histrionics. She has ideas. But she's circuitous. And she wants us to be like those Chinese gods who can't proceed except in a straight line. Sad. But let's try makin' a turn. The situation is something like this: An unhappy lady slips out through the butler's pantry and presents herself on the roof-garden, hopin' to attract our attention. Having succeeded, she informs us that she has proved conclusively that a certain Mr. Kroon has done away with Swift because of amorous jealousy. That's the straight line—the longest distance between two points.—Now for the curve. The lady herself, let us assume, is the spurned and not the spurner. She resents it.

She has a temper and is vengeful—and she comes to the roof here for the sole purpose of convincing us that Kroon is guilty. She's not beyond that sort of thing. She'd be jolly well glad to see Kroon suffer, guilty or not."

"But her story is plausible enough," said Markham aggressively. "Why try to find hidden meanings in obvious facts? Kroon could have done it. And your psychological theory regarding the woman's motives eliminates him entirely."

"My dear Markham—oh, my dear Markham! It doesn't eliminate him at all. It merely tends to involve the lady in a rather unpleasant bit of chicanery. The fact is, her little drama here on the roof may prove most illuminatin'."

Vance stretched his legs out before him and sank deeper into his chair.

"Curious situation. Y' know, Markham, Kroon deserted the party about fifteen or twenty minutes before the big race— legal matters to attend to for a maiden aunt, he explained—and he didn't appear again until after I had phoned you. Assumed immediately that Swift had shot himself. Also mentioned a couple of accurate details. All of which could have been either the result of actual knowledge or mere guesswork. Doubt inspired me to converse with the elevator boy. I learned that Kroon had not gone down or up in the elevator since his arrival here early in the afternoon..."

"What's that!" Markham exclaimed. "That's more than suspicious—taken with what we have just heard from this Miss Weatherby."

"I dare say." Vance was unimpressed. "The legal mind at work. But from my gropin' amateur point of view, I'd want more—oh, much more. However,"—Vance rose and meditated a moment—"I admit that a bit of lovin' communion with Mr. Kroon is definitely indicated." He turned to Heath. "Send the chappie up, will you, Sergeant? And be sweet to him. Don't annoy him. *La politesse.* No need to put him on his guard."

Heath nodded and started toward the door.

"I get you, Mr. Vance."

"And Sergeant," Vance halted him; "you might question the elevator boy and find out if there is anyone else in the building whom Kroon is in the habit of calling on. If so, follow it up with a few discreet inquiries."

Heath vanished down the stairs, and a minute or so later Kroon sauntered into the study with the air of a man who is bored and not a little annoyed.

"I suppose I'm in for some more tricky questions," he commented, giving Markham and Snitkin a fleeting contemptuous glance and letting his eyes come to rest on Vance with a look of resentment. "Do I take the third-degree standing or sitting?"

"Just as you wish," Vance returned mildly; and Kroon, after glancing about him, sat down leisurely at one end of the davenport. The man's manner, I could see, infuriated Markham, who leaned forward and asked in cold anger:

"Have you any urgent reasons for objecting to give us what assistance you can in our investigation of this murder?"

Kroon raised his eyebrows and smoothed the waxed ends of his mustache.

"None whatever," he said with calm superiority. "I might even be able to tell you who shot Woody."

"That's most interestin'," murmured Vance, studying the man indifferently. "But we'd much rather find out for ourselves, don't y' know. Much more sportin', what? And there's always the possibility that our own findin's might prove more accurate than the guesses of others."

Kroon shrugged maliciously and said nothing.

"When you deserted the party this afternoon, Mr. Kroon," Vance went on in an almost lackadaisical manner, "you gratuitously informed us that you were headed for a legal conference of some kind with a maiden aunt. I know we've been over this before, but I ask again: would you object to giving us, merely as a matter of record, the name and address of your aunt, and the nature of the legal documents which lured you so abruptly away from the Rivermont Handicap, after you had wagered five hundred dollars on the outcome?"

"I most certainly would object," returned Kroon coolly. "I thought you were investigating a murder; and I assure you my aunt had nothing to do with it. I fail to see why you should be interested in my family affairs."

"Life is full of surprises, don't y' know," murmured Vance. "One never knows where family affairs and murder overlap."

Kroon chuckled mirthlessly, but checked himself with a cough.

"In the present instance, I am happy to inform you that, so far as I am concerned, they do not overlap at all."

Markham swung round toward the man.

"That's for us to decide," he snapped. "Do you intend to answer Mr. Vance's question?"

Kroon shook his head.

"I do not! I regard that question as incompetent, irrelevant, and immaterial. Also frivolous."

"Yes, yes." Vance smiled at Markham. "It could be, don't y' know. However, let it pass, Markham. Present status: Name and address of maiden aunt, unknown; nature of legal documents, unknown; reason for the gentleman's reticence, also unknown."

Markham resentfully mumbled a few unintelligible words and resumed smoking his cigar while Vance continued the interrogation.

"I say, Mr. Kroon, would you also consider it irrelevant—and the rest of the legal verbiage—if I asked you by what means you departed and returned to the Garden apartment?"

Kroon appeared highly amused.

"I'd consider it irrelevant, yes; but since there is only one sane way I could have gone and come back, I'm perfectly willing to confess to you that I took a taxicab to and from my aunt's."

Vance gazed up at the ceiling as he smoked.

"Suppose," he said, "that the elevator boy should deny that he took you either down or up in the car since your first arrival here this afternoon. What would you say?"

Kroon jerked himself up to attention.

"I'd say that he had lost his memory—or was lying."

"Yes, of course. The obvious retort. Quite." Vance's eyes moved slowly to the man on the davenport. "You will probably have the opportunity of saying just that on the witness stand."

Kroon's eyes narrowed and his face reddened. Before he could speak, Vance went on.

"And you may also have the opportunity of officially giving or withholding your aunt's name and address. The fact is, you may find yourself in the most distressin' need of an alibi."

Kroon sank back on the davenport with a supercilious smile.

"You're very amusing," he commented lightly. "What next? If you'll ask me a reasonable question, I'll be only too happy to answer. I'm a highly esteemed citizen of these States—always willing, not to say anxious, to assist the authorities—to aid in the cause of justice, and all that sort of rot." There was an undercurrent of venom in his contumelious tone.

"Well, let's see where we stand." Vance suppressed an amused smile. "You left the apartment at approximately a quarter to four, took the elevator downstairs and then a taxi, went to your aunt's to fuss a bit with legal documents, drove back in a taxi, and took the elevator upstairs. Bein' gone a little over half an hour. During your absence Swift was shot. Is that correct?"

"Yes." Kroon was curt.

"But how do you account for the fact that when I met you in the hall on your return, you seemed miraculously cognizant of the details of Swift's passing?"

"We've been over that, too. I knew nothing about it. You told me Swift was dead, and I merely surmised the rest."

"Yes—quite. No crime in accurate surmisals. Deuced queer coincidence, however. Taken with other facts. As likely as a five-horse win parlay. Extr'ordin'ry."

"I'm listening with great interest." Kroon had again assumed his air of superiority. "Why don't you stop beating about the bush?"

"Worthwhile suggestion." Vance crushed out his cigarette and, drawing himself up in his chair, leaned forward and rested his elbows on his knees. "What I was leadin' up to was the fact that someone has definitely accused you of murdering Swift."

Kroon started, and his face went pale. After a few moments he forced a harsh guttural noise intended for a laugh.

"And who, may I ask, has accused me?"

"Miss Madge Weatherby."

One corner of Kroon's mouth went up in a sneer of hatred.

"She would! And she probably told you that it was a crime of passion—caused by an uncontrollable jealousy."

"Just that," nodded Vance. "It seems you have been forcing your unwelcome attentions upon her, with dire threats; whereas, all the time, she was madly enamored of Mr. Swift. And so, when the strain became too great, you eliminated your rival. Incidentally, she has a very pretty theory which fits the known facts, and which your own refusal to answer my questions bolsters up considerably."

"Well, I'll be damned!" Kroon got to his feet slowly and thrust his hands deep into his pockets. "I see what you're driving at. Why didn't you tell me this in the first place?"

"Waitin' for the final odds," Vance returned. "You hadn't laid your bet. But now that I've told you, do you care to give us the name and address of your maiden aunt and the nature of the legal documents you had to sign?"

"That's all damned nonsense," Kroon spluttered. "I don't need an alibi. When the time comes—"

At this moment Heath appeared at the door, and walking directly to Vance, handed him a page torn from his notebook, on which were several lines of handwriting.

Vance read the note rapidly as Kroon looked on with malignant resentment. Then he folded the paper and slipped it into his pocket.

"When the time comes..." he murmured. "Yes—quite." He raised his eyes lazily to Kroon. "As you say. When the time comes. The time has now come, Mr. Kroon."

The man stiffened, but did not speak. I could see that he was aggressively on his guard.

"Do you, by any chance," Vance continued, "know a lady named Stella Fruemon? Has a snug little apartment on the seventeenth floor of this building—only two floors below. Says you were visitin' her around four o'clock today. Left her at exactly four-fifteen. Which might account for your not using the elevator. Also for your reluctance to give us your aunt's name and address. Might account for other things as well... Do you care to revise your story?"

Kroon appeared to be thinking fast. He walked nervously up and down the study floor.

"Puzzlin' and interestin' situation," Vance went on. "Gentleman leaves this apartment at—let's say—ten minutes to four. Family documents to sign. Doesn't enter the elevator. Appears in apartment two floors below within a few minutes— been a regular visitor there. Remains till four-fifteen. Then departs. Shows up again in this apartment at half-past four. In the meantime, Swift is shot through the head—exact time unknown. Gentleman is apparently familiar with various details of the shooting. Refuses to give information regarding his whereabouts during his absence. A lady accuses him of the murder, and demonstrates how he could have accomplished it., Also kindly supplies the motive. Fifteen minutes of gentleman's absence—namely, from four-fifteen to four-thirty—unaccounted for."

Vance drew on his cigarette.

"Fascinatin' assortment of facts. Add them up. Mathematically speakin', they make a total... I say, Mr. Kroon, any suggestions?"

Kroon came to a sudden halt and swung about.

"No!" he blurted. "Damn your mathematics! And you people hang men on such evidence!" He sucked in a deep noisy breath and made a despairing gesture. "All right, here's the story. Take it or leave it. I've been mixed up with Stella Fruemon for the past year. She's nothing but a gold-digger and blackmailer. Madge Weatherby got on to it. She's the jealous member of this combination—not me. And she cared about as much for Woode Swift as I did. Anyway, I got involved with Stella Fruemon. It came to a show-down, and I had to pay through the nose. To avoid scandal for my family, of course. Otherwise, I'd have thrown her through the window and called it my boy scout's good deed for the day. At any rate, we each got our lawyers, and a settlement was reached. She finally named a stiff figure and agreed to sign a general release from all claims. In the circumstances, I had no alternative. Four o'clock today was the time set for the completion of the transaction. My lawyer and hers were to be at her apartment. The certified check and the papers were ready. So I went down there a little before four to clean up the whole dirty business. And I cleaned it up and got out. I had walked down the two flights of stairs to her apartment, and at four-fifteen, when the hold-up was over, I told the lady she could go to hell, and I walked back up the stairs."

Kroon took a deep breath and frowned.

"I was so furious—and relieved—that I kept on walking without realizing where I was going. When I opened the door which I thought led into the public hallway outside the Garden apartment, I found I was out on the terrace of the roof." He cocked an angry eye at Vance. "I suppose that fact is suspicious too—walking up three flights of stairs instead of two—after what I'd been through?"

"No. Oh, no." Vance shook his head. "Quite natural. Exuberant spirits. Weight off the shoulders, and all that. Three flights of stairs seemin' like two. Light impost, so to speak. Horses run better that way. Don't feel the extra furlong, as it were. Quite comprehensible... But please proceed."

"Maybe you mean that—and maybe you don't." Kroon spoke truculently. "Anyway, it's the truth... When I saw where I was I thought I'd come through the garden and go down the stairway there. It was really the natural thing to do..."

"You knew about the gate leading into the garden, then?"

"I've known about it for years. Everybody who's been up
here knows about it. On summer nights Floyd used to leave the
gate open and we'd walk up and down the terrace. Anything
wrong with my knowing about the gate?"

"No. Quite natural. And so, you opened the gate and
entered the garden?"

"Yes."

"And that would be between a quarter after four and
twenty minutes after four?"

"I wasn't holding a stopwatch on myself, but I guess
that's close enough... When I entered the garden I saw Swift
slumped down in his chair. His position struck me as funny, but
I paid no attention to it until I spoke to him and got no answer.
Then I approached and saw the revolver lying on the tiles, and
the hole in his head. It gave me a hell of a shock, I can tell you,
and I started to run downstairs to give the alarm. But I realized it would look bad for me. There I was, alone on the roof
with a dead man..."

"Ah, yes. Discretion. So you played safe. Can't say that I
blame you entirely—if your chronology is accurate. So, I take
it, you reentered the public stairway and came down to the
front door of the Garden apartment."

"That's just what I did." Kroon's tone was as vigorous as it
was resentful.

"By the by, during the brief time you were on the roof, or
even after you returned to the stairway, did you hear a shot?"

Kroon looked at Vance in obvious surprise.

"A shot? I've told you the fellow was already dead when I
first saw him."

"Nevertheless," said Vance, "there was a shot. Not the one
that killed him, but the one that summoned us to the roof.
There were two shots, don't y' know—although no one seems
to have heard the first."

Kroon thought a moment.

"By George! I did hear something, now that you put it
that way. I thought nothing of it at the time, since Woody was

already dead. But just as I reentered the stairway there was an explosion of some kind outside. I thought it was a car back-firing down in the street, and paid no attention to it."

Vance nodded with a puzzled frown.

"That's very interestin…" His eyes drifted off into space. "I wonder…" After a moment he returned his gaze to Kroon. "But to continue your tale. You say you left the roof immedi-ately and came downstairs. But there were at least ten minutes from the time you left the garden to the time I encountered you entering the apartment at the front door. How and where did you spend these ten intervening minutes?"

"I stayed on the landing of the stairs and smoked a couple of cigarettes. I was trying to pull myself together. After what I had been through, and then finding Woody shot, I was in a hell of a mental state."

Heath stood up quickly, one hand in his outside coat pocket, and thrust out his jaw belligerently toward the agitated Kroon.

"What kind of cigarettes do you smoke?" he barked.

The man looked at the Sergeant in bewilderment, and then said: "I smoke gold-tipped Turkish cigarettes. What about it?"

Heath drew his hand from his pocket and looked at some-thing which he held on his palm.

"All right," he muttered. Then he addressed Vance. "I got the stubs here. Picked 'em up on the landing when I came up from the dame's apartment. Thought maybe they might have some connection."

"Well, well," sneered Kroon. "So the police actually found something!… What more do you want?" he demanded of Vance.

"Nothing for the moment, thank you," Vance returned with exaggerated courtesy. "You have done very well by your-self this afternoon, Mr. Kroon. We won't need you any more… Sergeant, give instructions to Hennessey that Mr. Kroon may leave the apartment."

Kroon went to the door without a word.

"Oh, I say." Vance delayed him at the threshold. "Do you, by any chance, possess a maiden aunt?"

Kroon looked back over his shoulder with a vicious grin.

"No, thank God!" And he slammed the door noisily behind him.

CHAPTER TEN

The $10,000 Bet
(Saturday, April 14; 6:15 p. m.)

"**A** GOOD STORY," Markham commented dryly when Kroon had gone.

"Yes, yes. Good. But reluctant." Vance appeared disturbed.

"Do you believe it?"

"My dear Markham, I keep an open mind, neither believin' nor disbelievin'. Prayin' for facts. But no facts yet. Drama everywhere, but no substance. Kroon's story is at least consistent. One of the reasons why I'm skeptical. Always distrust consistency. Too easy to manufacture. And Kroon's shrewd no end."

"Still," put in Markham, "those cigarette butts which Heath found check with his story."

"Yes. Oh, yes." Vance nodded and sighed. "I don't doubt he smoked two cigarettes on the stair landing. But he could have smoked them just as well if he'd done the johnnie in. At the moment I'm suspectin' everyone here. Lot of angles protrudin' from this case."

"On the other hand," objected Markham, "with that entrance from the main stairway to the door open to anybody, why couldn't an outsider have killed Swift?"

Vance looked up at him with a melancholy air.

"Oh, Markham—my dear Markham! The legalistic intelligence at work. Ever lookin' for loopholes. The prosecutin' attorney hopin' for the best. No. Oh, no. No outsider. Too many sound objections. The murder was too perfectly timed. Only someone present could have executed it so fittingly. Moreover, it was committed in yon vault. Only someone thoroughly familiar with the Garden household and the exact situation here this afternoon could have done it…"

There was a rustle in the passageway, and Madge Weatherby came rushing into the study, with Heath following and protesting vigorously. It was obvious that Miss Weatherby had dashed up the stairs before anyone could interfere with her.

"What's the meaning of this?" she demanded imperiously. "You're letting Cecil Kroon go, after what I've told you? And I"—she indicated herself with a dramatic gesture—"I am being held here, a prisoner."

Vance rose wearily and offered her a cigarette. She brushed the proffered case aside and sat down rigidly.

"The fact is, Miss Weatherby," said Vance, returning to his chair, "Mr. Kroon explained his brief absence this afternoon lucidly and with impellin' logic. It seems that he was doing nothing more reprehensible than conferring with Miss Stella Fruemon and a brace of attorneys."

"Ah!" The woman's eyes glared with venom.

"Quite so. He was breaking off with the lady for ever and ever. Also getting a release from her and from her heirs, executors, administrators, and assigns, from the beginning of the world to the day of the date of these presents—I believe that is the correct legal phraseology. Really, y' know, he never cared for her. He assured us she was quite a nuisance. Was rather vehement about it. No woman would ever dominate and blackmail him—or brave words to that effect. The Cézanne slogan modified: *Pas une gonzesse ne me mettra le grappin dessus.*"

"Is that the truth?" Miss Weatherby straightened in her chair.

"Yes, yes. No subterfuge. Kroon said you were jealous of Stella. Thought I'd relieve your mind."

"Why didn't he tell me, then?"

"There's always the possibility you didn't give him a chance."

The woman nodded vigorously.

"Yes, that's right. I wouldn't speak to him when he returned here this afternoon."

"Care to revamp your original theory?" asked Vance. "Or do you still think that Kroon is the culprit?"

"I—I really don't know now," the woman answered hesitantly. "When I last spoke to you I was terribly upset… Maybe it was all my imagination."

"Imagination—yes. Terrible and dangerous thing. Causes more misery than actuality. Especially imagination stimulated by jealousy. 'Not poppy, nor mandragora, nor all the drowsy syrups of the world'…" He looked at the woman quizzically. "Since you're not so sure that Kroon did the deed, have you any other suggestions?"

There was a tense silence. Miss Weatherby's face seemed to contract: she drew in her lips. Her eyes almost closed.

"Yes!" she exploded, leaning toward Vance with a new enthusiasm. "It was Zalia Graem who killed Woody! She had the motive, as you call it. She's capable of such things, too. She's breezy and casual enough on the outside. But inside she's a demon. She'd stop at nothing. There was something between her and Woody. Then she chucked him over. But he wouldn't let her alone. He kept on annoying her, and she ignored him. He didn't have enough money to suit her. You saw the way they acted toward each other today."

"Have you any idea as to how she managed the crime?" Vance asked quietly.

"She was out of the drawing room long enough, wasn't she? Supposed to be telephoning. But does anyone really know where she was, or what she was doing?"

"Poignant question. Situation very mysterious." Vance rose slowly and bowed to the woman. "Thanks awfully—we're most grateful. And we shall not hold you prisoner any longer. If we should need you later, we'll communicate with you."

When she had gone Markham grinned sourly.

"The lady is well equipped with suspects. What do you make of this new accusation?"

Vance was frowning.

"Animosity shunted from Monsieur Kroon to La Graem. Yes. Queer situation. Logically speakin', this new accusation is more reasonable than her first. It has its points… If only I could get that disconnected buzzer out of my mind. It must fit somewhere… And that second shot—the one we all heard."

"Couldn't it have been a mechanism of some kind?" suggested Markham. "It's not difficult to effect, a detonation by electric wires."

Vance nodded apathetically.

"I'd thought of that. But there's nothing about the buzzer to indicate that a gadget might have been attached to it. I looked carefully while the telephone man was working on it."

Vance again moved to the buzzer and inspected it with care. Then he gave his attention to the book-shelves surrounding it. He took down a dozen or so volumes and scrutinized the empty shelves and the uprights. Finally he shook his head and returned to his chair.

"No. Nothing there. The dust behind the books is thick and shows no signs of recent disturbance. No powder marks anywhere. And no indications of a mechanism."

"It could have been removed before the repair man arrived," theorized Markham without enthusiasm.

"Yes, another possibility. I had thought of that too. But the opportunity was lacking. I came in here immediately after I had found the johnnie shot…" He took the cigarette from his lips and straightened up, "By Jove! Someone might have slipped in here when we all dashed upstairs after the shot. Remote chance, though. And yet... Another curious thing, Markham: three or four different people tried to storm this aerie while I was in the den with Garden. All of them wished to be with the corpse for *post-mortem* communion—that sort of morbid rigmarole. I wonder... However, it's too late to work from that point now. Nothing to do but to jot down those facts for future reference."

"Does the buzzer connect with any other room besides the den?"

Vance shook his head.

"No. That's the only connection."

"Didn't you say there was someone in the den at the time you heard this shot?"

Vance's gaze swept past Markham, and it was several moments before he answered.

"Yes. Zalia Graem was there. Ostensibly telephonin'." His voice, I thought, was a little bitter; and I could see that his mind had gone off on a new line of thought.

Heath squinted and moved his head up and down.

"Well, Mr. Vance, that gets us places."

Vance stared at him.

"Does it really, Sergeant? Where? It merely fuddles up the case—until we get some more information along the same line."

"We might get more information from the young woman herself," Markham put in sarcastically.

"Oh, yes. Quite. Obvious procedure. But I have a few queries to put to Garden first. Pavin' the way, as it were. I say, Sergeant, collect Floyd Garden and bring him here."

Garden came into the room uneasily and looking slightly haggard.

"What a mess!" he sighed, sinking dismally into a chair. He packed his pipe shakily. "Any light on the case?"

"A few fitful illuminations," Vance told him. "By the by, it seems that your guests walk in and out the front door without the formality of ringing or being announced. Is this practice custom'ry?"

"Oh, yes. But only when we're playing the races. Much more convenient. Saves annoyance and interruptions."

"And another thing: when Miss Graem was phoning in the den and you suggested that she tell the gentleman to call back later, did you actually know that it was a man she was talking to?"

Garden opened his eyes in mild surprise.

"Why, no. I was merely ragging her. Hadn't the faintest idea. But, if it makes any difference, I'm sure Sneed could give you the information, if Miss Graem won't. Sneed answered the phone, you know."

"It's of no importance." Vance brushed the matter aside. "It might interest you to know, however, that the buzzer in this room failed to function because someone had carefully disconnected the wires."

"The devil you say!"

"Oh, yes. Quite." Vance fixed Garden with a significant look. "This buzzer, if I understand it correctly, is operated only from the den, and when we heard the shot, Miss Graem was in the den. Incidentally, the shot we all heard was not the shot that killed Swift. The fatal shot had been fired at least five minutes before that. Swift never even knew whether he had won or lost his bet."

Garden's gaze was focused on Vance with wide-eyed awe. A smothered exclamation escaped his half-parted lips. Quickly he drew himself together and, standing up, let his eyes roam vaguely about the room.

"Good God, man!" He shook his head despondently. "This thing's getting hellish. I see your implication about the buzzer and the shot we heard. But I can't see just how the trick was done." He turned to Vance with an appealing look. "Are you sure about those disconnected wires and what you say was a second shot?"

"Quite sure," Vance's tone was casual. "Sad, what? By the by, Miss Weatherby tried to convince us that Miss Graem shot Swift."

"Has she any grounds for such an accusation?"

"Only that Miss Graem had a grudge of some kind against Swift and detested him thoroughly, and that, at the supposed time of his demise, Miss Graem was absent from the drawing room. Doubts that she was in the den phoning all the time. Thinks she was up here, busily engaged in murder."

Garden drew rapidly on his pipe and seemed to be thinking.

"Of course, Madge knows Zalia pretty well," he admitted with reluctance. "They go about a great deal together. Madge may know the inside story of the clash between Zalia and Woody. I don't. Zalia might have thought she had sufficient cause to end Woody's career. She's an amazing girl. One never quite knows what she will do next."

"Do you yourself regard Miss Graem as capable of a cold-blooded, skilfully planned murder?"

Garden pursed his lips and frowned. He coughed once or twice, as if to gain time; then he spoke.

"Damn it, Vance! I can't answer that question. Frankly, I don't know who is and who isn't capable of murder. The younger set today are all bored to death, intolerant of every restraint, living beyond their means, digging up scandal, seeking sensations of every type. Zalia is little different from the rest, as far as I can see. She always seems to be stepping on the gas and exceeding the speed limits. How far she would actually go, I'm not prepared to say. Who is, for that matter? It may be merely a big circus parade with her, or it may be fundamental—a violent reaction from respectability. Her people are eminently respectable. She was brought up strictly—even forced into a convent for a couple of years, I believe. Then broke loose and is now having her fling..."

"A vivid, though not a sweet, character sketch," murmured Vance. "One might say offhand that you are rather fond of her but don't approve."

Garden laughed awkwardly.

"I can't say that I dislike Zalia. Most men do like her—though I don't think any of them understand her. I know I don't.

There's some impenetrable wall around her. And the curious thing is, men like her although she doesn't make the slightest effort to gain their esteem or affection. She treats them shabbily—actually seems to be annoyed by their attentions."

"A poisonous, passive Dolores, so to speak."

"Yes, something like that, I should say. She's either damned superficial or deep as hell—I can't make up my mind which. As to her status in this present situation...well, I don't know. It wouldn't surprise me in the least if Madge was right about her. Zalia has staggered me a couple of times—can't exactly explain it. You remember, when you asked me about father's revolver, I told you Zalia had discovered it in that desk and staged a scene with it in this very room. Well, Vance, my blood went cold at the time. There was something in the way she did it, and in the tone of her voice, that made me actually fear that she was fully capable of shooting up the party and then walking about the room to chuckle at the corpses. No reason for my feelings, perhaps; but, believe me, I was damned relieved when she put the gun back and shut the drawer... All I can say," he added, "is that I don't wholly understand her."

"No. Of course not. No one can wholly understand another person. If anyone could he'd understand everything. Not a comfortin' thought... Thanks awfully for the recital of your fears and impressions. You'll look after matters downstairs for a while, won't you?"

Garden seemed to breathe more freely on being dismissed, and, with a mumbled acquiescence, moved toward the door.

"Oh, by the by," Vance called after him. "One other little point I wish to ask you about."

Garden waited politely.

"Why," asked Vance, blowing a ribbon of smoke toward the ceiling, "didn't you place Swift's bet on Equanimity?"

The man gave a start, and his jaw dropped. He barely rescued his pipe from falling to the floor.

"You didn't place it, don't y' know," Vance went on dulcetly, gazing at Garden with dreamy, half-closed eyes.

"Rather interestin' point, in view of the fact that your cousin was not destined to live long enough to collect the wager, even if Equanimity had won. And, in the circumstances, had you placed it, you would now be saddled with a ten-thousand-dollar debt—since Swift is no longer able to settle."

"God Almighty, stop it, Vance!" Garden exploded. He sank limply into a chair. "How the hell do you know I didn't place Woode's bet?"

Vance regarded the man with searching eyes.

"No bookie would take a bet of that size five minutes before post time. He couldn't absorb it. He would have to lay a lot of it off—he might even have to place some of it out of town—Chicago or Detroit. He'd need time, don't y' know. A ten-thousand-dollar bet would usually have to be placed at least an hour before the race was run. I've done a bit of hobnobbin' with bookies and racetrack men."

"But Hannix—"

"Don't make a Wall-Street financier of Hannix for my benefit," Vance admonished quietly. "I know these gentlemen of the chalk and eraser as well as you do. And another thing: I happened to be sitting in a strategic position near your table when you pretended to place Swift's bet. You very deftly pulled the cord taut over the plunger of the telephone when you picked up the receiver. You were talking into a dead phone."

Garden drew himself together and capitulated with a weary shrug.

"All right, Vance," he said. "I didn't place the bet. But if you think, for one moment, that I had any suspicion that Woody was going to be shot this afternoon, you're wrong."

"My dear fellow!" Vance sighed with annoyance. "I'm not thinkin'. Higher intelligence not at work at the moment. Mind a blank. Only tryin' to add up a few figures. Ten thousand dollars is a big item. It changes our total—eh, what?... But you haven't told me why you didn't place the bet. You could have placed it. You had sufficient indication that Swift was going to wager a large sum on Equanimity, and it would only have been necess'ry to inform him that the bet had to be placed early."

Garden rose angrily, but beneath his anger was a great perturbation.

"I didn't want him to lose the money," he asserted aggressively. "I knew what it would mean to him."

"Yes, yes. The Good Samaritan. Very touchin'. But suppose Equanimity had won, and your cousin had survived—what about the payoff?"

"I was fully prepared to run that risk. It wasn't a hell of a lot. What did the old oat-muncher pay, anyway?—less than two to one. A dollar and eighty cents to the dollar, to be exact. I would have been out eighteen thousand dollars. But there wasn't a chance of Equanimity's coming in—I was quite certain of that. I took the chance for Woody's sake. I was being decent—or weak—I don't know which. If the horse had won, I'd have paid Woody myself—and he would never have known that it wasn't Hannix's money."

Vance looked at the man thoughtfully.

"Thanks for the affectin' confession," he murmured at length. "I think that will be all for the moment."

As he spoke, two men with a long coffin-like wicker basket bustled into the passageway. Heath was at the door in two strides.

"The Public Welfare boys after the body," he announced over his shoulder.

Vance stood up.

"I say, Sergeant, have them go down the outside stairway. No use returning through the apartment." He addressed Garden again. "Would you mind showing them the way?"

Garden nodded morosely and went out on the roof. A few moments later the two carriers, with Garden leading the way, disappeared through the garden gate with their grim burden.

CHAPTER ELEVEN

The Second Revolver
(Saturday, April 14; 6:25 p. m.)

Markham REGARDED VANCE with dismal concern.

"What's the meaning of Garden's not placing that bet?"

Vance sighed.

"What's the meaning of anything? Yet, it's from just such curious facts as this that some provisional hypothesis may evolve."

"I certainly can't figure out what bearing Garden's conduct has on the case, unless—"

Vance interrupted him quickly.

"No. Puzzlin' situation. But everything we have learned so far might mean something. Provided, of course, we could read the meanin'. Emotion may be the key."

"Don't be so damned occult," snapped Markham. "What's on your mind?"

"My dear Markham! You're too flatterin'. Nothing whatever. I'm seekin' for something tangible. The other gun, for instance. The one that went off somewhere when the chappie was already dead. It should be here or hereabouts..." He turned to Heath. "I say, Sergeant, could you and Snitkin take a look for it? Suggested itiner'ry: the roof-garden and the flowerbeds, the terrace, the public stairs, the lower hallway. Then the apartment proper. Assumption: anyone present may have had it. Follow up all the known local migrations of everyone downstairs. If it's here it'll probably be in some tempor'ry hidin' place, awaitin' further disposal. Don't ransack the place. And don't be too dashed official. Sweetness and light does it."

Heath grinned. "I know what you mean, Mr. Vance."

"And, Sergeant, before you start reconnoiterin', will you fetch Hammle. You'll probably find him at the bar downstairs, ingesting a Scotch-an-soda."

When Heath had gone, Vance turned to Markham.

"Hammle may have some good counsel to offer, and he may not. I don't like the man—sticky sort. We might as well get rid of him—at least tempor'rily. The place is frightfully cluttered..."

Hammle strutted pompously into the study and was cursorily presented to Markham. Through the window, in the gathering dusk, I could catch glimpses of Heath and Snitkin moving along the flower boxes.

Vance waved Hammle to a chair and studied him a moment with a melancholy air, as if endeavoring to find an excuse for the man's existence.

The interview was brief and, as it turned out, of peculiar significance. The significance lay, not so much in what Hammle said, as in the result of the curiosity which Vance's questions aroused in the man. It was this curiosity which enabled him later to supply Vance with important information.

"It is not our desire to keep you here any longer than necess'ry, Mr. Hammle,"—Vance began the interview with marked distaste—"but it occurred to me to ask you if you have any ideas that might be helpful to us in solving Swift's murder."

Hammle coughed impressively and appeared to give the matter considerable thought.

"No, I have none," he at length admitted. "None whatever. But of course one can never tell about these things. The most insignificant facts can really be interpreted seriously, provided one has given them sufficient thought. As for myself, now, I haven't duly considered the various approaches to the subject."

"Of course," Vance agreed, "there hasn't been a great deal of time for serious thought concerning the situation. But I thought there might be something in the relationships of the various people here this afternoon—and I am assuming that you are fairly familiar with them all—that might inspire you to make a suggestion."

"All I can say," returned Hammle, carefully weighing his words, "is that there were many warring elements in the gathering—that is to say, many peculiar combinations. Oh, nothing criminal." He waved his hand quickly in deprecation. "I would have you understand that absolutely. But there was a combination of this and that, which might lead to—well, to anything."

"To murder, for instance?"

Hammle frowned. "Now, murder is a very, very serious business." His tone bordered on the sententious. "But, Mr. Vance, you can take it from me, in all solemnity, I wouldn't put even murder past any of those present today. No, by Gad!"

"That's an amazin' indictment," muttered Vance; "but I'm glad to have your opinion and we'll consider it... By the by, didn't you notice anything irregular in Garden's placing Swift's large bet on Equanimity at the last minute?"

Hammle's countenance went quickly blank. He presented Vance momentarily with a perfect "poker face." Then, unable to withstand the direct scrutiny of Vance's cold gaze, he puckered up his mouth into a shrewd smile.

"Why deny it?" he chuckled. "The laying of that bet was not only irregular—it was damned near impossible. I don't know a book-maker in New York who would take such an amount when there was not even enough time to throw some 'come-back money' into the totalizator. A swell time this Hannix would have had trying to balance his book with a cloudburst like that at the last minute! The whole transaction struck me as damned peculiar. Couldn't imagine what Garden was up to."

Vance leaned forward, and his eyelids drooped as he focused his gaze on Hammle.

"That might easily have had some bearing on the situation here this afternoon, and I'd like very much to know why you didn't mention it."

For a brief moment the man seemed flustered; but almost immediately he settled back in his chair with a complacent look, and extended his hands, palms up.

"Why should I become involved?" he asked with cynical suavity. "I have never believed in bothering too much with other people's concerns. I've too many problems of my own to worry about."

"That's one way of looking at life," Vance drawled. "And it has its points. However…" He contemplated the tip of his cigarette, then asked: "Would your discretion permit you to comment on Zalia Graem?"

Hammle sat up with alacrity.

"Ah!" He nodded his head significantly. "That's something to think about. There are varied possibilities in that girl. You may be on the right track. A most likely suspect for the murder. You never can tell about women, anyway. And, come to think of it, the shooting must have taken place during the time she was out of the room. She's a good pistol shot, too. I recall once when she came out to my estate on Long Island—she did a bit of target practice that afternoon. Oh, she knows weapons as most women know bonnets, and she's as wild as a two-year-old filly at her first barrier."

Vance nodded and waited.

"But don't think, for a minute," Hammle hurried on, "that I am intimating that she had anything to do with Swift's death. Absolutely not! But the mention of her name gave me pause." As he finished speaking he nodded his head sagely.

Vance stood up with a stifled yawn.

"It's quite evident," he said, "you're not in the mood to be specific. I wasn't looking for generalities, don't y' know. Consequently I may want to have another chat with you. Where can you be reached later, should we need you?"

"If I am permitted to go now, I shall return to Long Island immediately," Hammle answered readily, glancing speculatively at his watch. "Is that all you wish at the moment?"

"That is all, thank you."

Hammle again referred to his watch, hesitated a moment, and then left us.

"Not a nice person, Markham," Vance commented dolefully when Hammle had gone. "Not at all a nice person. As you noticed, everyone, according, to him, is fitted for the rôle of killer—everyone except himself, of course. A smug creature. And that unspeakable waistcoat! And the thick soles of his shoes! And the unpressed clothes! Oh, very careless and sportin'—and very British. The uniform of the horse-and-dog gentry. Animals really deserve better associates."

He shrugged sadly and, going to the buzzer, pressed the button.

"Queer reports on that Graem girl." He walked back to his chair musingly. "The time has come to commune with the lady herself..."

Garden appeared at the door.

"Did you ring for me, Vance?"

"Yes." Vance nodded. "The buzzer is working now. Sorry to trouble you, but we would like to see Miss Graem. Would you do the honors?"

Garden hesitated, his eyes fixed sharply on Vance. He started to say something, changed his mind and, with a muttered "Right-o," swung about and returned downstairs.

Zalia Graem swaggered into the room, her hands in her jacket pockets, and surveyed us with breezy cynicism.

"My nose is all powdered for the inquisition," she announced with a twisted smile. "Is it going to take long?"

"You might better sit down." Vance spoke with stern politeness.

"Is it compulsory?" she asked.

Vance ignored the question, and she leaned back against the door.

"We're investigating a murder, Miss Graem,"—Vance's voice was courteous but firm—"and it will be necess'ry to ask you questions that you may deem objectionable. But please believe that it will be for your own good to answer them frankly."

"Am I a suspect? How thrilling!"

"Everyone I've talked to thus far thinks so." He looked at the girl significantly.

"Oh, so that's how the going is! I'm in for a sloppy track, and I can't mud. How perfectly beastly!" She frowned. "I thought I detected a vague look of fear in people's eyes. I think I will sit down, after all." She threw herself into a chair and gazed up with simulated dejection. "Am I to be arrested?"

"Not just at the minute. But certain matters must be straightened out. It may be worth your while to help us."

"It sounds ghastly. But go ahead."

"First," said Vance, "we'd like to know about the feud between you and Swift."

"Oh, the devil!" the girl exclaimed disgustedly. "Must that be raked up? There was really nothing to it. Woody bothered the life out of me. I felt sorry for him and went around with him a bit when he implored me to and threatened to resort to all the known forms of suicide if I didn't. Then it became too much for me, and I decided to draw a line across the page. But I'm afraid I didn't go about it in a nice way. I told him I was extravagant and cared only for luxuries, and that I could never marry a poor man. I had a silly notion it might snap him out of his wistful adoration. It worked, after a fashion. He got furious and said nasty things—which, frankly, I couldn't forgive. So he took the high road, and I took the low—or the other way round."

"And so, the conclusion we may draw is that he played the horses heavily in the forlorn hope of amassing a sufficient fortune to overcome your aversion to his poverty—and that his bet on Equanimity today was a last fling—"

"Don't say that!" the girl cried, her hands tightening over the arms of the chair. "It's a horrible idea, but—it might be true. And I don't want to hear it."

Vance continued to study her critically.

"Yes, as you say. It might be true. On the other hand... however, we'll let it pass." Then he asked quickly: "Who telephoned you today, just before the Rivermont Handicap?"

"Tartarin de Tarascon," the girl replied sarcastically.

"And had you instructed this eminent adventurer to call you at just that time?"

"What has that to do with anything?"

"And why were you so eager to take the call on the den phone and shut the door?"

The girl leaned forward and looked at Vance defiantly.

"What are you trying to get at?" she demanded furiously.

"Are you aware," Vance went on, "that the den downstairs is the only room directly connected by wires with this room up here?"

The girl seemed unable to speak. She sat pale and rigid, her eyes fixed steadily on Vance.

"And do you know," he continued, without change of intonation, "that the wires at this end of the line had been disconnected? And are you aware that the shot which we heard downstairs was not the one that ended Swift's life—that he was shot in the vault off the hall, several minutes before we heard the shot?"

"You're being ghastly," the girl cried. "You're making up nightmares—nightmares to frighten me. You're implying terrible things. You're trying to torture me into admitting things that aren't true, just because I was out of the room when Woody was shot..."

Vance held up his hand to stop her reproaches.

"You misinterpret my attitude, Miss Graem," he said softly. "I asked you, a moment ago, for your own sake, to answer my questions frankly. You refuse. In those circumstances, you should know the facts as they appear to others." He paused. "You and Swift were not on good terms. You knew, as did the others, that he usually went up to the roof before races. You knew where Professor Garden kept his revolver. You're familiar with guns and a good pistol shot. A telephone call for you is perfectly timed. You disappear. Within the next five minutes Swift is shot behind that steel door. Another five minutes pass; the race is over; and a shot is heard. That shot could conceivably have been fired by a mechanism. The buzzer wires up here had been disconnected, obviously for some specific purpose. At the time of the second shot you were at the other end of those wires. You almost fainted at the sight of Swift. Later you tried to go upstairs... Adding all this up: you had a motive, a sufficient knowledge of the situation, access to the criminal agent, the ability to act, and the opportunity." Vance paused again. "Now are you ready to be frank, or have you really something to hide?"

A change came over the girl. She relaxed, as if from a sudden attack of weakness. She did not take her eyes from Vance, and appeared to be appraising him and deciding what course to follow.

Before she managed to speak Heath stamped up the passageway and opened the study door. He carried a woman's black-and-white tweed top-coat over his arm. He cocked an eyebrow at Vance and nodded triumphantly.

"I take it, Sergeant," Vance drawled, "your quest has been successful. You may speak out." He turned to Zalia Graem and explained: "Sergeant Heath has been searching for the gun that fired the second shot."

The girl became suddenly animated and leaned forward attentively.

"I followed the route you suggested, Mr. Vance," Heath reported. "After going over the roof and the stairs and the hall of the apartment, I thought I'd look through the wraps hanging in the hall closet. The gun was in the pocket of this." He threw the coat on the davenport and took a .38 gun-metal revolver from his pocket. He broke it and showed it to Vance and Markham. "Full of blanks—and one of 'em has been discharged."

"Very good, Sergeant," Vance complimented him. "Whose coat is this, by the by?"

"I don't know yet, Mr. Vance; but I'm going to find out *pronto*."

Zalia Graem had risen and come forward.

"I can tell you whose coat that is," she said. "It belongs to Miss Beeton, the nurse. I saw her wearing it yesterday."

"Thanks awfully for the identification," returned Vance, his eyes resting dreamily on her.

She gave him a wry smile and returned to her chair.

"But there's a question still pending," Vance said; "—to wit: are you ready to be frank now?"

"All right." She focused her gaze on Vance again. "Lemmy Merritt, one of the various scions of the horsy aristocracy that infests our eastern seaboard, asked me to drive out to Sands Point with him for the polo game tomorrow. I thought I might dig up some more exciting engagement and told him to call me here this afternoon at half-past three for a final yes or no. I purposely stipulated that time, so I wouldn't miss the running of the Handicap. As you know, he didn't call till after four, with excuses about not having been able to get to a telephone. I tried to get rid of him in a hurry, but he was persistent—the only virtue he possesses, so far as I know. I left him dangling on the wire when I came out to listen to the race, and then went back for a farewell and have-a-nice-time-without-me. Just as I hung up I heard what sounded like a shot and came to the door, to find everyone hurrying along the hall. An idea went through my head that maybe Woody had shot himself—that's why I went mid-Victorian and almost passed out when I saw him. That's everything. I know nothing about wires, buzzers, or mechanical devices; and I haven't been in this room for a week. However, I'll incriminate myself to the extent of admitting that I didn't like Woody, and that on many occasions I had the desire to blow his brains out. And, as you say, I am a pretty good shot."

Vance rose and bowed.

"Thanks for your ultimate candor, Miss Graem. I'm deuced sorry I had to torture you to obtain it. And please ignore the nightmares you accused me of manufacturing. I'm really grateful to you for helping me fill in the pattern."

The girl frowned as her intense gaze rested on Vance.

"I wonder if you don't really know more about this affair than you pretend."

"My dear Miss Graem! I do not pretend to know anything about it." Vance went to the door and held it open for her. "You may go now, but we shall probably want to see you again tomorrow, and I must ask for your promise that you will stay at home where you will be available."

"Don't worry, I'll be at home." She shrugged and then added: "I'm beginning to think that maybe Ogden Nash had the right idea."

As she went out, Miss Beeton was coming up the passageway toward the study. The two women passed each other without speaking.

"I'm sorry to trouble you, Mr. Vance," the nurse apologized, "but Doctor Siefert has just arrived and asked me to inform you that he wished very much to see you as soon as possible. Mr. Garden," she added, "has told him about Mr. Swift's death."

At that moment her gaze fell on the tweed coat, and a slight puzzled frown lined her forehead. Before she could speak Vance said:

"The Sergeant brought your coat up here. He didn't know whose it was. We were looking for something." Then he added quickly: "Please tell Doctor Siefert that I will be very glad to see him at once. And ask him if he will be good enough to come here to the study."

Miss Beeton nodded and went out, closing the door softly behind her.

CHAPTER TWELVE

Poison Gas
(Saturday, April 14; 6:40 p. m.)

VANCE WENT TO the window and looked out for some time in silence. It was obvious he was deeply troubled. Markham respected his perturbation and did not speak.

It was Vance himself who at length broke the silence.

"Markham," he said, his eyes scanning the brilliant sunset colors across the river, "the more I see of this case the less I like it. Everyone seems to be trying to pin the posy of guilt on the other chap. And there's fear wherever I turn. Guilty consciences at work."

"But everyone," returned Markham, "seems pretty well agreed that this Zalia Graem had a hand in it."

Vance inclined his head.

"Oh, yes," he murmured. "I had observed that fact. I wonder..."

Markham studied Vance's back for several moments.

"Do you think Doctor Siefert will be of any help?" he asked.

"He might be, of course," Vance replied. "Evidently he wants to see me. But I imagine it's curiosity as much as anything else. However, there's little that anyone who was not actually here can tell us. The difficulty in this case, Markham, lies in trying to weed out a multiplicity of misleading items…"

There was a soft knock, and Vance turned from the window. He was confronted by Garden, who had opened the study door without waiting for a summons.

"Sorry, Vance," Garden apologized, "but Doc Siefert is downstairs and says he'd like to see you, if convenient, before he goes."

Vance looked at the man a moment and frowned.

"Miss Beeton informed me of the fact a few minutes ago. I asked her to tell the doctor I would be glad to see him at once. I can't understand his sending you also. Didn't the nurse give him the message?"

"I'm afraid not. I know Siefert sent Miss Beeton up here, and I assumed, as I imagine Siefert did, that you had detained her." He looked round the room with a puzzled expression. "The fact is, I thought she was still up here."

"You mean she hasn't returned downstairs?" Vance asked.

"No, she hasn't come down yet."

Vance took a step forward.

"Are you sure of that, Garden?"

"Yes, very sure." Garden nodded vigorously. "I've been in the front hall, near the foot of the stairs, ever since Doc Siefert arrived."

Vance walked thoughtfully to a small table and broke the ashes from his cigarette.

"Did you see any of the others come down?" he asked Garden.

"Why, yes," Garden told him. "Kroon came down and went out. And then Madge Weatherby also came down and went out. And shortly after the nurse had gone up with Siefert's message to you, Zalia came down and hurried away. But that's all. And, as I say, I've been down there in the front hall all the time."

"What about Hammle?"

"Hammle? No, I haven't seen anything of him. I thought he was still here with you."

"That's deuced queer." Vance moved slowly to a chair and sat down with a perplexed frown. "It's possible you missed him. However, it doesn't matter." He had lifted his head a little and was watching Garden speculatively. "Ask the doctor to come up, will you?"

When Garden had left us Vance sat smoking and staring at the ceiling. I knew from the droop of his eyelids that he was disturbed. He moved restlessly in his chair and finally leaned forward, resting his elbows on his knees.

"Deuced queer," he muttered again.

"For Heaven's sake, Vance," Markham commented irritably. "It's entirely possible Garden wasn't watching the stairs as closely as he imagines."

"Yes. Oh, yes." Vance nodded vaguely. "Everyone worried. No one on the alert. Normal mechanisms not functioning. Still, the stairs are visible half way up the hall, and the hall itself isn't very spacious…"

"It's quite possible Hammle went down the main stairs from the terrace, wishing, perhaps, to avoid the others."

"He hadn't his hat up here with him," Vance returned without looking up. "He would have had to enter the front hall and pass Garden to get it. No point in such silly manœuvres… But it isn't Hammle I'm thinking of. It's Miss Beeton. I don't like it…" He got up slowly and took out another cigarette. "She's not the kind of girl that would neglect taking my message to Siefert immediately, unless for a very good reason."

"A number of things might have happened—" Markham began, but Vance cut in.

"Yes, of course. That's just it. Too many things have happened here today already." He went to the north window and looked out into the garden. Then he returned to the center of the room and stood for a moment in tense meditation. "As you say, Markham." His voice was barely audible. "Something may have happened..." Suddenly he threw his cigarette into an ashtray and turned on his heel. "Oh, my word! I wonder... Come, Sergeant. We'll have to make a search—immediately."

He opened the door quickly and started down the hall. We followed him with vague apprehension, not knowing what was in his mind and with no anticipation of what was to follow. Vance peered out through the garden door. Then he turned back, shaking his head.

"No, it couldn't have been there. We would have been able to see." His eyes moved inquiringly up and down the hall, and after a moment a strange, startled look came into them. "It could be!" he exclaimed. "Oh, my aunt! Damnable things are happening here. Wait a second."

He rapidly retraced his steps to the vault door. Grasping the knob, he rattled it violently; but the door was now locked. Taking the key from its nail, he inserted it hurriedly into the lock. As he opened the heavy door a crack, a pungent, pene-trating odor assailed my nostrils. Vance quickly drew back.

"Out into the air!" he called over his shoulder, in our direction. "All of you!"

Instinctively we made for the door to the garden.

Vance held one hand over his nose and mouth and pushed the vault door further inward. Heavy amber-colored fumes drifted out into the hall, and I felt a stifling, choking sensation. Vance staggered back a short step, but kept his hand on the door-knob.

"Miss Beeton! Miss Beeton!" he called. There was no response; and I saw Vance put his head down and move forward into the dense fumes that were emanating from the open door. He sank to his knees on the threshold and leaned forward into the vault. The next moment he had straightened up and was dragging the limp body of the nurse out into the passageway.

The whole episode took much less time than is required to relate it. Actually no more than ten seconds had elapsed from the time he had inserted the key into the lock. I knew what an effort he was making, for even as I stood outside the garden door, where the fumes were comparatively thin, I felt half suffocated, and Markham and Heath were choking and coughing.

As soon as the girl was out of the vault, Vance took her up in his arms and carried her unsteadily out into the garden, where he placed her gently on the wicker settee. His face was deathly pale; his eyes were watering; and he had difficulty with his breathing. When he had released the girl, he leaned heavily against one of the iron posts which supported the awning. He opened his mouth wide and sucked the fresh air into his lungs.

The nurse was gasping stertorously and clutching her throat. Although her breast was rising and falling convulsively, her whole body was limp and lifeless.

At that moment Doctor Siefert stepped through the garden door, a look of amazement on his face. He had all the outward appearance of the type of medical man Vance had described to us the night before. He was about sixty, conservatively but modishly attired, and with a bearing studiously dignified and self-sufficient.

With a great effort Vance drew himself erect.

"Hurry, doctor," he called. "It's bromine gas." He made a shaky gesture with one hand toward the prostrate figure of the nurse.

Siefert came rapidly forward, moved the girl's body into a more comfortable position and opened the collar of her uniform.

"Nothing but the air can help her," he said, as he moved one end of the settee around so that it faced the cool breeze from the river. "How are you feeling, Vance?"

Vance was dabbing his eyes with a handkerchief. He blinked once or twice and smiled faintly.

"I'm quite all right." He went to the settee and looked down at the girl for a moment. "A close call," he murmured.

Siefert inclined his head gravely.

At this moment Hammle came strutting up briskly from a remote corner of the garden.

"Good Gad!" he exclaimed. "What's the matter?"

Vance turned to the man in angry surprise.

"Well, well," he greeted him. "The roll call is complete. I'll tell you later what's the matter. Or perhaps you will be able to tell me. Wait over there." And he jerked his head in the direction of a chair nearby.

Hammle glared in resentment and began spluttering; but Heath, who had come quickly to his side, took him firmly by the arm and led him diplomatically to the chair Vance had indicated. Hammle sat down meekly and took out a cigarette.

"I wish I'd taken the earlier train to Long Island," he muttered.

"It might have been better, don't y' know," murmured Vance, turning away from him.

The nurse's strangled coughing had abated somewhat. Her breathing was deeper and more regular, and the gasping had partly subsided. Before long she struggled to sit up.

Siefert helped her.

"Breathe as deeply and rapidly as you can," he said. "It's air you need."

The girl made an effort to follow instructions, one hand braced against the back of the settee, and the other resting on Vance's arm.

A few minutes later she was able to speak, but with considerable difficulty.

"I feel—better now. Except for the burning—in my nose and throat."

Siefert sent Heath for some water and when the Sergeant had fetched it Miss Beeton drank a glassful in choking gulps. In another two or three minutes she seemed to have recovered to a great extent. She looked up at Vance with frightened eyes.

"What happened?" she asked.

"We don't know yet." Vance returned her gaze with obvious distress. "We only know that you were poisoned with bromine gas in the vault where Swift was shot. We were hoping that you could tell us about it yourself."

She shook her head vaguely, and there was a dazed look in her eyes.

"I'm afraid I can't tell you very much. It all happened so unexpectedly—so suddenly. All I know is that when I went to tell Doctor Siefert he might come upstairs, I was struck on the head from behind, just as I passed the garden door. The blow didn't render me entirely unconscious, but it stunned me so that I was unaware of anything or anybody around me. Then I felt myself being caught from behind, turned about, and forced back up the passageway and into the vault. I have a faint recollection of the door being shut upon me, although I wasn't sufficiently rational to protest or even to realize what had happened. But I was conscious of the fact that inside the vault there was a frightful suffocating smell. I was leaning up against the wall and it was very painful to breathe... I felt myself sinking—and that's the last I remember..." She shuddered. "That's all I knew—until just now."

"Yes. Not a pleasant experience. But it could have been much worse." Vance spoke in a lowvoice and smiled gravely down at the girl. "There's a bad bruise on the back of your head. That too might have been worse, but the starched band of your cap probably saved you from more serious injury."

The girl had got to her feet and stood swaying a little as she steadied herself against Vance.

"I really feel all right now." She looked at Vance wistfully. "And I have you to thank—haven't I?"

Siefert spoke gruffly. "A few more minutes of that bromine gas would have proved fatal. Whoever found you and got you out here did so just in time."

The girl had not taken her eyes from Vance.

"How did you happen to find me so soon?" she asked him.

"Belated reasoning," he answered. "I should have found you several minutes before—the moment I learned that you had not returned downstairs. But at first it was difficult to realize that anything serious could have happened to you."

"I can't understand it even now," the girl said with a bewildered air.

"Neither can I—entirely," returned Vance. "But perhaps I can learn something more."

Going quickly to the pitcher of water Heath had brought, he dipped his handkerchief into it. Pressing the handkerchief against his face, he disappeared into the passageway. A minute or so later he returned. In his hand he held a jagged piece of thin curved glass, about three inches long.

It was part of a broken vial, and still clinging to it was a small paper label on which was printed the symbol "Br."

"I found this on the tiled floor, in the far corner of the vault. It was just beneath one of the racks which holds Professor Garden's assortment of chemicals. There's an empty space in the rack, but this vial of bromine couldn't have fallen to the floor accidentally. It could only have been taken out deliberately and broken at the right moment." He handed the fragment of glass to Heath. "Take this, Sergeant, and have it gone over carefully for fingerprints. But if, as I suspect, the same person that killed Swift handled it, I doubt if there will be any telltale marks on it. However…"

Heath accepted the bit of glass gingerly, rolled it in his handkerchief and thrust it into his pocket.

"If it does show any fingerprints," he grumbled, "it'll be the first we found around here."

Vance turned to Markham, who had been standing near the rock pool during the entire scene, looking on with aggressive bewilderment.

"Bromine," he explained, "is a common reagent. It's to be found in almost every chemist's laborat'ry. It's one of the halogens, and, though it's never found free in nature, it occurs in various compounds. Incidentally, it got its name from the Greek *bromos*, which means stench. It hasn't figured very often as a criminal agent, although accidental cases of bromine poisoning are numerous. But it was used extensively during the war in the manufacture of gas bombs, for it volatilizes on coming in contact with the air. And bromine gas is suffocating and deadly. Whoever planned this lethal chamber for Miss Beeton wasn't without cruelty."

"It was a dastardly thing, Vance," Siefert burst out, his eyes flashing.

Vance nodded and his eyes moved to the nurse.

"Yes. All of that, doctor. So was Swift's murder... How are you feeling now, Miss Beeton?"

"A little shaky," she answered with a weak smile. "But nothing more." She was leaning against one end of the settee.

"Then we'll carry on, what?"

"Of course," she returned in a low voice.

Floyd Garden stepped out from the hallway at this moment. He coughed and looked at us with blinking inquisitive eyes.

"What's this beastly odor in the hall?" he asked. "It's gotten downstairs, and Sneed is already crying like a lost baby. Is anything wrong?"

"Not now. No," Vance returned. "A little bromine gas a few minutes ago; but the air will be clear in a little while. No casualties. Everyone doing well... Did you want to see me?"

Garden looked round at the group on the roof with a puzzled air.

"Awfully sorry to interrupt you, Vance; but the fact is, I came for the doctor." His eyes rested on Siefert, and he smiled dryly. "It's the usual thing, doc," he said. "The mater seems almost in a state of collapse—she assured me vigorously that she hadn't an ounce of strength left. I got her to go to bed—which she seemed perfectly willing to do. But she insists on seeing you immediately. I never know when she means it and when she doesn't. But that's the message."

A worried look came into Siefert's eyes, and he took a slow deep breath before answering.

"I'll come at once, of course," he said. He looked at the nurse and then lifted his gaze to Vance. "Will you excuse me?"

Vance bowed. "Certainly, doctor. But I think Miss Beeton had better remain here in the air for a while longer."

"Oh, by all means. By all means. If I need her I'll send word. But I trust that won't be necessary." And Siefert left the roof reluctantly, with Garden following him.

Vance watched them until they turned through the door of the passageway; then he spoke to the nurse.

"Please sit here a few minutes, Miss Beeton. I want to have a talk with you. But first I'd like a minute or two with Mr. Hammle."

The nurse nodded her assent and sat down a little wearily on the settee.

Vance beckoned curtly to Hammle. "Suppose we go inside for a moment."

Hammle rose with alacrity. "I was wondering how much longer you gentlemen were going to keep me here."

Vance led the way into the study, and Markham and I followed behind Hammle.

"What were you doing on the roof, Mr. Hammle?" asked Vance. "I told you some time ago, after our brief interview, that you might go."

Hammle fidgeted. He was patently apprehensive and wary.

"There's no crime in going out into the garden for a while—is there?" He asked with unimpressive truculence.

"None whatever," Vance returned casually. "I was wonderin' why you preferred the garden to going home. Devilish things have been happening in the garden this afternoon."

"As I told you, I wish I had gone. How did I know—?"

"That's hardly the point, Mr. Hammle." Vance cut him short. "It doesn't answer my question."

"Well now, look here," Hammle explained fulsomely; "I had just missed a train to Long Island, and it was more than an hour until the next one. When I went out of here and started to go downstairs, I suddenly said to myself, 'It'll be pleasanter waiting in the garden than in the Pennsylvania Station.' So I went out on the roof and hung around. And here I am."

Vance regarded the man shrewdly and nodded his head.

"Yes, as you say. Here you are. More or less in evidence. By the by, Mr. Hammle, what did you see while you were waiting in the garden for the next train?"

"Not a thing—absolutely!" Hammle's tone was aggressive. "I walked along the boxwood hedges, smoking, and was leaning over the parapet by the gate, looking out at the city, when I heard you come out carrying the nurse."

Vance narrowed his eyes: it was obvious he was not satisfied with Hammle's explanation.

"And you saw no one else either in the garden or on the terrace?"

"Not a soul," the man assured him.

"And you heard nothing?"

"Not until you gentlemen came out."

Vance stood regarding Hammle for several moments. Then he turned and walked toward the garden window.

"That will be all for the moment," he said brusquely. "But we shall probably want to see you tomorrow."

"I'll be at home all day. Glad to be of any service." Hammle shot a covert look at Vance, made his adieux quickly, and went out down the passageway.

CHAPTER THIRTEEN

The Azure Star
(Saturday, April 14; 7 p. m.)

VANCE RETURNED AT once to the garden. Miss Beeton drew herself up a little as he approached her.

"Do you feel equal to a few questions?" he asked her.

"Oh, yes." She smiled with more assurance now, and rose.

Dusk was settling rapidly over the city. A dull slate color was replacing the blue mist over the river. The skies beyond the Jersey hills were luminous with the vivid colors of the sunset, and in the distance tiny specks of yellow light were beginning to appear in the windows of the serried buildings. A light breeze was blowing from the north, and the air was cool.

As we crossed the garden to the balustrade, Miss Beeton took a deep breath and shuddered slightly.

"You'd better have your coat," Vance suggested. He returned to the study and brought it out to her. When he had helped her into it she turned suddenly and looked at him inquiringly.

"Why was my coat brought to the study?" she asked. "It's been worrying me frightfully...with all the terrible things that have been going on today."

"Why should it worry you?" Vance smiled at the girl. "A misplaced coat is surely not a serious matter." His tone was reassuring. "But we really owe you an explanation. You see, two revolvers figured in Swift's death. One of them we all saw on the roof here—that was the one with which the chap was killed. But no one downstairs heard the shot because the poor fellow met his end in Professor Garden's storeroom vault—"

"Ah! That was why you wanted to know if the key was in its place." The girl nodded.

"The shot we all heard," Vance went on, "was fired from another revolver after Swift's body had been carried from the vault and placed in the chair out here. We were naturally anxious to find that other weapon, and Sergeant Heath made a search for it..."

"But—but—my coat?" Her hand went out and she clutched at Vance's sleeve as a look of understanding came into her frightened eyes.

"Yes," Vance said, "the Sergeant found the revolver in the pocket of your top-coat. Someone had put it there as a tempor'ry hiding place."

She recoiled with a sudden intake of breath.

"How dreadful!" Her words were barely audible.

Vance put his hand on her shoulder.

"If you had not come to the study when you did and seen the coat, we would have returned it to the closet downstairs and saved you all this worry."

"But it's too terrible!.... And then this—this attempt on my life. I can't understand. I'm frightened."

"Come, come," Vance exhorted the girl. "It's over now, and we need your help."

She gazed directly into his eyes for several minutes. Then she gave him a faint smile of confidence.

"I'm very sorry," she said simply. "But this house—this family—they've been doing queer things to my nerves for the past month. I can't explain it, but there's something frightfully wrong here... I was in charge of an operating room in a Montreal hospital for six months, attending as many as six and eight operations a day; but that never affected me the way this household does. There, at least, I could see what was going on—I could help and know that I was helping. But here everything goes on in dark corners, and nothing I do seems to be of any use. Can you imagine a surgeon suddenly going blind in the middle of a laparotomy and trying to continue without his sight? That's how I feel in this strange place... But please don't think I am not ready to help—to do anything I can for you. You, too, always have to work in the dark, don't you?"

"Don't we all have to work in the dark?" Vance murmured, without taking his eyes from her. "Tell me who you think could have been guilty of the terrible things that have happened here."

All fear and doubt seemed to have left the girl. She moved toward the balustrade and stood looking over the river with an impressive calm and self-control.

"Really, I don't know," she answered with quiet restraint. "There are several possibilities, humanly speaking. But I haven't had time to think about it clearly. It all happened so suddenly..."

"Yes, quite," put in Vance. "Things like that usually do come suddenly and without previous warning."

"Woode Swift's death wasn't at all the sort of thing I would expect to happen here," the girl went on. "I wouldn't have been surprised at some act of impulsive violence, but this premeditated murder, so subtle and so carefully planned, seems alien to the atmosphere here. Besides, it isn't a loving family, except on the surface. Psychologically, everyone seems at cross purposes—full of hidden hatreds. No contacts anywhere— I mean, no understanding contacts. Floyd Garden is saner than the others. His interests are narrower, to be sure, but, on his own mental level, he has always impressed me as being straightforward and eminently human. He's dependable, too, I think. He's intolerant of subtleties and profundities, and has always taken the course of ignoring the existence of those qualities which have caused friction between the other members of the household. Maybe I'm wrong about it, but that has been my impression."

She paused and frowned.

"As for Mrs. Garden, I feel that by nature she is shallow and is deliberately creating for herself a deeper and more complex mode of life, which she doesn't in the least understand. That, of course, makes her unreasonable and dangerous. I have never had a more unreasonable patient. She has no consideration whatever for others. Her affection for her nephew has never seemed genuine to me. He was like a little clay model that she had made and prized highly. If she had an idea for another figurine, I feel that she would have wet the clay and remodeled it into a new object of adoration."

"And Professor Garden?"

"He's a researcher and scientist, of course, and, therefore, not altogether human, in the conventional sense. I have thought sometimes that he isn't wholly rational. To him people and things are merely elements to be converted into some new chemical combination. Do you understand what I am trying to say?"

"Yes, quite well," Vance assured her. "Every scientist imagines himself an *Ubermensch*. Power is his god. Many of the world's greatest scientists have been regarded as madmen. Perhaps they were. Yes. A queer problem. The possession of power induces weakness. Silly notion, what? The most dangerous agency in the world is science. Especially dangerous to the scientist himself. Every great scientific discoverer is a Frankenstein. However... What is your impression of the guests who were present today?"

"I don't feel competent to pass judgment on them," the girl replied seriously. "I can't entirely understand them. But each one strikes me as dangerous in his own way. They are all playing a game—and it seems to be a game without rules. To them the outcome justifies the methods they use. They seem to be mere seekers after sensation, trying to draw the veil of illusion over life's realities because they are not strong enough to face the facts."

"Yes, quite. You have clear vision." Vance scrutinized the girl beside him. "And you took up nursing because you are able to face the realities. You are not afraid of life—or of death."

The girl looked embarrassed.

"You're making too much of my profession. After all, I had to earn my living, and nursing appealed to me."

"Yes, of course. It would." Vance nodded. "But tell me, wouldn't you rather not have to work for your living?"

She looked up.

"Perhaps. But isn't it natural for every woman to prefer luxury and security to drudgery and uncertainty?"

"No doubt," said Vance. "And speakin' of nursing, just what do you think of Mrs. Garden's condition?"

Miss Beeton hesitated before she answered:

"Really, I don't know what to say. I can't understand it. And I rather suspect that Doctor Siefert himself is puzzled by it. Mrs. Garden is obviously a sick woman. She shows many of the symptoms of that nervous, erratic temperament exhibited by people suffering from cancer. Though she's much better some days than others, I know that she suffers a great deal. Doctor Siefert tells me she is really a neurological case; but I get the feeling, at times, that it goes much deeper—that an obscure physiological condition is producing the neurological symptoms she shows."

"That's most interestin'. Doctor Siefert mentioned something of the kind to me only a few days ago." Vance moved nearer to the girl. "Would you mind telling me something of your contacts with the members of the household?"

"There's very little to tell. Professor Garden practically ignores me—half the time I doubt if he even knows I am here.

Mrs. Garden alternates between periods of irritable admonition and intimate confidence. Floyd Garden has always been pleasant and considerate. He has wanted me to be happy here, and has often apologized for his mother's abominable treatment of me at times. I've rather liked him for his attitude."

"And what of Swift—did you see much of him?"

The girl seemed reluctant to answer and looked away; but she finally turned back to Vance.

"The truth is, Mr. Swift asked me several times to go to dinner and the theatre with him. He was never objectionable in his advances; but he did rather annoy me occasionally. I got the impression, though, that he was one of those unhappy men who feel their inferiority and seek to bolster themselves up with the affections of women. I think that he was really concerned with Miss Graem, and merely turned to me through pique."

Vance smoked for a few moments in silence. Then he said:

"What of the big race today? Had there been much discussion about it?"

"Oh, yes. For over a week I've heard little else here. A curious tension has been growing in the house. I heard Mr. Swift remark to Floyd Garden one evening that the Rivermont Handicap was his one remaining hope, and that he thought Equanimity would win. They immediately went into a furious argument regarding Equanimity's chances."

"Was it generally known to the other members of the afternoon gatherings how Swift felt about this race and Equanimity?"

"Yes, the matter was freely discussed for days. You see," the girl added in explanation, "it's impossible for me not to overhear some of these afternoon discussions; and Mrs. Garden herself often takes part in them and then discusses them with me later."

"By the by," asked Vance, "how did you come to bet on Azure Star?"

"Frankly," the girl confessed shyly, "I've been mildly interested in the horse-betting parties here, though I've never had any desire to make a wager myself. But I overheard you tell Mr. Garden that you had picked Azure Star, and the name was so appealing that I asked Mr. Garden to place that bet for me. It was the first time I ever bet on a horse."

"And Azure Star came in." Vance sighed. "Too bad. Actually you bet against Equanimity, you know—he was the favorite. A big gamble. Most unfortunate that you won. Beginner's luck, d' ye see, is always fatal."

The girl's face became suddenly sombre, and she looked steadily at Vance for several moments before she spoke again.

"Do you really think it will prove fatal?"

"Yes. Oh, yes. Inevitable. You won't be able to resist making other wagers. One doesn't stop with the first bet if one wins. And, invariably, one loses in the end."

Again the girl gave Vance a long and troubled look; then her gaze drifted to the darkening sky overhead.

"But Azure Star is a beautiful name, isn't it?" She pointed upward. "There's one now."

We all looked up. High above we saw a single bright star shining with blue luminosity in the cloudless sky. After a moment Vance moved toward the parapet and looked out over the waters of the river to the purpling hills and the still glowing sunset colors in the west. The sharp forms of the great gaunt buildings of the city to the south cut the empyrean like the unreal silhouettes on a theatrical drop.

"No city in the world," Vance said, "is as beautiful as New York seen from a vantage point like this in the early twilight." (I wondered at his sudden change of mood.)

He stepped up on the parapet and looked down into the great abyss of deep shadows and flickering lights far below. A curious chill of fear ran over me—the sort of fear I have always felt when I have seen acrobatic performers perilously balanced high above a circus arena. I knew Vance had no fear of heights and that he possessed an abnormal sense of equilibrium. But I nevertheless drew in an involuntary breath; my feet and lower limbs began to tingle; and for a moment I actually felt faint.

Miss Beeton was standing close to Markham, and she, too, must have experienced something of the sensation I felt, for I saw her face go suddenly pale. Her eyes were fixed on Vance with a look of apprehensive horror, and she caught at Markham's arm as if for support.

"Vance!" It was Markham's stern voice that broke the silence. "Come down from there!"

Vance jumped down and turned to us.

"Frightfully sorry," he said. "Height does affect most people. I didn't realize." He looked at the girl. "Will you forgive me?..."

As he spoke Floyd Garden stepped out on the roof through the passageway door.

"Sorry, Vance," he apologized, "but Doc Siefert wants Miss Beeton downstairs—if she feels equal to it. The mater is putting on one of her acts."

The nurse hurried away immediately, and Garden strolled up to Vance. He was again fussing with his pipe.

"A beastly mess," he mumbled. "And you've certainly put the fear of God and destruction into the hearts of the pious boys and girls here this afternoon. They all got the jitters after you talked with them." He looked up. "The fact is, Vance, if you should want to see Kroon or Zalia Graem or Madge Weatherby for any reason this evening, they'll be here. They've all asked to come. Must return to the scene of the crime, or something of that kind. Need mutual support. And, to tell you the truth, I'm damned glad they're coming. At least we can talk the thing over and drink highballs; and that's better than fussing and worrying about it all alone."

"Perfectly natural. Quite." Vance nodded. "I understand their feelings—and yours—perfectly... Beastly mess, as you say... And now suppose we go down."

Doctor Siefert met us at the foot of the stairs.

"I was just coming up for you, Mr. Vance. Mrs. Garden insists on seeing you gentlemen." Then he added in a low tone: "She's in a tantrum. A bit hysterical. Don't take anything she may say too seriously."

We entered the bedroom. Mrs. Garden, in a salmon-pink silk dressing gown, was in bed, bolstered up by a collection of pillows. Her face was drawn and, in the slanting rays of the nightlight, seemed flabby and unhealthy. Her eyes glared demoniacally as she looked at us, and her fingers clutched nervously at the quilt. Miss Beeton stood at the far side of the bed, looking down at her patient with calm concern; and Professor Garden leaned heavily against the windowsill opposite, his face a mask of troubled solicitude.

"I have something to say, and I want you all to hear it." Mrs. Garden's voice was shrill and strident. "My nephew has been killed today—and I know who did it!" She glared venomously at Floyd Garden who stood near the foot of the bed, his pipe hanging limply from the corner of his mouth. "*You* did it!" She pointed an accusing finger at her son. "You've always hated Woody. You've been jealous of him. No one else had any reason to do this despicable thing. I suppose I should lie for you and shield you. But to what end? So you could kill somebody else? Perhaps—perhaps even me, or your father. No! The time has come for the truth. You killed Woody, and I know you killed him. And I know why you did it…"

Floyd Garden stood through this tirade without moving and without perceptible emotion. He kept his eyes on his mother with cynical indifference. When she paused he took the pipe from his mouth and with a sad smile said:

"And why did I do it, mater?"

"Because you were jealous of him. Because you knew that I had divided my estate equally between you two—and you want it all for yourself. You always resented the fact that I loved Woody as well as you. And now you think that by having got Woody out of the way, you'll get everything when I die. But you're mistaken. You'll get nothing! Do you hear me? Nothing! Tomorrow I'm going to change my will." Her eyes were full of frantic gloating: she was like a woman who has suddenly gone out of her mind. "I'm going to change my will, do you understand? Woody's share will go to your father, with the stipulation that you will never get or inherit a dollar of it. And your share will go to charity." She laughed hysterically and beat the bed with her clenched fists.

Doctor Siefert had been watching the woman closely. He now moved a little nearer the bed.

"An ice-pack, immediately," he said to the nurse; and she went quickly from the room. Then he busied himself with his medicine case and deftly prepared a hypodermic injection.

"I won't let you give me that," the woman on the bed screamed. "There's nothing the matter with me. I'm tired of taking your drugs."

"Yes, I know. But you'll take this, Mrs. Garden." Doctor Siefert spoke with calm assurance.

The woman relaxed under his patient dictatorial scrutiny and permitted him to give her the injection. She lay back on the pillows, staring blankly at her son. The nurse returned to the room and arranged the ice-bag for her patient.

Doctor Siefert then quickly made out a prescription and turned to Miss Beeton.

"Have this filled at once. A teaspoonful every two hours until Mrs. Garden falls asleep."

Floyd Garden stepped forward and took the prescription.

"I'll phone the pharmacy," he said. "It'll take them only a few minutes to send it over." And he went out of the room.

After a few final instructions to Miss Beeton, the doctor led the way to the drawing room and the rest of us followed, leaving the nurse rearranging Mrs. Garden's pillows. Professor Garden, who during the painful scene had stood with his back to us, gazing out of the window into the night, still remained there, looking like a hunched gargoyle framed by the open casement.

As we passed the den door, we could hear Floyd Garden telephoning.

"I think Mrs. Garden will quiet down now," Doctor Siefert remarked to Vance when we reached the drawing room. "As I told you, you mustn't take her remarks seriously when she's in this condition. She will probably have forgotten about it by tomorrow."

"Her bitterness, however, did not seem entirely devoid of rationality," Vance returned.

Siefert frowned but made no comment on Vance's statement. Instead he said in his quiet, well-modulated voice, as he sat down leisurely in the nearest chair: "This whole affair is very shocking. Floyd Garden gave me but few details when I arrived. Would you care to enlighten me further?"

Vance readily complied. He briefly went over the entire case, beginning with the anonymous telephone message he had received the night before. (Not by the slightest sign did the doctor indicate any previous knowledge of that telephone call. He sat looking at Vance with serene attentiveness, like a specialist listening to the case history of a patient.) Vance withheld no important detail from him. He explained about the races and the wagers, Swift's withdrawal to the roof, the actions of the other members of the party, the shot, the finding of Swift's body, the discoveries in the vault, the matter of the disconnected buzzer wires, the substance of his various interviews with the members of the Garden family and their guests, and, finally, the finding of the second revolver in the nurse's coat.

"And the rest," Vance concluded, "you yourself have witnessed."

Siefert nodded very slowly two or three times, as if to infer that he had received a clear and satisfactory picture of the events of the afternoon.

"A very serious situation," he commented gravely, as if making a diagnosis. "Some of the things you have told me seem highly significant. A shrewdly conceived murder—and a vicious one. Especially the hiding of the revolver in Miss Beeton's coat and the attempt on her life with the bromine gas in the vault. I don't understand that phase of the situation."

Vance looked up quickly.

"Do you understand any other phase of the situation?"

"No, no. I did not mean to imply that," Siefert hastened to answer. "I was merely thinking that while Swift's death could conceivably be explained on rational grounds, I fail to see any possible reason for this dastardly attempt to involve Miss Beeton and then to end her life."

"But I seriously doubt," said Vance, "that the revolver was put in Miss Beeton's coat pocket with any intention of incriminating her. I imagine it was to have been taken out of the house at the first opportunity. But I agree with you that the bromine episode is highly mystifyin'." Vance, without appearing to do so, was watching the doctor closely. "When you asked to see me on your arrival here this afternoon," he went on, "I was hoping that you might have some suggestion which, coming from one who is familiar with the domestic situation here, might put us on the track to a solution."

Siefert solemnly shook his head several times.

"No, no. I am sorry, but I am completely at a loss myself. When I asked to speak to you and Mr. Markham it was because I was naturally deeply interested in the situation here and anxious to hear what you might have to say about it." He paused, shifted slightly in his chair, and then asked: "Have you formed any opinion from what you have been able to learn?"

"Yes. Oh, yes." Vance's gaze drifted from the doctor to the beautiful T'ang horse which stood on a nearby cabinet. "Frankly, however, I detest my opinion. I'd hate to be right about it. A sinister, unnatural conclusion is forcing itself upon me. It's sheer horror." He spoke with unwonted intensity.

Siefert was silent, and Vance turned to him again.

"I say, doctor, are you particularly worried about Mrs. Garden's condition?"

A cloud overspread Siefert's countenance, and he did not answer at once.

"It's a queer case," he said at length, with an obvious attempt at evasion. "As I recently told you, it has me deeply puzzled. I'm bringing Kattelbaum* up tomorrow."

---

*   *Hugo Kattelbaum, though a comparatively young man, was one of the country's leading authorities on cancer, and his researches on the effect of radium on the human viscera had, for the past year, been receiving considerable attention in the leading medical journals.*

"Yes. As you say. Kattelbaum." Vance looked at the doctor dreamily. "My anonymous telephone message last night mentioned radioactive sodium. But equanimity is essential. Yes. By all means. Not a nice case, doctor—not at all a nice case... And now I think we'll be toddlin'." Vance rose and bowed with formal brusqueness. Siefert also got up.

"If there is anything whatever that I can do for you..." he began.

"We may call on you later," Vance returned, and walked toward the archway.

Siefert did not follow us, but turned and moved slowly toward one of the front windows, where he stood looking out, with his hands clasped behind him. We reentered the hallway and found Sneed waiting to help us with our coats.

We had just reached the door leading out of the apartment when the strident tones of Mrs. Garden's voice assailed us again. Floyd Garden was standing just inside the bedroom door, looking over at his mother.

"Your solicitude won't do you any good, Floyd," Mrs. Garden cried. "Being kind to me now, are you? Telephoning for the prescription—all attention and loving kindness. But don't think you're pulling the wool over my eyes. It won't make any difference. Tomorrow I change my will! Tomorrow..."

We continued on our way out, and heard no more.

But Mrs. Garden did not change her will. The following morning she was found dead in bed.

CHAPTER FOURTEEN

Radioactive Sodium
(Sunday, April 15; 9 a. m.)

SHORTLY AFTER NINE o'clock the next morning there was a telephone call from Doctor Siefert. Vance was still abed when the telephone rang, and I answered it. (I had been up for several hours: the events of the preceding day had stirred me deeply, and I had been unable to sleep.) The doctor's voice was urgent and trouble when he asked that I summon Vance immediately. I had a premonition of further disaster as I roused Vance. He seemed loath to get up and complained cynically about people who rise early in the morning. But he finally slipped into his Chinese robe and sandals and, lighting a *Régie*, went protestingly into the anteroom.

It was nearly ten minutes before he came out again. His resentment had given way, and as he stepped across to the table and rang for Currie, there was a look of keen interest in his eyes.

"Breakfast at once," he ordered when his old butler appeared. "And put out a sombre suit and my black Homburg.

And, by the by, Currie, a little extra coffee. Mr. Markham will be here soon and may want a cup."

Currie went out, and Vance turned back to his bedroom. At the door he stopped and turned to me with a curious look.

"Mrs. Garden was found dead in her bed this morning," he drawled. "Poison of some kind. I've phoned Markham, and we'll be going to the Garden apartment as soon as he comes. A bad business, Van—very bad. There's too much betting going on in that house." And he went on into the bedroom.

Markham arrived within half an hour. In the meantime Vance had dressed and was finishing his second cup of coffee.

"What's the trouble now?" Markham demanded irritably, as he came into the library. "Perhaps now that I'm here, you'll be good enough to forgo your cryptic air."

"My dear Markham—oh, my dear Markham!" Vance looked up and sighed. "Do sit down and have a cup of coffee while I enjoy this cigarette. Really, y' know, it's deuced hard to be lucid on the telephone." He poured a cup of coffee, and Markham reluctantly sat down. "And please don't sweeten the coffee," Vance went on. "It has a delightfully subtle bouquet, and it would be a pity to spoil it with saccharine."

Markham, frowning defiantly, put three lumps of sugar in the cup.

"Why am I here?" he growled.

"A profoundly philosophical question," smiled Vance. "Unanswerable, however. Why are any of us here? Why anything? But, since we are all here without knowing the reason therefor, I'll pander to your pragmatism." He drew deeply on his cigarette and settled back lazily in his chair. "Siefert phoned me this morning, just before I called you. Explained he didn't know your private number at home and asked me to apologize to you for not notifying you direct."

"Notifying me?" Markham set down his cup.

"About Mrs. Garden. She's dead. Found so this morning in bed. Probably murdered."

"Good God!"

"Yes, quite. Not a nice situation. No. The lady died some time during the night—exact hour unknown as yet. Siefert says it might have been caused by an overdose of the sleeping medicine he prescribed for her. It's all gone. And he says there was enough of it to do the trick. On the other hand, he admits it might have been something else. He's very noncommittal. No external signs he can diagnose. Craves our advice and succor. Hence his summons."

Markham pushed his cup aside with a clatter and lighted a cigar.

"Where's Siefert now?" he asked.

"At the Gardens'. Very correct. Standing by, and all that. The nurse phoned him shortly after eight this morning—it was she who made the discovery when she took Mrs. Garden's breakfast in. Siefert hastened over and after viewing the remains and probing round a bit called me. Said that, in view of yesterday's events, he didn't wish to go ahead until we got there."

"Well, why don't we get along?" snapped Markham, standing up.

Vance sighed and rose slowly from his chair.

"There's really no rush. The lady can't elude us. And Siefert won't desert the ship. Moreover, it's a beastly hour to drag one out of bed. Y' know, Markham, an entertainin' monograph could be written about the total lack of consideration on the part of murderers. They think only of themselves. No fellow feelin'. Always upsettin' the normal routine. And they never declare a holiday—not even on a Sunday morning… However, as you say. Let's toddle."

"Hadn't we better notify Heath?" suggested Markham.

"Yes—quite," returned Vance, as we went out. "I called the Sergeant just after I phoned you. He's been up half the night working on the usual police routine. Stout fella, Heath. Amazin' industry. But quite futile. If only such energy led anywhere beyond steel filing cabinets. I always think tenderly of Heath as a perpetuator of archives…"

Miss Beeton admitted us to the Garden apartment. She looked drawn and worried, but she gave Vance a faint smile of greeting which he returned.

"I'm beginning to think this nightmare will never end, Mr. Vance," she said.

Vance nodded sombrely, and we went on into the drawing room where Doctor Siefert, Professor Garden, and his son were awaiting us.

"I'm glad you've come, gentlemen," Siefert greeted us, coming forward.

Professor Garden sat at one end of the long davenport, his elbows resting on his knees, his face in his hands. He barely acknowledged our presence. Floyd Garden got to his feet and nodded abstractedly in our direction. A terrible change seemed to have come over him. He looked years older than when we had left him the night before, and his face, despite its tan, showed a greenish pallor. His eyes moved vaguely about the room; he was visibly shaken.

"What a hell of a situation!" he mumbled, focusing watery eyes on Vance. "The mater accuses me last night of putting Woody out of the way, and then threatens to cut me off in her will. And now she's dead! And it was I who took charge of the prescription. The doc says it could have been the medicine that killed her."

Vance looked at the man sharply.

"Yes, yes," he said in a low, sympathetic tone. "I thought of all that, too, don't y' know. But it certainly won't help you to be morbid about it. How about a Tom Collins?"

"I've had four already," Garden returned dispiritedly, sinking back into his chair. But almost immediately he sprang to his feet again. He pointed a finger at Vance, and his eyes filled with apprehension and entreaty.

"For God's sake," he burst out, "it's up to you to find out the truth. I'm on the spot—what with my going out of the room with Woody yesterday, my failure to place his bet, then the mater's accusation, and that damned will of hers, and the medicine. You've got to find out who's guilty..."

As he was talking the door bell had rung, and Heath came up the hallway.

"Sure, we're gonna find out," came the pugnacious voice of the Sergeant from the archway. "And it ain't gonna be so well with you when we do."

Vance turned quickly round. "Oh, I say, Sergeant. Less animation, please. This is hardly the time. Too early in the morning." He went to Garden and, putting a hand on the man's shoulder, urged him back into his chair. "Come, buck up," he said; "we'll need your help, and if you work up a case of jitters you'll be useless."

"But don't you see how deeply involved I am?" Garden protested weakly.

"You're not the only one involved," Vance returned calmly. He turned to Siefert. "I think, doctor, we should have a little chat. Possibly we can get the matter of your patient's death straightened out a bit. Suppose we go upstairs to the study, what?"

As we stepped through the archway into the hall, I glanced back. Young Garden was staring after us with a hard, determined look. The professor had not moved, and took no more notice of our going than he had of our coming.

In the study Vance went directly to the point.

"Doctor, the time has come when we must be perfectly frank with each other. The usual conventional considerations of your profession must be temporarily put aside. A matter far more urgent is involved now, and it requires more serious consideration than the accepted relationship between doctor and patient. Therefore, I shall be altogether candid with you and trust that you can see your way to being equally candid with me."

Siefert, who had taken a chair near the door, looked at Vance a trifle uneasily.

"I regret that I do not understand what you mean," he said in his suavest manner.

"I merely mean," replied Vance coolly, "that I am fully aware that it was you who sent me the anonymous telephone message Friday night."

Siefert raised his eyebrows slightly.

"Indeed! That's very interesting."

"Not only interestin'," drawled Vance, "but true. How I know it was you need not concern us at the moment. I only beg of you to admit that it is so, and to act accordingly. The fact has a direct bearing on this tragic case, and unless you will assist us with a frank statement, a grave injustice may be done—an injustice that could not be squared with any existing code of medical ethics."

Siefert hesitated for several moments. He withdrew his eyes hastily from Vance and looked thoughtfully out of the window toward the west.

"Assuming, for the sake of argument," he said with deliberation, like a man carefully choosing his words, "that it was I who phoned you Friday night, what then?"

Vance watched the man with a faint smile.

"It might be, don't y' know," he said, "that you were cognizant of the situation here, and that you had a suspicion—or let us say, a fear—that something tragic was impending." Vance took out his cigarette case and lighted a cigarette. "I fully understood the import of that message, doctor—as you intended. That is why I happened to be here yesterday afternoon. The significance of your reference to the *Æneid* and the inclusion of the word 'equanimity' did not escape me. I must say, however, that your advice to investigate radioactive sodium was not entirely clear—although I think I now have a fairly lucid idea as to the implication. However, there were some deeper implications in your message, and this is the time, d' ye see, when we should face this thing together with complete honesty."

Siefert brought his eyes back to Vance in a long appraising glance, and then shifted them to the window again. After a minute or two he stood up, clasped his hands behind him, and strode across the room. He looked out over the Hudson with troubled concern. Then he turned and, nodding as if in answer to some question he had put to himself, said:

"Yes, I did send you that message. Perhaps I was not entirely loyal to my principles when I did so, for I had little doubt that you would guess who sent it and would understand what I was trying to convey to you. But I realize that nothing can be gained now by not being frank with you... The situation in this household has bothered me for a long time, and lately I've had a sense of imminent disaster. All of the factors of late have been ripening for this final outburst. And I felt so strongly about them that I could not resist sending an anonymous message to you, in the hope that the vague eventualities I anticipated might be averted."

"How long have you felt this vague premonition?" asked Vance.

"For the past three months, I should say. Although I have acted as the Gardens' physician for many years, it was not until last fall that Mrs. Garden's changing condition came to my notice. I thought little of it at first, but, as it grew worse and I found myself unable to diagnose it satisfactorily, a curious suspicion forced itself on me that the change was not entirely natural. I began coming here much more frequently than had been my custom, and during the last couple of months I had felt many subtle undercurrents in the various relationships of the household, which I had never sensed before. Of course, I knew that Floyd and Swift never got along particularly well—that there was some deep animosity and jealousy between them. I also knew the conditions of Mrs. Garden's will. Furthermore, I knew of the gambling on the horses that had become part of the daily routine here. Neither Floyd nor Woode kept anything from me—you see, I have always been their confidant as well as their physician—and their reactions toward their personal affairs—which, unfortunately, included horse-racing—were well known to me."

Siefert paused with a frown.

"As I say, it has been only recently that I have felt something deeper and more significant in all this interplay of temperaments; and this feeling grew to such proportions that

I actually feared a violent climax of some kind—especially as Floyd told me only a few days ago that his cousin intended to stake his entire remaining funds on Equanimity in the big race yesterday. So overpowering was my feeling in regard to the whole situation here that I decided to do something about it, if I could manage it without divulging any professional confidences. But you saw through my subterfuge, and, to be wholly candid with you, I'm rather glad you did."

Vance nodded. "I appreciate your scruples in the matter, doctor. I only regret that I was unable to forestall these tragedies. That, as it happened, was beyond human power." Vance looked up quickly. "By the by, doctor, did you have any definite suspicions when you phoned me Friday night?"

Siefert shook his head with emphasis. "No. Frankly, I was baffled. I merely felt that some sort of explosion was imminent. But I hadn't the slightest idea in what quarter that explosion would occur."

"Can you say from what quarter the causes for your apprehension arose?"

"No. Nor can I say whether my feeling had to do with Mrs. Garden's state of health alone, or whether I was influenced also by the subtle antagonism between Floyd and Woode Swift. I asked myself the question many times, without finding a satisfactory answer. At times, however, I could not resist the impression that the two factors were in some way closely related. Hence my phone message, in which, by inference, I called your attention to both Mrs. Garden's peculiar illness and the tense atmosphere that had developed round the daily betting on the races."

Vance smoked a while in silence. "And now, doctor, will you be so good as to give us the full details about this morning?"

Siefert drew himself up in his chair.

"There's practically nothing to add to the information I gave you over the phone. Miss Beeton called me a little after eight o'clock and informed me that Mrs. Garden had died some time during the night. She asked for instructions, and I told her that I would come at once. I was here half an hour or so later. I could find no determinable cause for Mrs. Garden's death, and assumed it might have been her heart until Miss Beeton called my attention to the fact that the bottle of medicine sent by the druggist was empty..."

"By the by, doctor, what was, the prescription you made out for your patient last night?"

"A simple barbital solution."

"Why did you not prescribe one of the ordin'ry barbiturate compounds?"

"Why should I?" Siefert asked with obvious annoyance. "I always prefer to know exactly what my patient is getting. I'm old-fashioned enough to take little stock in proprietary mixtures."

"And I believe you told me on the telephone that there was sufficient barbital in the prescription to have caused death."

"Yes." The doctor nodded. "If taken at one time."

"And Mrs. Garden's death was consistent with barbital poisoning?"

"There was nothing to contradict such a conclusion," Siefert answered. "And there was nothing to indicate any other cause."

"When did the nurse discover the empty bottle?"

"Not until after she had phoned me, I believe."

"Could the taste of the solution be detected if it were given to a person without his knowledge?"

"Yes—and no," the doctor replied judicially. "The taste is a bit acrid; but it is a colorless solution, like water, and if it were drunk fast the taste might go unnoticed."

Vance nodded. "Therefore, if the solution had been poured into a glass and water had been added, Mrs. Garden might conceivably have drunk it all without complaining about the bitter taste?"

"That's wholly possible," the doctor told him. "And I cannot help feeling that something of that kind took place last night. It was because of this conclusion that I called you immediately."

Vance, smoking lazily, was watching Siefert from under speculative eyelids. Moving slightly in his chair and crushing out his cigarette in a small jade ashtray at his side, he said:

"Tell me something of Mrs. Garden's illness, doctor, and why radioactive sodium should have suggested itself to you."

Siefert brought his eyes sharply back to Vance.

"I was afraid you would ask me that. But this is no time for squeamishness. I must trust wholly to your discretion." He paused, as if determining how he might best approach a matter which was obviously distasteful to him. "As I've already said, I don't know the exact nature of Mrs. Garden's ailment. The symptoms have been very much like those accompanying radium poisoning. But I have never prescribed any of the radium preparations for her—I am, in fact, profoundly skeptical of their efficacy. As you may know, we have had many untoward results from the haphazard, unscientific administration of these radium preparations."*

He cleared his throat before continuing.

"One evening while reading the reports of the researches made in California on radioactive sodium, or what might be called artificial radium, which has been heralded as a possible medium of cure for cancer, I suddenly realized that Professor Garden himself was actively interested in this particular line of research and had done some very creditable work in the field. The realization was purely a matter of association, and I gave it little thought at first. But the idea persisted, and before long some very unpleasant possibilities began to force themselves upon me."

---

*   *Doctor Siefert was undoubtedly alluding to recent distressing stories in the press of radium poisoning—one of the death of a prominent steel manufacturer and sportsman, presumably resulting from the continued use of a radioactive water extensively advertised as a cure for various ailments; and another of the painful and fatal poisoning of several women and girls whose occupation was painting so-called radiolite watch-dials.*

Again the doctor paused, a troubled look on his face.

"About two months ago I suggested to Doctor Garden that, if it were at all feasible, he put Miss Beeton on his wife's case. I had already come to the conclusion that Mrs. Garden required more constant attention and supervision than I could afford her, and Miss Beeton, who is a registered nurse, had, for the past year or so, been working with Doctor Garden in his laboratory—in fact, it was I who had sent her to him when he mentioned his need of a laboratory assistant. I was particularly anxious to have her take Mrs. Garden's case, rather than some other nurse, for I felt that from her observations some helpful suggestions might result. The girl had been on several difficult cases of mine, and I was wholly familiar with her competency and discretion."

"And have Miss Beeton's subsequent observations been helpful to you, doctor?" asked Vance.

"No, I can't say that they have," Siefert admitted, "despite the fact that Doctor Garden still availed himself of her services occasionally in the laboratory, thereby giving her an added opportunity of keeping an eye on the entire situation. But, on the other hand, neither have they tended to dissipate my suspicions."

"I say, doctor," Vance asked after a moment, "could this new radioactive sodium be administered to a person without his knowing it?"

"Oh, quite easily," Siefert assured him. "It could, for instance, be substituted in a shaker for ordinary salt and there would be nothing to arouse the slightest suspicion."

"And in quantities sufficient to produce the effects of radium poisoning?"

"Undoubtedly."

"And how long would it be before the effects of such administrations proved fatal?"

"That's impossible to say."

Vance was studying the tip of his cigarette. Presently he asked: "Has the nurse's presence in the house resulted in any information regarding the general situation here?"

"Nothing that I had not already known. In fact, her observations have merely substantiated my own conclusions. It's quite possible, too, that she herself may unwittingly have augmented the animosity between young Garden and Swift, for she has intimated to me once or twice that Swift had annoyed her occasionally with his attentions; and I have a very strong suspicion that she is personally interested in Floyd Garden."

Vance looked up with augmented interest.

"What, specifically, has given you that impression, doctor?"

"Nothing specific," Siefert told him. "I have, however, observed them together on several occasions, and my impression was that some sentiment existed there. Nothing that I can put my finger on, though. But one night when I was walking up Riverside Drive I happened to see them together in the park—undoubtedly a stroll together."

"By the by, doctor, have young Garden and the nurse been acquainted only since she came here to take care of his mother?"

"Oh, no," said Siefert. "But their previous acquaintance was, I imagine, more or less casual. You see, during the time Miss Beeton was Doctor Garden's laboratory assistant she had frequent occasion to come to the apartment here to work with the professor in his study—stenographic notes and transcription, records, and the like. And she naturally became acquainted with Floyd and Woode Swift and Mrs. Garden herself..."

The nurse appeared at the door at that moment to announce the arrival of the Medical Examiner, and Vance asked her to bring Doctor Doremus up to the study.

"I might suggest," said Siefert quickly, "that, with your consent, it would be possible to have the Medical Examiner accept my verdict of death due to an accidental overdose of barbital and avoid the additional unpleasantness of an autopsy."

"Oh, quite." Vance nodded. "That was my intention." He turned to the District Attorney. "All things considered, Markham," he said, "I think that might be best. There's nothing to be gained from an autopsy. We have enough facts, I think, to proceed without it. Undoubtedly Mrs. Garden's death was caused by the barbital solution. The radioactive sodium is a separate and distinct issue."

Markham nodded in reluctant acquiescence as Doremus was led into the room by Miss Beeton. The Medical Examiner was in vile humor and complained bitterly about having been summoned personally on a Sunday morning. Vance placated him somewhat and introduced him to Doctor Siefert. After a brief interchange of explanations and comments Doremus readily agreed to Markham's suggestion that the case be regarded as resulting from an overdose of barbital solution.

Doctor Siefert rose and looked hesitantly at Vance. "You will not need me further, I trust."

"Not at the moment, doctor." Vance rose also and bowed formally. "We may, however, communicate with you later. Again our thanks for your help and your candor... Sergeant, will you accompany Doctor Siefert and Doctor Doremus below and take care of any necess'ry details... And, Miss Beeton, please sit down for a moment. There are a few questions I want to ask you."

The girl came forward and seated herself in the nearest chair, as the three men went down the passageway.

CHAPTER FIFTEEN

Three Visitors
(Sunday, April 15, 10:45 a. m.)

"**I** DON'T MEAN to trouble you unduly, Miss Beeton," said Vance; "but we should like to have a firsthand account of the circumstances surrounding the death of Mrs. Garden."

"I wish there was something definite I could tell you," the nurse replied readily in a business-like manner, "but all I know is that when I arose this morning, a little after seven, Mrs. Garden seemed to be sleeping quietly. After dressing I went to the dining room and had my breakfast; and then I took a tray in to Mrs. Garden. She always had tea and toast at eight o'clock, no matter how late she may have retired the night before. It wasn't until I had drawn up the shades and closed the windows, that I realized something was wrong. I spoke to her and she didn't answer me; and when I tried to rouse her I got no response. I saw then that she was dead. I called Doctor Siefert at once, and he came over as quickly as he could."

"You sleep, I believe, in Mrs. Garden's room?"

The nurse inclined her head. "Yes. You see, Mrs. Garden frequently needed some small service in the night."

"Had she required your attention at any time during the night?"

"No. The injection Doctor Siefert gave her before he left her seemed to have quieted her and she was sleeping peacefully when I went out—"

"You went out last night... What time did you leave the house?" asked Vance.

"About nine o'clock. Mr. Floyd Garden suggested it, assuring me that he would be here and that he thought I needed a little rest. I was very glad of the opportunity, for I was really fatigued and unnerved."

"Had you no professional qualms about leaving a sick patient at such a time?"

"Ordinarily I might have had," the girl returned resentfully; "but Mrs. Garden had never shown *me* any consideration. She was the most selfish person I ever knew. Anyway, I explained to Mr. Floyd Garden about giving his mother a teaspoonful of the medicine if she should wake up and show any signs of restlessness. And then I went out into the park."

"At what time did you return, Miss Beeton?"

"It must have been about eleven," she told him. "I hadn't intended to stay out so long, but the air was invigorating, and I walked along the river almost to Grant's tomb. When I got back I went immediately to bed."

"Mrs. Garden was asleep when you came in?"

The girl turned her eyes to Vance before answering.

"I—I thought—she was asleep," she said hesitantly. "Her color was all right. But perhaps—even then—"

"Yes, yes. I know," Vance put in quickly. "However..." He inspected his cigarette for a moment. "By the by, did you notice anything changed—anything, let us say, out of place—in the room, on your return?"

The nurse shook her head slowly.

"No. Everything seemed the same to me. The windows and shades were just as I had left them, and—Wait, there was something. The glass I had left on the night-table with drinking water was empty. I refilled it before going to bed."

Vance looked up quickly. "And the bottle of medicine?"

"I didn't particularly notice that; but it must have been just as I had left it, for I remember a fleeting sense of relief because Mrs. Garden hadn't needed a dose of the medicine."

Vance seemed profoundly puzzled and said nothing for some time. Then he glanced up suddenly.

"How much light was there in the room?"

"Only a dim shaded nightlight by my bed."

"In that case, you might conceivably have mistaken an empty bottle for one filled with a colorless fluid."

"Yes, of course," the nurse returned reluctantly. "That must have been the case. Unless…" Her voice trailed off.

Vance nodded and finished the sentence for her. "Unless Mrs. Garden drank that medicine deliberately some time later." He studied the girl a moment. "But that isn't altogether reasonable. I don't care for the theory. Do you?"

She returned his gaze with complete frankness, and made a slight negative gesture of the head.

"No," she said. Then she added quickly: "But I wish it were true."

"Quite," agreed Vance. "It would be somewhat less terrible."

"I know what you mean." She took a deep tremulous breath and shuddered slightly.

"Tell me, when did you discover that all the medicine was gone?" Vance asked.

"Shortly before Doctor Siefert arrived this morning. I moved the bottle when I was arranging the table, and realized it was empty."

"I think that will be all just now, Miss Beeton." Vance glanced at the girl sombrely and then turned away. "Really, y' know, I'm deuced sorry. But you'd better not plan on leaving here just yet. We will undoubtedly want to see you again today."

As she got up her eyes rested on Vance with an enigmatic look. She seemed about to say something further, but instead she turned quickly and went from the room.

Heath must have been waiting in the passageway for the girl's dismissal, for just as she was going out, he came in to report that Siefert and Doremus had departed, and that Floyd Garden had made the arrangements for the removal of his mother's body.

"And what do we do now, Mr. Vance?" Heath asked.

"Oh, we carry on, Sergeant." Vance was unusually serious. "I want to talk to Floyd Garden first. Send him up. And call one of your men; but stay on the job downstairs yourself till he arrives. We may get this affair cleared up today."

"That wouldn't make me sore, Mr. Vance," returned Heath fervently, as he went toward the door.

Markham had risen and was pacing the floor, drawing furiously on his cigar.

"Evidently you see some light in this damnable situation," he grumbled to Vance. "I wish I could." He stopped and turned. "Are you serious about the possibility of getting this thing cleared up today?"

"Oh, quite. It could be, don't y' know." Vance cocked an eye whimsically at Markham. "Not legally, of course. Not a case for the law. No. Legal technicalities quite useless in such an emergency. Deeper issues involved. Human issues, d' ye see?"

"You're talking nonsense," Markham muttered. "You and your damned pseudo-subtle moods!"

"I can change the mood," Vance offered cheerfully. "I'm frank to confess that I like the situation even less than you do. But there's no other procedure indicated. The law is helpless against it at present. And, frankly, I'm not interested in your law. I want justice."

Markham snorted. "And just what do you intend to do?"

Vance looked past Markham into some remote world of his own imagining. "I shall try to stage a tragic drama," he said evenly. "It may be effective. If it fails, I'm afraid there's no help for us."

Markham snorted again. "Philo Vance—impresario!"

"Quite," Vance nodded. "Impresario. As you say. Aren't we all?"

Markham looked at him steadily for a while. "When does the curtain go up?"

"Anon."

Footsteps sounded in the passageway, and Floyd Garden entered the study. He appeared deeply shaken. "I can't stand much today. What do you want?" His tone was unduly resentful. He sat down and seemed to ignore us entirely as he fussed nervously with his pipe.

"We understand just how you feel," Vance said. "It was not my intention to bother you unnecess'rily. But if we are to get at the truth, we must have your cooperation."

"Go ahead, then," Garden mumbled, his attention still on his pipe.

Vance waited until the man got his pipe going. "We must have as many details as possible about last night. Did your expected guests come?"

Garden nodded cheerlessly. "Oh, yes. Zalia Graem, Madge Weatherby, and Kroon."

"And Hammle?"

"No, thank Heaven!"

"Didn't that strike you as a bit odd?"

"It didn't strike me as odd at all," Garden grumbled. "It struck me only as a relief. Hammle's all right, but he's a frightful bore—cold-blooded, self-sufficient. I never feel that the man has any real blood in him. Horses, dogs, foxes, game—anything but human beings. If one of his damned hounds had died he'd have taken it more to heart than Woody's death. I was glad he didn't show up."

Vance nodded with understanding. "Was there anyone else here?"

"No, that was all."

"Which of your visitors arrived first?"

Garden took the pipe from his mouth and looked up swiftly. "Zalia Graem. She came at half-past eight, I should say. Why?"

"Merely garnerin' facts," Vance replied indifferently. "And how long after Miss Graem came in did Miss Weatherby and Kroon arrive?"

"About half an hour. They came a few minutes after Miss Beeton had gone out."

Vance returned the man's steady scrutiny.

"By the by, why did you send the nurse out last night?"

"She looked as if she needed some fresh air," Garden answered with a show of complete frankness. "She'd had a tough day. Moreover, I didn't think there was anything seriously wrong with the mater. And I was going to be here myself and could have got her anything she might have needed." His eyes narrowed slightly. "Shouldn't I have let the nurse go out?"

"Yes. Oh, yes. Quite humane, don't y' know. A tryin' day for her."

Garden shifted his gaze heavily to the window, but Vance continued to study the man closely.

"What time did your guests depart?" he asked.

"A little after midnight. Sneed brought in sandwiches about half-past eleven. Then we had another round of highballs…" The man turned his eyes sharply back to Vance. "Does it matter?"

"I don't know. Perhaps not. However, it could… Did they all depart at the same time?"

"Yes. Kroon had his car below, and offered to drop Zalia at her apartment."

"Miss Beeton had returned by then, of course?"

"Yes, long before that. I heard her come in about eleven."

"And after your guests had gone, what did you do?"

"I sat up for half an hour or so, had another drink and a pipe; then I shut up the front of the house and turned in."

"Your bedroom is next to your mother's, I believe."

Garden nodded. "Father's been sharing it with me since the nurse has been here."

"Had your father retired when you went to your bedroom?"

"No. He rarely turns in before two or three in the morning. He works up here in the study till all hours."

"Was he up here last night?"

Garden looked a little disturbed.

"I imagine so. He couldn't very well have been anywhere else. He certainly didn't go out."

"Did you hear him when he came to bed?"

"No."

Vance lighted another cigarette, took several deep inhalations on it, and settled himself deeper in his chair.

"To go back a bit," he said casually. "The sleeping medicine Doctor Siefert prescribed for your mother seems to constitute a somewhat crucial point in the situation. Did you have occasion to give her a dose of it while the nurse was out?"

Garden drew himself up sharply and set his jaw.

"No, I did not," he said through his teeth.

Vance took no notice of the change in the man's manner.

"The nurse, I understand, gave you explicit instructions about the medicine before she went out. Will you tell me exactly where this was?"

"In the hall," Garden answered with a puzzled frown. "Just outside the den door. I had left Zalia in the drawing room and had gone to tell Miss Beeton she might go out for a while. I waited to help her on with her coat. It was then she told me what to do in case the mater woke up and was restless."

"And when she had gone you returned to the drawing room?"

"Yes, immediately." Garden still looked puzzled. "That's exactly what I did. And a few minutes later Madge and Kroon arrived."

There was a short silence during which Vance smoked thoughtfully.

"Tell me, Garden," he said at length, "did any of your guests enter your mother's room last night?"

Garden's eyes opened wide: color came back into his face, and he sprang to his feet.

"Good God, Vance! Zalia was in mother's room!"

Vance nodded slowly. "Very interestin'. Yes, quite… I say, do sit down. Light your beastly pipe, and tell us about it."

Garden hesitated a moment. He laughed harshly and resumed his seat.

"Damn it! You take it lightly enough," he complained.

"That may be the whole explanation."

"One never knows, does one?" Vance returned indifferently. "Carry on."

Garden had some difficulty getting his pipe going again. For a moment or two he sat with clouded, reminiscent eyes gazing out of the east window.

"It must have been about ten o'clock," he said at length. "The mater rang the little bell she keeps on the table beside her bed, and I was about to answer it when Zalia jumped up and said she would see what the mater wanted. Frankly, I was glad to let her go, after the scene you witnessed here yesterday—I had a feeling I might still be *persona non grata* there. Zalia came back in a few minutes and casually reported that the mater only wanted to have her water glass refilled."

"And did you yourself go into your mother's room at any time during Miss Beeton's absence?"

"No, I did not!" Garden looked defiantly at Vance.

"And you're sure that no one else entered your mother's room during the nurse's absence?"

"Absolutely."

I could tell by Vance's expression that he was not satisfied with Garden's answers. He broke the ashes from his cigarette with slow deliberation. His eyelids drooped a little with puzzled speculation. Without looking up, he asked:

"Were Miss Weatherby and Kroon in the drawing room with you during their entire visit?"

"Yes—with the exception of ten minutes or so, when they walked out on the balcony."

"And you and Miss Graem remained in the drawing room?"

"Yes. I was in no particular mood to view the nocturnal landscape—nor, apparently, was Zalia."

"About what time did Miss Weatherby and Kroon go out on the balcony?"

Garden thought a moment. "I'd say it was shortly before the nurse returned."

"And who was it," Vance went, "that first suggested going home?"

Garden pondered the question.

"I believe it was Zalia."

Vance got up.

"Awfully good of you, Garden, to let us bother you with these queries at such a time," he said kindly. "We're deuced grateful… You won't be leaving the house today?"

Garden shook his head as he stood up.

"Hardly," he said. "I'll stay in with father. He's pretty well broken up. By the way, would you care to see him?"

Vance waved his hand negatively.

"No. That won't be necess'ry just now."

Garden went morosely from the room, his head down, like a man weighted with a great mental burden.

When he had gone Vance stood for a moment in front of Markham, eyeing him with cynical good nature.

"Not a nice case, Markham. As I said. Frankly speakin', do you see any titbit for the law to get its teeth into?"

"No, damn it!" Markham blurted angrily. "No two things hang together. There's no straight line in any direction. Every thread in the case is tangled with every other thread. Heaven knows, there are enough motives and opportunities. But which are we to choose as a starting point?… And yet," he added grimly, "a case could be made out—"

"Oh, quite," Vance interrupted. "A case against any one of various persons. And one case as good—or as bad—as another. Everyone has acted in a perfect manner to bring suspicion upon himself." He sighed. "A sweet situation."

"And fiendish," supplemented Markham. "If it weren't for that fact, I'd be almost inclined to call it two suicides and let it go at that."

"Oh, no, you wouldn't," countered Vance with an affectionate shake of the head. "Neither would I. Really, y' know, that's not the way to be humane." He moved toward the window and looked out. "But I have things pretty well in hand. The pattern is shaping itself perfectly. I've fitted together all the pieces, Markham—all but one. And I hold that piece too, but I don't know where it goes, or how it fits into the ensemble."

Markham looked up. "What's the piece that's bothering you, Vance?"

"Those disconnected wires on the buzzer. They bother me frightfully. I know they have a bearing on the terrible things that have been going on here..." He turned from the window and walked up and down the room several times, his head down, his hands thrust deep into his pockets. "Why should those wires have been disconnected?" he murmured, as if talking to himself. "How could they have been related to Swift's death or to the shot we heard? There was no mechanism. No, I'm convinced of that. After all, the wires merely connect two buzzers...a signal...a signal between upstairs and downstairs... a signal—a call—a line of communication..."

Suddenly he stopped his meditative pacing. He was now facing the door into the passageway and he stared at it as if it were something strange—as if he had never seen it before.

"Oh, my aunt!" he exclaimed. "My precious aunt! It was too obvious." He wheeled about to Markham, a look of self-reproach on his face. "The answer was here all the time," he said. "It was simple—and I was looking for complexities... The picture is complete now, Markham. Everything fits. Those disconnected wires mean that there's another murder contemplated—a murder that was intended from the first, but that did not come off." He took a deep breath. "This business must be cleared up today. Yes..."

He led the way downstairs. Heath was smoking gloomily in the lower hall.

"Sergeant," Vance said to him, "phone Miss Graem, Miss Weatherby, Kroon—and Hammle. Have them all here late this afternoon—say six o'clock. Floyd Garden can help you in getting in touch with them."

"They'll be here, all right, Mr. Vance," Heath assured him.

"And Sergeant, as soon as you have taken care of this, telephone me. I want to see you this afternoon. I'll be at home. But wait here for Snitkin and leave him in charge. No one is to come here but those I've asked you to get, and no one is to leave the apartment. And, above all, no one is to be permitted to go upstairs either to the study or the garden... I'm staggerin' along now."

"I'll be phoning you by the time you get home, Mr. Vance."

Vance went to the front door but paused with his hand on the knob.

"I think I'd better speak to Garden about the gathering before I go. Where is he, Sergeant?"

"He went into the den when he came downstairs," Heath told him with a jerk of the head.

Vance walked up the hall and opened the den door. I was just behind him. As the door swung inward and Vance stepped over the threshold, we were confronted by an unexpected tableau. Miss Beeton and Garden were standing just in front of the desk, outlined against the background of the window. The nurse's hands were pressed to her face, and she was leaning against Garden, sobbing. His arms were about her.

At the sound of Vance's entry they drew away from each other quickly. The girl turned her head to us with a sudden motion, and I could see that her eyes were red and filled with tears. She caught her breath and, turning with a start, half ran through the connecting door into the adjoining bedroom.

"I'm frightfully sorry," Vance murmured. "Thought you were alone."

"Oh, that's all right," Garden returned, although it was painfully evident the man was embarrassed. "But I do hope, Vance," he added with a forced smile, "that you won't misunderstand. Everything, you know, is in an emotional upheaval here. I imagine Miss Beeton had all she could stand yesterday and today, and when I found her in here she seemed to break down, and—put her head on my shoulder. I was merely trying to comfort her. I can't help feeling sorry for the girl."

Vance raised his hand in good-natured indifference.

"Oh, quite, Garden. A harassed lady always welcomes a strong masculine shoulder to weep on. Most of them leave powder on one's lapel, don't y' know; but I'm sure Miss Beeton wouldn't be guilty of that... Dashed sorry to interrupt you, but I wanted to tell you before I went that I have instructed Sergeant Heath to have all your guests of yesterday here by six o'clock this afternoon. Of course, we'll want you and your father here, too. If you don't mind, you might help the Sergeant with the phone numbers."

"I'll be glad to, Vance," Garden returned, taking out his pipe and beginning to fill it. "Anything special in mind?"

Vance turned toward the door.

"Yes. Oh, yes. Quite. I'm hopin' to clear this matter up later on. Meanwhile I'm running along. Cheerio." And he went out, closing the door.

As we walked down the outer hall to the elevator, Vance said to Markham somewhat sadly: "I hope my plan works out. I don't particularly like it. But I don't like injustice, either..."

CHAPTER SIXTEEN

Through the Garden Door
(Sunday, April 15; afternoon.)

We HAD BEEN home but a very short time when Sergeant Heath telephoned as he had promised. Vance went into the anteroom to answer the call and closed the door after him. A few minutes later he rejoined us and, ringing for Currie, ordered his hat and stick.

"I'm running away for a while, old dear," he said to Markham. "In fact, I'm joining the doughty Sergeant at the Homicide Bureau. But I sha'n't be very long. In the meantime, I've ordered lunch for us here."

"Damn the lunch!" grumbled Markham. "What are you meeting Heath for?"

"I'm in need of a new waistcoat," Vance told him lightly.

"That explanation's a great help," Markham snorted.

"Sorry. It's the only one I can offer at present," Vance returned.

Markham stared at him, disgruntled, for several minutes.

"Why all this mystery?" he demanded.

"Really, y' know, Markham, it's necess'ry." Vance spoke seriously. "I'm hoping to work out this beastly affair tonight."

"For Heaven's sake, Vance, what are you planning?" Markham stood up in futile desperation.

Vance took a pony of brandy and lighted a *Régie*. Then he looked at Markham affectionately.

"I'm plannin' to entice the murderer into making one more bet—a losing bet... Cheerio." And he was gone.

Markham fumed and fretted during Vance's absence. He showed no inclination to talk, and I left him to himself. He tried to interest himself in Vance's library, but evidently found nothing to hold his attention. Finally he lit a cigar and settled himself in an easy chair before the window, while I busied myself with some notes I was preparing for Vance.

It was a little after half-past two when Vance returned to the apartment.

"Everything is in order," he announced as he came in. "There are no horses running today, of course, but nevertheless I'm looking forward to a big wager being laid this evening. If the bet isn't placed, we're in for it, Markham. Everyone will be present, however. The Sergeant, with Garden's help, has got in touch with all those who were present yesterday, and they will foregather again in the Garden drawing room at six o'clock. I myself have left a message for Doctor Siefert, and I hope he gets it in time to join us. I think he should be there..." He glanced at his watch and, ringing for Currie, ordered a bottle of 1919 Montrachet chilled for our lunch.

"If we don't tarry too long at table," he said, "we'll be able to hear the second half of the Philharmonic programme. Melinoff is doing Grieg's piano concerto, and I think it might do us all a bit of spiritual good. A beautiful climax, Markham— one of the most stirring in all music—simple, melodious, magistral. Curious thing about Grieg: it's taken the world a long time to realize the magnitude of the man's genius. One of the truly great composers..."

But Markham did not go with us to the concert. He pleaded an urgent political appointment at the Stuyvesant Club, but promised to meet us at the Garden apartment at six o'clock. As if by tacit agreement, no word regarding the case was spoken during lunch. When we had finished Markham excused himself and departed for the club, while Vance and I drove to Carnegie Hall. Melinoff gave a competent, if not an inspired, performance, and Vance seemed in a more relaxed frame of mind as we started for home.

Sergeant Heath was waiting for us when we reached the apartment.

"Everything's set, sir," he said to Vance; "I got it here."

Vance smiled a little sadly. "Excellent, Sergeant. Come into the other room with me while I get out of these Sunday togs."

Heath picked up a small package wrapped in brown paper, which he had evidently brought with him, and followed Vance into the bedroom. Ten minutes later they both came back into the library. Vance was now wearing a heavy dark tweed sack suit; and on Heath's face was a look of smug satisfaction.

"So long, Mr. Vance," he said, shaking hands. "Good luck to you." And he lumbered out.

We arrived at the Garden apartment a few minutes before six o'clock. Detectives Hennessey and Burke were in the front hall. As soon as we were inside Burke came up and, putting his hand to his mouth, said to Vance *sotto voce*:

"Sergeant Heath told me to tell you everything's all right. He and Snitkin are on the job."

Vance nodded and started up the stairs.

"Wait down here for me, Van," he said over his shoulder. "I'll be back immediately."

I wandered into the den, the door of which was ajar, and walked aimlessly about the room, looking at the various pictures and etchings. One behind the door attracted my attention—I think it was a Blampied—and I lingered before it for several moments. Just then Vance entered the room. As he came in he threw the door open wider, half pocketing me in the corner behind it, where I was not immediately noticeable. I was about to speak to him, when Zalia Graem came in.

"Philo Vance." She called his name in a low, tremulous voice.

He turned and looked at the girl with a quizzical frown. "I've been waiting in the dining room," she said. "I wanted to see you before you spoke to the others."

I realized immediately, from the tone of her voice, that my presence had not been noticed, and my first impulse was to step out from the corner. But, in the circumstances, I felt there could be nothing in her remarks which would be beyond the province of my privilege of hearing, and I decided not to interrupt them.

Vance continued to look squarely at the girl, but did not speak. She came very close to him now.

"Tell me why you have made me suffer so much," she said.

"I know I have hurt you," Vance returned. "But the circumstances made it imperative. Please believe that I understand more of this case than you imagine I do."

"I am not sure that I understand." The girl spoke hesitantly. "But I want you to know that I trust you." She looked up at him, and I could see that her eyes were glistening. Slowly she bowed her head. "I have never been interested in any man," she went on—and there was a quaver in her voice. "The men I have known have all made me unhappy and seemed always to lead me away from the things I longed for..." She caught her breath. "You are the one man I have ever known whom I could—care for."

So suddenly had this startling confession come, that I did not have time to make my presence known, and after Miss Graem finished speaking I remained where I was, lest I cause her embarrassment.

Vance placed his hands on the girl's shoulders and held her away from him.

"My dear," he said, with a curiously suppressed quality in his voice, "I am the one man for whom you should not care." There was no mistaking the finality of his words.

Behind Vance the door to the adjoining bedroom opened suddenly, and Miss Beeton halted abruptly on the threshold. She was no longer wearing the nurse's uniform, but a plain tailored tweed suit, severe in cut.

"I'm sorry," she apologized. "I thought Floyd—Mr. Garden—was in here."

Vance looked at her sharply.

"You were obviously mistaken, Miss Beeton."

Zalia Graem was staring at the nurse with angry resentment.

"How much did you hear," she asked, "before you decided to open the door?"

Miss Beeton's eyes narrowed and there was a look of scorn in her steady gaze.

"You perhaps have something to hide," she answered coldly, as she walked across the room to the hall door and went toward the drawing room.

Zalia Graem's eyes followed her as if fascinated, and then she turned back to Vance.

"That woman frightens me," she said. "I don't trust her. There's something dark—and cruel—back of that calm self-sufficiency of hers... And you've been so kind to her—but you have made *me* suffer."

Vance smiled wistfully at the girl.

"Would you mind waiting in the drawing room a little while?..."

She gave him a searching look and, without speaking, turned and went from the den.

Vance stood for some time gazing at the door with a frown of indecision, as if loath to proceed with whatever plans he had formulated. Then he turned to the window.

I took this opportunity to come out from my corner, and just as I did so Floyd Garden appeared at the hall door.

"Oh, hello, Vance," he said. "I didn't know you had returned until Zalia just told me you were in here. Anything I can do for you?"

Vance swung around quickly.

"I was just going to send for you. Everyone here?"

Garden nodded gravely. "Yes, and they're all frightened to death—all except Hammle. He takes the whole thing as a lark. I wish somebody had shot him instead of Woody."

"Will you send him in here," Vance asked. "I want to talk to him. I'll see the others presently."

Garden walked up the hall, and at that moment I heard Burke speaking to Markham at the front door. Markham immediately joined us in the den.

"Hope I haven't kept you waiting," he greeted Vance.

"No. Oh, no." Vance leaned against the desk. "Just in time. Everyone's here except Siefert, and I'm about to have Hammle in here for a chat. I think he'll be able to corroborate a few points I have in mind. He hasn't told us anything yet. And I may need your moral support."

Markham had barely seated himself when Hammle strutted into the den with a jovial air. Vance nodded to him brusquely and omitted all conventional preliminaries.

"Mr. Hammle," he said, "we're wholly familiar with your philosophy of minding your own business and keeping silent in order to avoid all involvements. A defensible attitude—but not in the present circumstances. This is a criminal case, and in the interest of justice to everyone concerned, we must have the whole truth. Yesterday afternoon you were the only one in the drawing room who had even a partial view down the hallway. And we must know everything you saw, no matter how trivial it may seem to you."

Hammle, assuming his poker expression, remained silent; and Markham leaned forward glowering at him.

"Mr. Hammle"—he spoke with cold, deadly calm—"if you don't wish to give us here what information you can, you will be taken before the Grand Jury and put under oath."

Hammle gave in. He spluttered and waved his arms.

"I'm perfectly willing to tell you everything I know. You don't have to threaten me. But to tell you the truth," he added suavely, "I didn't realize how serious the matter was." He sat down with pompous dignity and assumed an air which was obviously meant to indicate that for the time being he was the personification of law, order, and truth.

"First of all, then," said Vance, without relaxing his stern gaze, "when Miss Graem left the room, ostensibly to answer a telephone call, did you notice exactly where she went?"

"Not exactly," Hammle returned; "but she turned to the left, toward the den. You understand, of course, that it was impossible for me to see very far down the hall, even from where I sat."

"Quite." Vance nodded. "And when she came back to the drawing room?"

"I saw her first opposite the den door. She went to the hall closet where the hats and wraps are kept, and then came back to stand in the archway until the race was over. After that I didn't notice her either coming or going, as I had turned to shut off the radio."

"And what about Floyd Garden?" asked Vance. "You remember he followed Swift out of the room. Did you notice which way they went, or what they did?"

"As I remember, Floyd put his arm around Swift and led him into the dining room. After a few moments they came out. Swift seemed to be pushing Floyd away from him, and then he disappeared down the hall toward the stairs. Floyd stood outside the dining room door for several minutes, looking after his cousin, and then went down the hall after him; but he must have changed his mind, for he came back into the drawing room in short order."

"And you saw no one else in the hall?"

Hammle shook his head ponderously. "No. No one else."

"Very good." Vance took a deep inhalation on his cigarette. "And now let's go to the roof-garden, figuratively speaking. You were in the garden, waiting for a train, when the nurse was almost suffocated with bromine gas in the vault. The door into the passageway was open, and if you had been looking in that direction you could easily have seen who passed up and down the corridor." Vance looked at the man significantly. "And I have a feelin' you were looking through that door, Mr. Hammle. Your reaction of astonishment when we came out on the roof was a bit overdone. And you couldn't have seen much of the city from where you had been standing, don't y' know."

Hammle cleared his throat, and grinned.

"You have me there, Vance," he admitted with familiar good humor. "Since I couldn't make my train, I thought I'd satisfy my curiosity and stick around for a while to see what happened. I went out on the roof and stood where I could look through the door into the passageway—I wanted to see who was going to get hell next, and what would come of it all."

"Thanks for your honesty." Vance's face was coldly formal. "Please tell us now exactly what you saw through that doorway while you were waiting, as you've confessed, for something to happen."

Again Hammle cleared his throat.

"Well, Vance, to tell you the truth, it wasn't very much. Just people coming and going. First I saw Garden go up the passageway toward the study; and almost immediately he went back downstairs. Then Zalia Graem passed the door on her way to the study. Five or ten minutes later the detective—Heath, I think his name is—went by the door, carrying a coat over his arm. A little later—two or three minutes, I should say—Zalia Graem and the nurse passed each other in the passageway, Zalia going toward the stairs, and the nurse toward the study. A couple of minutes after that Floyd Garden passed the door on his way to the study again—"

"Just a minute," Vance interrupted. "You didn't see the nurse return downstairs after she passed Miss Graem in the passageway?"

Hammle shook his head emphatically. "No. Absolutely not. The first person I saw after the two girls was Floyd Garden going toward the study. And he came back past the door in a minute or so..."

"You're quite sure your chronology is accurate?"

"Absolutely."

Vance seemed satisfied and nodded.

"That much checks accurately with the facts as I know them," he said. "But are you sure no one else passed the door, either coming or going, during that time?"

"I would swear to that."

Vance took another deep puff on his cigarette.

"One more thing, Mr. Hammle: while you were out there in the garden, did anyone come out on the roof from the terrace gate?"

"Absolutely not. I didn't see anybody at all on the roof."

"And when Garden had returned downstairs, what then?"

"I saw you come to the window and look out into the garden. I was afraid I might be seen, and the minute you turned away I went over to the far corner of the garden, by the gate. The next thing I knew, you gentlemen were coming out on the roof with the nurse."

Vance moved forward from the desk against which he had been resting.

"Thank you, Mr. Hammle. You've told me exactly what I wanted to know. It may interest you to learn that the nurse informed us she was struck over the head in the passageway, on leaving the study, and forced into the vault which was full of bromine fumes."

Hammle's jaw dropped and his eyes opened. He grasped the arms of his chair and got slowly to his feet.

"Good Gad!" he exclaimed. "So that's what it was! Who could have done it?"

"A pertinent question," returned Vance casually. "Who could have done it, indeed? However, the details of your secret observations from the garden have corroborated my private suspicions, and it's possible I may be able to answer your question before long. Please sit down again."

Hammle shot Vance an apprehensive look and resumed his seat. Vance turned from the man and looked out of the window at the darkening sky. Then he swung about to Markham. A sudden change had come over his expression, and I knew, by his look, that some deep conflict was going on within him.

"The time has come to proceed, Markham," he said reluctantly. Then he went to the door and called Garden.

The man came from the drawing room immediately. He seemed nervous, and eyed Vance with inquisitive anxiety.

"Will you be so good as to tell everyone to come into the den?" Vance requested.

With a barely perceptible nod Garden turned back up the hall; and Vance crossed the room and seated himself at the desk.

CHAPTER SEVENTEEN

An Unexpected Shot
(Sunday, April 15; 6:20 p. m.)

ZALIA GRAEM WAS the first to enter the den. There was a strained, almost tragic look on her drawn face. She glanced at Vance appealingly and seated herself without a word. She was followed by Miss Weatherby and Kroon, who sat down uneasily beside her on the davenport. Floyd Garden and his father came in together. The professor appeared dazed, and the lines on his face seemed to have deepened during the past twenty-four hours. Miss Beeton was just behind them and stopped hesitantly in the doorway, looking uncertainly at Vance.

"Did you want me too?" she asked diffidently.

"I think it might be best, Miss Beeton," said Vance. "We may need your help."

She gave him a nod of acquiescence and, stepping into the room, sat down near the door.

At that moment the front door bell rang, and Burke ushered Doctor Siefert into the den.

"I just got your message, Mr. Vance, and came right over." He looked about the room questioningly and then brought his eyes back to Vance.

"I thought you might care to be present," Vance said, "in case we can reach some conclusion about the situation here. I know you are personally interested. Otherwise I wouldn't have telephoned you."

"I'm glad you did," said Siefert blandly, and walked across to a chair before the desk.

Vance lighted a cigarette with slow deliberation, his eyes moving aimlessly about the room. There was a tension over the assembled group. But as future events indicated, no one could have known what was in Vance's mind or his reason for bringing them all together.

The taut silence was broken by Vance's voice. He spoke casually, but with a curious emphasis.

"I have asked you all to come here this afternoon in the hope that we could clear up the very tragic situation that exists. Yesterday Woode Swift was murdered in the vault upstairs. A few hours later I found Miss Beeton locked in the same vault, half suffocated. Last night, as you all know by now, Mrs. Garden died from what we have every reason to believe was an overdose of barbital prescribed by Doctor Siefert. There can be no question that these three occurrences are closely related—that the same hand participated in them all. The pattern and the logic of the situation point indisputably to that assumption. There was, no doubt, a diabolical reason for each act of the murderer—and the reason was fundamentally the same in each instance. Unfortunately, the stage setting for this multiple crime was so confused that it facilitated every step of the murderer's plan, and at the same time tended to disperse suspicion among many people who were entirely innocent."

Vance paused for a moment.

"Luckily, I was present when the first murder was committed, and I have since been able to segregate the various facts connected with the crime. In that process of segregation I may have seemed unreasonable and, perhaps, harsh to several persons present. And during the process of my brief investigation, it has been necess'ry for me to withhold any expression of my personal opinions for fear of providing the perpetrator with an untimely warning. This, of course, would have proved fatal, for so cleverly was the whole plot conceived, so fortuitous were many of the circumstances connected with it, that we would never have succeeded in bringing the crime home to the true culprit. Consequently, an interplay of suspicion between the innocent members and guests of this household was essential. If I have offended anyone or seemed unjust, I trust that, in view of the abnormal and terrible circumstances, I may be forgiven—"

He was interrupted by the startling sound of a shot ominously like that of the day before. Everyone in the room stood up quickly, aghast at the sudden detonation. Everyone except Vance. And before anyone could speak, his calm authoritative voice was saying:

"There is no need for alarm. Please sit down. I expressly arranged that shot for all of you to hear—it will have an important bearing on the case…"

Burke appeared suddenly at the door.

"Was that all right, Mr. Vance?"

"Quite all right," Vance told him. "The same revolver and blanks?"

"Sure, just like you told me. And from where you said. Wasn't it like you wanted it?"

"Yes, precisely," nodded Vance. "Thanks, Burke."

The detective grinned broadly and moved away down the hall.

"That shot, I believe," resumed Vance, sweeping his eyes lazily over those present, "was similar to the one we heard yesterday afternoon—the one that summoned us to Swift's dead body. It may interest you to know that the shot just fired by Detective Burke was fired from the same revolver, with the same cartridges, that the murderer used yesterday—*and from about the same spot.*"

"But this shot sounded as if it were fired down here some-where," cut in Siefert.

"Exactly," said Vance with satisfaction. "It was fired from one of the windows on this floor."

"But I understood that the shot yesterday came from upstairs." Siefert looked perplexed.

"That was the general, but erroneous, assumption," explained Vance. "Actually it did not. Yesterday, because of the open roof door and the stairway, and the closed door of the room from which the shot was fired, and mainly because we were psychologically keyed to the idea of a shot from the roof, it gave us all the impression of coming from the garden. We were misled by our manifest, but unformulated, fears."

"By George, you're right, Vance!" It was Floyd Garden who spoke almost excitedly. "I remember wondering at the time of the shot where it could have come from, but naturally my mind went immediately to Woody, and I assumed it came from the garden."

Zalia Graem turned quickly to Vance.

"The shot yesterday didn't sound to me as if it came from the garden. When I came out of the den I wondered why you were all hurrying upstairs."

Vance returned her gaze squarely.

"No, it must have sounded much closer to you," he said. "But why didn't you mention that important fact yesterday when I talked with you about the crime?"

"I—don't know," the girl stammered. "When I saw Woody dead up there, I naturally thought I'd been mistaken."

"But you couldn't have been mistaken," returned Vance, half under his breath. His eyes drifted off into space again. "And after the revolver had been fired yesterday from a downstairs window, it was surreptitiously placed in the pocket of Miss Beeton's top-coat in the hall closet. Had it been fired from upstairs it could have been hidden to far better advantage somewhere on the roof or in the study. Sergeant Heath, having searched both upstairs and down, later found it in the hall closet." He turned again to the girl. "By the by, Miss Graem, didn't you go to that closet after answering your telephone call here in the den?"

The girl gasped.

"How—how did you know?"

"You were seen there," explained Vance. "You must remember that the hall closet is visible from one end of the drawing room."

"Oh!" Zalia Graem swung around angrily to Hammle. "So it was you who told him!"

"It was my duty," returned Hammle, drawing himself up righteously.

The girl turned back to Vance with flashing eyes.

"I'll tell you why I went to the hall closet. I went to get a handkerchief I had left in my handbag. Does that make me a murderer?"

"No. Oh, no." Vance shook his head and sighed. "Thank you for the explanation... And will you be so good as to tell me exactly what you did last night when you answered Mrs. Garden's summons?"

Professor Garden, who had been sitting with bowed head, apparently paying no attention to anyone, suddenly looked up and let his hollow eyes rest on the girl with a slight show of animation.

Zalia Graem glared defiantly at Vance.

"I asked Mrs. Garden what I could do for her, and she requested me to fill the water glass on the little table beside her bed. I went into the bathroom and filled it; then I arranged her pillows and asked her if there was anything else she wanted. She thanked me and shook her head; and I returned to the drawing room."

Professor Garden's eyes clouded again, and he sank back in his chair, once more oblivious to his surroundings.

"Thank you," murmured Vance, nodding to Miss Graem and turning to the nurse. "Miss Beeton," he asked, "when you returned last night, was the bedroom window which opens on the balcony bolted?"

The nurse seemed surprised at the question. But when she answered, it was in a calm, professional tone.

"I didn't notice. But I know it was bolted when I went out—Mrs. Garden always insisted on it. I'm sorry I didn't look at the window when I returned. Does it really matter?"

"No, not particularly." Vance then addressed Kroon. "I understand you took Miss Weatherby out on the balcony last night. What were you doing there during the ten minutes you remained outside?"

Kroon bristled. "If you must know, we were fighting about Miss Fruemon—"

"We were not!" Miss Weatherby's shrill voice put in. "I was merely asking Cecil—"

"That's quite all right." Vance interrupted the woman sharply and waved his hand deprecatingly. "Questions or recriminations—it really doesn't matter, don't y' know." He turned leisurely to Floyd Garden. "I say, Garden, when you left the drawing room yesterday afternoon, to follow Swift on your errand of mercy, as it were, after he had given you his bet on Equanimity, where did you go with him?"

"I led him into the dining room." The man was at once troubled and aggressive. "I argued with him for a while, and then he came out and went down the hall to the stairs. I watched him for a couple of minutes, wondering what else I might do about it, for, to tell you the truth, I didn't want him to listen in on the race upstairs. I was pretty damned sure Equanimity wouldn't win, and he didn't know I hadn't placed his bet. I was rather worried about what he might do. For a minute I thought of following him upstairs, but changed my mind. I decided there was nothing more to be done about it except to hope for the best. So I returned to the drawing room."

Vance lowered his eyes to the desk and was silent for several moments, smoking meditatively.

"I'm frightfully sorry, and all that," he murmured at length, without looking up; "but the fact is, we don't seem to be getting any forrader. There are plausible explanations for everything and everybody. For instance, during the commission of the first crime, Doctor Garden was supposedly at the library or in a taxicab. Floyd Garden, according to his own statement, and with the partial corroboration of Mr. Hammle here, was in the dining room and the lower hallway. Mr. Hammle himself, as well as Miss Weatherby, was in the drawing room. Mr. Kroon explains that he was smoking somewhere on the public stairway, and left two cigarette butts there as evidence. Miss Graem, so far as we can ascertain, was in the den here, telephoning. Therefore assuming—merely as a hypothesis— that anyone here could be guilty of the murder of Swift, of the apparent attempt to murder Miss Beeton, and of the possible murder of Mrs. Garden, there is nothing tangible to substantiate an individual accusation. The performance was too clever, too well conceived, and the innocent persons seem unconsciously and involuntarily to have formed a conspiracy to aid and abet the murderer."

Vance looked up and went on. "Moreover, nearly everyone has acted in a manner which conceivably would make him appear guilty. There have been an amazing number of accusations. Mr. Kroon was the first victim of one of these unsubstantiated accusations. Miss Graem has been pointed out to me as the culprit by several persons. Mrs. Garden last night directly accused her son. In fact, there has been a general tendency to involve various people in the criminal activities here. From the human and psychological point of view the issue has been both deliberately and unconsciously clouded, until the confusion was such that no clear-cut outline remained. And this created an atmosphere which perfectly suited the murderer's machinations, for it made detection extremely difficult and positive proof almost impossible... And yet," Vance added, "someone in this room is guilty."

He rose dejectedly. I could not understand his manner: it was so unlike the man as I had always known him. All of his assurance seemed gone, and I felt that he was reluctantly admitting defeat. He turned and looked out of the window into the gathering dusk. Then he swung round quickly, and his eyes swept angrily about the room, resting for a brief moment on each one present.

"Furthermore," he said with a staccato stress on his words, "*I know who the guilty person is!*"

There was an uneasy stir in the room and a short tense silence which was broken by Doctor Siefert's cultured voice.

"If that is the case, Mr. Vance—and I do not doubt the sincerity of your statement—I think it your duty to name that person."

Vance regarded the doctor thoughtfully for several moments before answering. Then he said in a low voice: "I think you are right, sir." Again he paused and, lighting a fresh cigarette, moved restlessly up and down in front of the window. "First, however," he said, stopping suddenly, "there's something upstairs I wish to look at again—to make sure... You will all please remain here for a few minutes." And he moved swiftly toward the door. At the threshold he hesitated and turned to the nurse. "Please come with me, Miss Beeton. I think you can help me."

The nurse rose and followed Vance into the hall. A moment later we could hear them mounting the stairs.

A restlessness swept over those who remained below. Professor Garden got slowly to his feet and went to the window, where he stood looking out. Kroon threw a half-smoked cigarette away and, taking out his case offered it to Miss Weatherby. As they lighted their cigarettes they murmured something to each other which I could not distinguish. Floyd Garden shifted uncomfortably in his chair and resumed his nervous habit of packing his pipe. Siefert moved around the room, pretending to inspect the etchings, and Markham's eyes followed his every move. Hammle cleared his throat loudly several times, lighted a cigarette, and busied himself with various papers which he took from his pocket folder. Only Zalia Graem remained unruffled. She leaned her head against the back of the davenport and, closing her eyes, smoked languidly. I could have sworn there was the trace of a smile at the corners of her mouth...

Fully five minutes passed, and then the tense silence of the room was split by a woman's frenzied and terrifying cry for help, from somewhere upstairs. As we reached the hallway the nurse came stumbling down the stairs, holding with both hands to the bronze railing. Her face was ghastly pale, and there was a wild, frightened look in her eyes.

"Mr. Markham! Mr. Markham!" she called hysterically. "Oh, my God! The most terrible thing has happened!"

She had just reached the foot of the stairs when Markham came up to her. She stood clutching the railing for support.

"It's Mr. Vance!" she panted excitedly. "He's—gone!"

A chill of horror passed over me, and everyone in the hall seemed stunned. I noticed—as something entirely apart from my immediate perceptions—Heath and Snitkin and Peter Quackenbush, the official police photographer, step into the hall through the main entrance. Quackenbush had his camera and tripod with him; and the three men stood calmly just inside the door, detached from the amazed group around the foot of the stairs. I vaguely wondered why they were accepting the situation with such smug indifference...

In broken phrases, interspersed with gasping sobs, the nurse was explaining to Markham.

"He went over—Oh, God, it was horrible! He said he wanted to ask me something, and led me out into the garden. He began questioning me about Doctor Siefert, and Professor Garden, and Miss Graem. And while he talked he moved over to the parapet—you remember where he stood last night. He got up there again, and looked down. I was frightened—the way I was yesterday. And then—and then—while I was talking to him—he bent over, and I could see—oh, God!—he had lost his balance." She stared at Markham wild-eyed. "I reached toward him...and suddenly he wasn't there any more... He had gone over!..."

Her eyes lifted suddenly over our heads and peered past us transfixed. A sudden change came over her. Her face seemed contorted into a hideous mask. Following her horrified gaze, we instinctively turned and glanced up the hallway toward the drawing room...

There, near the archway, looking calmly toward us, was Vance.

I have had many harrowing experiences, but the sight of Vance at that moment, after the horror I had been through, affected me more deeply than any shock I can recall. A numbness overcame me, and I could feel cold perspiration breaking out all over my body. The sound of Vance's voice merely tended to upset me further.

"I told you last night, Miss Beeton," he was saying, his eyes resting sternly on the nurse, "that no gambler ever quits with his first winning bet, and that in the end he always loses." He came forward a few steps. "You won your first gamble, at long odds, when you murdered Swift. And your poisoning of Mrs. Garden with the barbital also proved a winning bet. But when you attempted to add me to your list of victims, because you suspected I knew too much—you lost. That race was fixed—you hadn't a chance."

Markham was glaring at Vance in angry amazement.

"What is the meaning of all this?" he fairly shouted, despite his obvious effort to suppress his excitement.

"It merely means, Markham," explained Vance, "that I gave Miss Beeton an opportunity to push me over the parapet to what ordinarily would have been certain death. And she took that opportunity. This afternoon I arranged for Heath and Snitkin to witness the episode; and I also arranged to have it permanently recorded."

"Recorded? Good God! What do you mean?" Markham seemed half dazed.

"Just that," returned Vance calmly. "An official photograph taken with a special lens adapted to the semi-light—for the Sergeant's archives." He looked past Markham to Quackenbush. "You got the picture, I hope," he said.

"I sure did," the man returned with a satisfied grin. "At just the right angle too. A pippin."

The nurse, who had been staring at Vance as if petrified, suddenly relaxed her hold on the stair railing, and her hands went to her face in a gesture of hopelessness and despair. Then her hands dropped to her sides to reveal a face of haggard defeat. "Yes!" she cried at Vance; "I tried to kill you. Why shouldn't I? You were about to take everything—*everything*— away from me."

She turned quickly and ran up the stairs. Almost simultaneously Vance dashed forward.

"Quick, quick!" He called out. "Stop her before she gets to the garden."

But before any of us realized the significance of his words, Vance was himself on the stairs. Heath and Snitkin were just behind him, and the rest of us, stupefied, followed. As I came out on the roof, I could see Miss Beeton running toward the far end of the garden, with Vance immediately behind her. Twilight had nearly passed, and a deep dusk had settled over the city. As the girl leaped up on the parapet at the same point where Vance had stood the night before, she was like a spectral silhouette against the faintly glowing sky. And then she disappeared down into the deep shadowy abyss, just before Vance could reach her...

CHAPTER EIGHTEEN

The Scratch Sheet
(Sunday, April 15; 7:15 p. m.)

A HALF HOUR LATER we were all seated in the den again. Heath and the detectives had gone out immediately after the final catastrophe to attend to the unpleasant details occasioned by Miss Beeton's suicide.

Vance was once more in the chair at the desk. The tragic termination of the case seemed to have saddened him. He smoked gloomily for a few minutes. Then he spoke.

"I asked all of you to stay because I felt you were entitled to an explanation of the terrible events that have taken place here, and to hear why it was necess'ry for me to conduct the investigation in the manner I did. To begin with, I knew from the first that I was dealing with a very shrewd and unscrupulous person, and I knew it was someone who was in the house yesterday afternoon. Therefore, until I had some convincing proof of that person's guilt, it was imperative for me to appear to doubt everyone present. Only in an atmosphere of mutual

suspicion and recrimination—in which I myself appeared to
be as much at sea as anyone else—was it possible to create in
the murderer that feeling of security which I felt would lead to
his final undoing.

"I was inclined to suspect Miss Beeton almost from the
first, for, although everyone here had, through some act, drawn
suspicion upon himself, only the nurse had the time and the
unhampered opportunity to commit the initial crime. She was
entirely unobserved when she put her plan into execution; and
so thoroughly familiar was she with every arrangement of the
household, that she had no difficulty in timing her every step
so as to insure this essential privacy. Subsequent events and
circumstances added irresistibly to my suspicion of her. For
instance, when Mr. Floyd Garden informed me where the key
to the vault was kept, I sent her to see if it was in place, without
indicating to her where its place was, in order to ascertain if
she knew where the key hung. Only someone who knew exactly
how to get into the vault at a moment's notice could have been
guilty of killing Swift. Of course, the fact that she did know was
not definite proof of her guilt, as there were others who knew;
but at least it was a minor factor in the case against her. If she
had not known where the key was kept, she would have been
automatically eliminated. My request that she look for the key
was made with such casualness and seeming indifference that
it apparently gave her no inkling of my ulterior motive.

"Incidentally, one of my great difficulties in the case has
been to act in such a way, at all times, that her suspicions would
not be aroused at any point. This was essential because, as I
have said, I could hope to substantiate my theory of her guilt
only by making her feel sufficiently secure to do or say something which would give her away.

"Her motive was not clear at first, and, unfortunately, I
thought that by Swift's death alone she had accomplished her
purpose. But after my talk with Doctor Siefert this morning,
I was able to understand fully her whole hideous plot. Doctor
Siefert pointed out definitely her interest in Floyd Garden,

although I had had hints of it before. For instance, Floyd Garden was the only person here about whom she spoke to me with admiration. Her motive was based on a colossal ambition—the desire for financial security, ease and luxury; and mixed with this overweening desire was a strange twisted love. These facts became clear to me only today."

Vance glanced at young Garden.

"It was you she wanted," he continued. "And I believe her self-assurance was such that she did not doubt for a minute that she would be successful in attaining her goal."

Garden sprang to his feet.

"Good God, Vance!" he exclaimed. "You're right. I see the thing now. She has been making up to me for a long time; and, to be honest with you, I may have said and done things which she could have construed as encouragement—God help me!" He sat down again in dejected embarrassment.

"No one can blame you," Vance said kindly. "She was one of the shrewdest women I have ever encountered. But the point of it all is, she did not want only you—she wanted the Garden fortune as well. That's why, having learned that Swift would share in the inheritance, she decided to eliminate him and leave you sole beneficiary. But this murder did not, by any means, constitute the whole of her scheme."

Vance again addressed us in general.

"Her whole terrible plot was clarified by some other facts that Doctor Siefert brought out this morning during my talk with him. The death, either now or later, of Mrs. Garden was also an important integer of that plot; and Mrs. Garden's physical condition had, for some time, shown certain symptoms of poisoning. Of late these symptoms have increased in intensity. Doctor Siefert informed me that Miss Beeton had been a laborat'ry assistant to Professor Garden during his experiments with radioactive sodium, and had often come to the apartment here for the purpose of typing notes and attending to other duties which could not conveniently be performed at the University. Doctor Siefert also informed me that she had actually entered the household here about two months ago, to take personal charge of Mrs. Garden's case. She had, however, continued to assist Professor Garden occasionally in his work and naturally had access to the radioactive sodium he had begun to produce; and it was since she had come here to live that Mrs. Garden's condition had grown worse—the result undoubtedly of the fact that Miss Beeton had greater and more frequent opportunities for administering the radioactive sodium to Mrs. Garden. Her decision to eliminate Mrs. Garden, so that Floyd Garden would inherit her money, undoubtedly came shortly after she had become the professor's assistant and had, through her visits to the apartment become acquainted with Floyd Garden and familiar with the various domestic arrangements here."

Vance turned his eyes to Professor Garden.

"And you too, sir," he said, "were, as I see it, one of her intended victims. When she planned to shoot Swift I believe she planned a double murder—that is, you and Swift were to be shot at the same time. But, luckily, you had not returned to your study yesterday afternoon at the time fixed for the double shooting, and her original plan had to be revised."

"But—but," stammered the professor, "how could she have killed me and Woody too?"

"The disconnected buzzer wires gave me the answer this morning," explained Vance. "Her scheme was both simple and bold. She knew that, if she followed Swift upstairs before the big race, she would have no difficulty in enticing him into the vault on some pretext or other—especially in view of the fact that he had shown a marked interest in her. Her intention was to shoot him in the vault, just as she did, and then go into the study and shoot you. Swift's body would then have been placed in the study, with the revolver in his hand. It would appear like murder and suicide. As for the possibility of the shot in the study being heard downstairs, I imagine she had tested that out beforehand under the very conditions obtaining yesterday afternoon. Personally, I am of the opinion that a shot in the study could not be heard down here during the noise and excitement of a race broadcast, with the study door and windows shut. For the rest, her original plan would have proceeded just as her revised one did. She would merely have fired two blanks out of the bedroom window instead of one. In the event that you should have guessed her intent when she entered the study, and tried to summon help, she had previously disconnected the wires of the buzzer just behind your chair at the desk."

"But, good Lord!" exclaimed Floyd Garden in an awed tone. "It was she herself who told Sneed about the buzzer being out of order."

"Precisely. She made it a point to be the one to discover that fact, in order to draw suspicion entirely away from herself; for the natural assumption, she must have reasoned, would be that the person who had disconnected the wires for some criminal purpose would be the last one to call attention to them. It was a bold move, but it was quite in keeping with her technique throughout."

Vance paused. After a moment he went on.

"As I say, her plan had to be revised somewhat because Doctor Garden had not returned. She had chosen the Rivermont Handicap as the background for her manœuvres, for she knew Swift was placing a large bet on the race—and if he lost, it would give credence to the theory of suicide. As for the shooting of Doctor Garden, that would, of course, be attributed to his attempt to thwart his nephew's suicide. And, in a way, Doctor Garden's absence helped her, though it required quick thinking on her part to cover up this unexpected gap in her well-laid plans. Instead of placing Swift in the study, as she originally intended, she placed him in his chair on the roof. She carefully wiped up the blood in the vault so that no trace of it remained on the floor. A nurse with operating-room experience in removing blood from sponges, instruments, operating table and floor, would have known how. Then she came down and fired a blank shell out of the bedroom window just as soon as the outcome of the race had been declared official. Substantiatin' suicide.

"Of course, one of her chief difficulties was the disposal of the second revolver—the one she fired down here. She was confronted with the necessity either of getting rid of the revolver—which was quite impossible in the circumstances—or of hiding it safely till she could remove it from the apartment; for there was always the danger that it might be discovered and the whole technique of the plot be revealed. Since she was the person apparently least under suspicion, she probably considered that placing it temporarily in the pocket of her own top-coat, would be sufficiently safe. It was not an ideal hiding place; but I have little doubt that she was frustrated in an attempt to hide it somewhere on the roof or on the terrace upstairs, until she could take it away at her convenience without being observed. She had no opportunity to hide the revolver upstairs after we had first gone to the roof and discovered Swift's body. However, I think it was her intention to do just this when Miss Weatherby saw her on the stairs and resentfully called my attention to the fact. Naturally, Miss Beeton denied having been on the stairs at all. And the significance of the situation did not occur to me at the moment; but I believe that she had the revolver on her person at the time Miss Weatherby saw her. She evidently thought she would have sufficient time while I was in the den, to run to the roof and hide the revolver; but when she had barely started upstairs, Miss Weatherby came unexpectedly out of the drawing room with the intention of going to the garden herself. It was immediately after that, no doubt, that she dropped the revolver into her coat pocket in the hall closet..."

"But why," asked Professor Garden, "didn't she fire the revolver upstairs in the first place—it would certainly have made the shot sound more realistic—and then hide it in the garden before coming down?"

"My dear sir! That would have been impossible, as you can readily see. How would she have got back downstairs? We were ascending the stairs a few seconds after we heard the shot, and would have met her coming down. She could, of course, have come down by the public stairs and reentered the apartment at the front door without being seen, but in that event she could not have established her presence down here at the time the shot was fired—and this was of utmost importance to her. When we reached the foot of the stairs, she was standing in the doorway of Mrs. Garden's bedroom, and she made it clear that she had heard the shot. It was, of course, a perfect alibi, provided the technique of the crime had not been revealed by the evidence she left in the vault... No. The shot could not have been fired upstairs. The only place she could have fired it and still have established her alibi, was out of the bedroom window."

He turned to Zalia Graem.

"Now do you see why you felt so definitely that the shot did not sound as if it came from the garden? It was because, being in the den, you were the person nearest to the shot when it was fired and could more or less accurately gauge the direction from which it came. I'm sorry I could not explain that fact to you when you mentioned it, but Miss Beeton was in the room, and it was not then the time to reveal my knowledge to her."

"Well, anyway, you were horrid about it," the girl complained. "You acted as if you believed the reason I heard the shot so distinctly was that I had fired it."

"Couldn't you read between the lines of my remarks? I was hoping you would."

She shook her head. "No, I was too worried at the time; but I'll confess that when you asked Miss Beeton to go to the roof with you, the truth dawned on me."

(The moment she made this remark I recalled that she was the only person in the room who was entirely at ease when Vance had gone upstairs.)

There was another brief silence in the room, which was broken by Floyd Garden.

"There's one point that bothers me, Vance," he said. "If Miss Beeton counted on our accepting the suicide theory, what if Equanimity had won the race?"

"That would have upset her entire calculations," answered Vance. "But she was a great gambler. And, remember, she was playing for the highest stakes. She was practically betting her life. I'll warrant it was the biggest wager ever made on Equanimity."

"Good God!" Floyd Garden murmured. "And I thought Woody's bet was a big one?"

"But, Mr. Vance," put in Doctor Siefert, frowning, "your theory of the case does not account for the attempt made on her own life."

Vance smiled faintly.

"There was no attempt on her life, doctor. When Miss Beeton left the study, a minute or so after Miss Graem, to take my message to you, she went instead into the vault, shut the door, making sure this time that the lock snapped, and gave herself a superficial blow on the back of the head. She had reason to believe, of course, that it would be but a short time before we looked for her; and she waited till she heard the key in the lock before she broke the vial of bromine. It is possible that when she went out of the study she had begun to fear that I might have some idea of the truth, and she enacted this little melodrama to throw me off the track. Her object undoubtedly was to throw suspicion on Miss Graem."

Vance looked at the girl sympathetically.

"I think when you were called from the drawing room to the phone, Miss Graem—at just the time Miss Beeton was on her way upstairs to shoot Swift—she decided to use you, should it be necess'ry to save herself. Undoubtedly, she knew of your feud with Swift, and capitalized on it; and she also undoubtedly realized that you would be a suspect in the eyes of the others who were here yesterday. That is why, my dear, I sought to lead her on by seeming to regard you as the culprit. And it had its effect... I hope you can find it in your heart to forgive me for having made you suffer."

The girl did not speak—she seemed to be struggling with her emotions.

Siefert had leaned forward and was studying Vance closely.

"As a theory, that may be logical," he said with skeptical gravity. "But, after all, it is only a theory."

Vance shook his head slowly.

"Oh, no, doctor. It's more than a theory. And you should be the last person to put that name on it. Miss Beeton herself—and in your presence—gave the whole thing away. Not only did she lie to us, but she contradicted herself when you and I were on the roof and she was recovering from the effects of the bromine gas—effects, incidentally, which she was able to exaggerate correctly as the result of her knowledge of medicine."

"But I don't recall—"

Vance checked him. "Surely, doctor, you remember the story she told us. According to her voluntary account of the episode, she was struck on the head and forced into the vault; and she fainted immediately as the result of the bromine gas; then the next thing she knew was that she was lying on the settee in the garden, and you and I were standing over her."

Siefert inclined his head.

"That is quite correct," he said, frowning at Vance.

"And I am sure you also remember, doctor, that she looked up at me and thanked me for having brought her out into the garden and saved her, and also asked me how I came to find her so soon."

Siefert was still frowning intently at Vance.

"That also is correct," he admitted. "But I still don't understand wherein she gave herself away."

"Doctor," asked Vance, "if she had been unconscious, as she said, from the time she was forced into the vault to the time she spoke to us in the garden, how could she possibly have known who it was that had found her and rescued her from the vault? And how could she have known that I found her soon after she had entered the vault?... You see, doctor, she was never unconscious at all: she was taking no chances whatever of dying of bromine gas. As I have said, it was not until I had started to unlock the door that she broke the vial of bromine; and she was perfectly aware who entered the vault and carried her out to the garden. Those remarks of hers to me were a fatal error on her part."

Siefert relaxed and leaned back in his chair with a faint wry smile.

"You are perfectly right, Mr. Vance. That point escaped me entirely."

"But," Vance continued, "even had Miss Beeton not made the mistake of lying to us so obviously, there was other proof that she alone was concerned in that episode. Mr. Hammle here conclusively bore out my opinion. When she told us her story of being struck on the head and forced into the vault, she did not know that Mr. Hammle had been in the garden observing everyone who came and went in the passageway. And she was alone in the corridor at the time of the supposed attack. Miss Graem, to be sure, had just passed her and gone downstairs; and the nurse counted on that fact to make her story sound plausible, hoping, of course, that it would produce the effect she was striving for—that is, to make it appear that Miss Graem had attacked her."

Vance smoked in silence for a moment.

"As for the radioactive sodium, doctor, Miss Beeton had been administering it to Mrs. Garden, content with having her die slowly of its cumulative effects. But Mrs. Garden's threat to erase her son's name from her will necessitated immediate action, and the resourceful girl decided on an overdose of the barbital last night. She foresaw, of course, that this death could easily be construed as an accident or as another suicide. As it happened, however, things were even more propitious for her, for the events of last night merely cast further suspicion on Miss Graem.

"From the first I realized how difficult, if not impossible, it would be to prove the case against Miss Beeton; and during the entire investigation I was seeking some means of trapping her. With that end in view, I mounted the parapet last night in her presence, hoping that it might suggest to her shrewd and cruel mind a possible means of removing me from her path, if she became convinced that I had guessed too much. My plan to trap her was, after all, a simple one. I asked you all to come here this evening, not as suspects, but to fill the necess'ry rôles in my grim drama."

Vance sighed deeply before continuing.

"I arranged with Sergeant Heath to equip the post at the far end of the garden with a strong steel wire such as is used in theatres for flying and levitation acts. This wire was to be just long enough to reach as far as the height of the balcony on this floor. And to it was attached the usual spring catch which fastens to the leather equipment worn by the performer. This equipment consists of a heavy cowhide vest resembling in shape and cut the old Ferris waist worn by young girls in post-Victorian days, and even later. This afternoon Sergeant Heath brought such a leather vest—or what is technically known in theatrical circles as a 'flying corset'—to my apartment, and I put it on before I came here... You might be interested in seeing it. I took it off a little while ago, for it's frightfully uncomfortable..."

He rose and went through the door into the adjoining bedroom. A few moments later he returned with the leather "corset." It was made of very heavy brown leather, with a soft velour finish, and was lined with canvas. The sides, instead of being seamed, were held together by strong leather thongs laced through brass eyelets. The closing down the middle was effected by a row of inch-wide leather straps and steel buckles by which the vest was tightened to conform to the contour of the person who wore it. There were adjustable shoulder straps of leather, and thigh straps strongly made and cushioned with thick rolls of rubber.

Vance held up this strange garment.

"Here it is," he said. "Ordinarily, the buckles and straps are in front and the attachment for the spring catch is in back.

But for my purpose this had to be reversed. I needed the rings in front because the wire had to be attached at this point when my back was turned to Miss Beeton." He pointed to two heavy overlapping iron rings, about two inches in diameter, held in place by nuts and bolts in a strip of canvas, several layers in thickness, in the front of the corset.

Vance threw the garment on the desk.

"This waistcoat, or corset," he said, "is worn under the actor's costume; and in my case I put on a loose tweed suit today so that the slightly protruding rings in front would not be noticeable.

"When I took Miss Beeton upstairs with me, I led her out into the garden and confronted her with her guilt. While she was protesting, I mounted the parapet, standing there with my back to her, ostensibly looking out over the city, as I had done last evening. In the semi-darkness I snapped the wire to the rings on the front of my leather vest without her seeing me do so. She came very close to me as she talked, but for a minute or so I was afraid she would not take advantage of the situation. Then, in the middle of one of her sentences, she lurched toward me with both hands outstretched, and the impact sent me over the parapet. It was a simple matter to swing myself over the balcony railing. I had arranged for the drawing room door to be unlatched, and I merely disconnected the suspension wire, walked in, and appeared in the hallway. When Miss Beeton learned that I had witnesses to her act, as well as a photograph of it, she realized that the game was up.

"I admit, however, that I had not foreseen that she would resort to suicide. But perhaps it is just as well. She was one of those women who through some twist of nature—some deep-rooted wickedness—personify evil. It was probably this perverted tendency which drew her into the profession of nursing, where she could see, and even take part in, human suffering."

Vance leaned back in his chair and smoked abstractedly. He seemed to be deeply affected, as were all of us. Little more was said—each of us, I think, was too much occupied with his own thoughts for any further discussion of the case. There were a few desultory questions, a few comments, and then a long silence.

Doctor Siefert was the first to take his departure. Shortly afterward the others rose restlessly.

I felt shaken from the sudden let-down of the tension through which I had been going, and walked into the drawing room for a drink of brandy. The only light in the room came through the archway from the chandelier in the hall and from the afterglow of the sky which faintly illumined the windows, but it was sufficient to enable me to make my way to the little cabinet bar in the corner. I poured myself a pony of brandy and, drinking it quickly, stood for a moment looking out of the window over the slaty waters of the Hudson.

I heard someone enter the room and cross toward the balcony, but I did not look round immediately. When I did turn back to the room I saw the dim form of Vance standing before the open door to the balcony, a solitary, meditative figure. I was about to speak to him when Zalia Graem came softly through the archway and approached him.

"Good-by, Philo Vance," she said.

"I'm frightfully sorry," Vance murmured, taking her extended hand. "I was hoping you would forgive me when you understood everything."

"I do forgive you," she said. "That's what I came to tell you."

Vance bowed his head and raised her fingers to his lips.

The girl then withdrew her hand slowly and, turning, went from the room.

Vance watched her till she had passed through the archway. Then he moved to the open door and stepped out on the balcony.

When Zalia Graem had gone, I went into the den where Markham sat talking with Professor Garden and his son. He looked up at me as I entered, and glanced at his watch.

"I think we'd better be going, Van," he said. "Where's Vance?"

I went reluctantly back into the drawing room to fetch him. He was still standing on the balcony, gazing out over the city with its gaunt spectral structures and its glittering lights.

To this day Vance has not lost his deep affection for Zalia Graem. He has rarely mentioned her name, but I have noted a subtle change in his nature, which I attribute to the influence of that sentiment. Within a fortnight after the Garden murder case, Vance went to Egypt for several months; and I have a feeling that this solitary trip was motivated by his interest in Miss Graem. One evening after his return from Cairo he remarked to me: "A man's affections involve a great responsibility. The things a man wants most must often be sacrificed because of this exacting responsibility." I think I understood what was in his mind. With the multiplicity of intellectual interests that occupied him, he doubted (and I think rightly so) his capacity to make any woman happy in the conventional sense.

As for Zalia Graem, she married Floyd Garden the following year, and they are now living on Long Island, only a few miles distant from Hammle's estate. Miss Weatherby and Kroon are still seen together; and there have been rumors from time to time that she is about to sign a contract with a Hollywood motion-picture producer. Professor Garden is still living in his penthouse apartment, a lonely and somewhat pathetic figure, completely absorbed in his researches.

A year or so after the tragedies at the Garden apartment, Vance met Hannix, the book-maker, at Bowie. It was a casual meeting, and I doubt if Vance remembered it afterward. But Hannix remembered. One day, several months later, when Vance and I were sitting in the downstairs dining hall of the clubhouse at Empire, Hannix came over and drew up a chair.

"What's happened to Floyd Garden, Mr. Vance?" he asked. "I haven't heard from him for over a year. Given up the horses?"

"It's possible, don't y' know," Vance returned with a faint smile.

"But why?" demanded Hannix. "He was a good sport, and I miss him."

"I dare say." Vance nodded indifferently. "Perhaps he grew a bit weary of contributing to your support."

"Now, now, Mr. Vance." Hannix assumed an injured air and extended his hands appealingly. "That was a cruel remark. I never held out with Mr. Garden for the usual bookie maximum. Believe me, I paid him mutuel prices on any bet up to half a hundred... By the way, Mr. Vance,"—Hannix leaned forward confidentially—"the Butler Handicap is coming up in a few minutes, and the slates are all quoting Only One at eight. If you like the colt, I'll give you ten on him. He's got a swell chance to win."

Vance looked at the man coldly and shook his head. "No, thanks, Hannix. I'm already on Discovery."

Discovery won that race by a length and a half. Only One, incidentally, finished a well-beaten second.